GHOST BRAND OF THE WISHBONES

GHOST BRAND OF THE WISHBONES

PETER DAWSON

SAGEBRUSH
Large Print Westerns

First published in Great Britain by Gunsmoke
First published in the United States by Five Star

Published in Large Print 2014 by ISIS Publishing Ltd.,
7 Centremead, Osney Mead, Oxford OX2 0ES
by arrangement with
Golden West Literary Agency

CIP data is available for this title from the British Library

ISBN 978–0–7531–5364–2 (pb)

Printed and bound in Great Britain by
T. J. International Ltd., Padstow, Cornwall

Table of Contents

HELL'S HALF ACRE

Jonathan Glidden published all of his fiction under the *nom de plume* Peter Dawson, a name originally given him by his agent, Marguerite Harper. This short novel, which he had titled "One Man Holdout", became his fifty-first published magazine story when it appeared under the title "A Gun-Champion for Hell's Half Acre" in *Complete Western Book Magazine* (10/39), a Red Circle pulp magazine published by Newsstand Publications, Inc. It was sold to the magazine on June 29, 1939. The author was paid $135.00 for it at the rate of a cent a word. For its first book appearance, the title has been somewhat modified from the rather garish title given it by Ward Marshall who edited *Complete Western Book Magazine* at the time.

CHAPTER
ONE

The locomotive rumbled past them in a swirl of dust and cinders and escaping steam that laid a fog in under the glare of the unshaded lantern that hung from the Sands station awning. The two men waiting there squinted their eyes against the flying particles and stared far down the dark tracks toward the oncoming red lantern of the caboose.

Above the rumble of the string of freight cars rushing up out of the darkness, the shorter of the two shouted angrily: "Here's your last chance, Sheriff. Let me handle this." His blunt and freckled face was set doggedly, and the glance he turned on his companion was belligerent.

The other, a five-pointed star pinned to the open vest over his narrow and flat chest, merely let down the corners of his thin mouth under his corn-silk mustache as his answer. The screeching brakes had slowed the train now, and he was watching a tall man carrying a suitcase swing down off the caboose's step fifty yards below the station. The speed of the train carried the tall man on at a run for a few strides. Then both watchers saw him raise a hand in parting salute to the brakeman, who leaned out from the caboose's platform and swung his brass lantern in a highball to the engineer.

Far ahead the locomotive's exhaust took up its interrupted pound, and the last two cars swept on past the station and left a sudden stillness in comparison with the rush of sound of a moment ago. The tall man must have seen the waiting pair, for he paused momentarily to transfer his battered fiber suitcase from right hand to left before he came on again. There was a certain effortless quality in his long stride unusual in a man so tall. When he had stepped well within the circle of light, his face showed aquiline and lean and with a certain smiling gravity beneath its weathered bronze. He was outfitted in a black broadcloth suit and a white shirt, the tight collar of which was obviously uncomfortable to him. A pair of well-worn boots accentuated his tallness.

He stopped ten feet out from the waiting pair, set his suitcase down, and drawled: "You're like two crows, waitin' to make a meal off a dyin' rabbit. Sheriff, it's past your bedtime. Why the reception committee?"

The sheriff's thin face took on a deeper scowl. "I come along to make sure Gault tried," he said.

"Tried what?"

Gault, the short man, said scornfully: "To get you to take the side road out o' town, Ed."

Ed's brown eyes lost a trifle of their amusement. "What's wrong with the street, Tom?" he asked.

"You tell him, Sheriff," Tom Gault said. "You were so damned anxious to come along and make sure I didn't start anything!"

4

The lawman said flatly: "Kip Ison's at the Gem. Him and three of his crew."

"I still don't get it," Ed said.

"They're waitin' for you," Gault put in. "Uhling probably sent 'em in."

"Why?"

"Things have happened since you been gone," Gault explained. "Our beloved neighbors have made a dicker with that sheep company to sell out the Basin. Uhling's threatened to tar and feather the first sheepman that sets foot on this range."

"And what's that got to do with me?"

"Plenty," Sheriff Peers muttered. His watery blue eyes fixed a hard stare on Ed January. "Uhling knows where the other Basin outfits stand, knows they're sellin' for a better price than he can lay on the line for their spreads. He don't know about you. He aims to make sure. So he's sent in his understrapper to make you another offer."

"He made me an offer before I went away. I told him it was no dice." Ed laughed, a laugh that wasn't reflected in his surface-glinted blue eyes. "But if this is the way he wants it, it'll be a pleasure to talk to friend Ison."

"You think it will," Peers said acidly. "Start anything and I'll jug the lot of you."

Ed January's brows came up in mock surprise. "It'd be worth it just to see how long you could hold Kip Ison in that jail of yours, Sheriff. You've been in office long enough to know who keeps you there."

The official mask of Sheriff Peers's face was broken for a moment by a real and sudden anger. "Any man that says I play along with Uhling is a liar!" he stated flatly. "You need takin' down a peg or two, January!"

"You takin' over the job?" Ed drawled.

Tom Gault said hastily: "Pull in your horns, you two! Peers, we won't start anything unless we're prodded into it. And we ain't walkin' around anything, either."

The hot flush that had clouded the lawman's face gradually receded. After a moment in which his hostile stare held to Ed, he growled — "Don't say I didn't warn you." — and walked off.

They waited until the choppy tread of his boots had passed out of hearing around the far corner of the station. Then Ed said: "He's makin' it mighty plain. That puts about the whole pack against us, don't it?"

"You could pull out of it."

"And let Uhling claim he ran me out?" Ed slowly shook his head. "No thanks. I worked ten years to earn the money for that layout. I'll hang onto it."

"Lines you up square in the middle, don't it? The Basin outfits hatin' you because no sheep company can operate without a right of way through your place to summer graze in the mountains. And Uhling not trustin' you not to sell out him and the rest of the cattlemen. Well, you have one more chance before they touch off the fireworks. If you're smart, you'll take it."

"Uhn-uh. I stay."

"Why? There's a hundred other places you could go for a new start. Uhling's offer is fair."

Ed smiled thinly. "If you're through singin' your psalms, we might get on up the street and see Ison," he drawled.

Tom Gault's homely face broke into a wide grin. "It was worth tryin', anyway," he said, a little sheepishly. He picked up Ed's suitcase and led the way around the freight platform and back to a hitch rail where two ponies, a chestnut and a roan, stood tied. He unlaced the pouch to the chestnut's saddle and lifted out a heavy shell belt and a holster, handing them across to Ed and saying: "Thought you might need this." He wore his own weapon, a .44 Colt, rammed through the waistband of his faded blue Levi's.

Ed took off his coat and hung it on the saddle horn. He removed a shoulder-holster that hung at his armpit and transferred the weapon — a Colt single-action .38 — to the other holster which he cinched about his waist and thonged low on his right thigh. Then, getting into his coat again, he asked: "Is Les Pace the one that's bringin' in this sheep outfit?"

Gault nodded, swore roundly. "Damned if I can figure that man. You'd swear he was born with a brandin' iron in his hand. Yet, he'll sell out a cattle range like this. No wonder Uhling's riled."

They started out along the cinder-surfaced path that led from the station to the town's main thoroughfare, marked in the darkness by a shadowed line of poplars and cottonwoods. Into the brief silence, Gault said: "Did you buy that blooded stock you went after?"

Ed nodded. "They're due in three weeks."

Gault let out a gusty sigh: "Well, you must know what you're doin'."

They turned into the street and in under the trees, heading for the meager sprinkling of lights that showed at the town's center. Ed ignored his friend's uneasiness, asked: "Any other news?"

"Old Bill Atwood cashed in. Him and his mule fell through a rotten ledge in the brakes north of the layout."

Ed's lean face showed a definite shock. It took him several seconds to say, incredulously: "Bill dead?" Then, as the full realization came, he mused aloud: "The good ones always seem to go first. I hope it was clean and quick. That's the way he'd want to go."

They were silent from there on, to the end of the first path and until they'd stepped up onto the first stretch of awninged plank walk that fronted the stores. They both looked obliquely up and across the street toward the lights of the Gem Saloon. It lay fifty yards ahead now, and the wash of orange lights from its windows showed vaguely four figures that had the walk in front to themselves.

One man stood alone at the edge of the walk. He leaned indolently against an awning post, a big man, solid looking, his cross-legged stance giving a hint of studied arrogance. Behind him, in the shadow of the adobe wall, stood three others.

Ed stopped before the lighted window of a restaurant and reached into a coat pocket and took out a sack of tobacco dust. He sifted some of the weed onto a wheat-straw paper and offered the makings to Gault.

Gault said: "No thanks." Then, urgently: "Ed, there's three others behind Ison over there. No one'll blame you if you turn and go back."

"You're spooky, Tom."

"The hell I am! I've got sense. They're hardcases. If you go in there, they'll carry you out on a shutter. Four against two is bad odds any way you figure it."

"One, not two," Ed said. "You're not drawin' your forty a month to mix in on my troubles."

"That's up to me, ain't it? I tell you it's a fool's play to head across there."

Ed looked back over his shoulder and in at the restaurant window. His eyes all at once showed a live interest. "Who's the redhead?" he asked.

Gault turned irritably to face the window and see the girl inside behind the counter. "Bill Atwood's daughter. She took that money Bill left her and bought this . . ." He was abruptly aware that Ed had changed the subject and said savagely: "Use your brains, Ed. Odds is odds, but . . ."

"Pretty, isn't she?" Ed drawled. He turned his back to the window, flicked alight a match, lit his smoke, and then said: "Remember, stay set." He started out across the walk.

Gault let him go, knowing that further talk was wasted. He was for the first time in many years really afraid, yet his glance was touched with open admiration as he watched Ed's tall figure fade into the half light of the street. He knew what he was doing, and he waited where he was, catching his breath as Ed reappeared opposite to step in between two ponies tied at the hitch rail and up onto the walk within ten feet of Kip Ison.

He heard Ed's cool, drawling voice say — "Like a drink, Kip?" — and Ison's answer, long in coming: "Why not?"

He saw Ed step on across the walk and in through the swing doors, plainly ignoring Ison's three men. Then Ed was out of sight. Kip Ison's solid shape followed. It seemed an eternity of time to Gault before the three others filed in through the doors. Once they'd disappeared, his right hand lifted to the handles of his Colt, and he started across the street.

Inside the Gem, Ed sauntered to the polished pine bar. A quick and cursory inspection of the room showed him that it was empty, probably through Kip Ison's foresight. His half-amused glance took in Pinto Mundorff, the dour-visaged owner who was tending bar.

He told Mundorff — "Two glasses and a bottle that isn't watered, Pinto." — smiling a little at the drawn tautness of Pinto's face. Pinto had worked for Simon Uhling years ago. There was no doubt as to where his sympathies would lie if anyone started anything.

Kip Ison stepped in alongside Ed at the bar, putting his elbows on it, a booted foot on the brass rail, and letting his two big hands rest palm down on the polished wood. The greatest contrast between the two men seemed to be that Ed's hair was blond, his eyes light, while Ison was dark, with smoky black eyes constantly alive.

10

Ison said, with a touch of rancor in his voice: "Pace got a wire from Tucson today. The sheep company's sendin' a buyer in here Thursday . . . tomorrow. Looks like they're expectin' you to sell out with the others." He waited, got no comment from Ed, who was filling two glasses from the bottle Pinto had set before him, so he went on. "The boss' last offer still stands, January. That's final."

Ed pushed one of the filled shot glasses across to Ison. "I'm not sellin'," he said. "That's final, too."

Kip Ison's face turned hard as rimrock, took on a down-lipped grimace. Then, glancing down at his whiskey glass, a shrewdness crept into his look. He leaned over and, without touching the glass, sniffed at it and made a wry face. Then he picked up the whiskey and turned sideways to the counter so that he faced Ed.

He drawled tonelessly: "Y'know, I've found out a thing or two about whiskey." The hand holding the glass crossed in front of him to the edge of the bar. "One is that it takes on the smell of anything it gets close to." The glass came out over the counter edge, and Ison's hand tipped it. "Right then, before I picked this up, I'd have swore it had the stink o' polecat!"

His hand tipped the glass farther, and Ed was seeing the amber liquid spill in a broken line into the spittoon at Ison's feet. It splashed against the metal with a liquid sound that was loud against the stillness.

Ed glanced into the bar mirror, taking in Ison's three crewmen standing to one side of the swing doors along the front wall. Then he was pushing out from the bar, his move calculatingly slow.

When he had arm room, and with elbows still cocked, he lashed out with his open left hand and the back of it caught Ison hard across the mouth and drove him a full step to the side in a stumbling lurch. As he moved, Ed's right hand streaked up to his thigh to brush aside his coat. He pivoted. He palmed up the long-barreled Colt. The move was fast, effortless, and smooth, and he wheeled as he made it.

His weapon swung in a tight arc and arrested the furtive move of one of Ison's men by the doors. He said tonelessly: "Kip, fill that glass and drink it down!"

Ison stood three feet out from the bar now, fists knotted and feet spread. Even though Ed wasn't looking at him, he hesitated in making the lunge he was set for.

"Like hell!" he rasped.

"I'll count to ten, to myself, Kip. Have that drink poured before I finish."

The stillness that settled down over the room was potent, ready to explode. Ison's men stood in a paralysis of caution, watching for their chance. They were a hard-bitten trio, all wearing double belts. Ed's glance clung to them unwinkingly. Then, after a long five seconds, Ison stepped sullenly to the bar and sloshed some whiskey from the bottle into the glass and raised it.

Ed heard a stealthy move behind him. Even before that hint of sound had telegraphed its complete warning, he was whirling to face the bar. The hard, down-slashing blow of Pinto Mundorff's shot-filled blackjack grazed his shoulder. He leaned far back over the bar and slugged Pinto a quick glancing blow with his six-gun. The saloon owner's eyes took on a stupid vacant stare, his knees buckled, and he slumped down behind the counter. Ed was already wheeling away from him.

Ed's Colt's jumped into line with one of the only two lights in the room, an ornate cut-glass bracket lamp in a holder at one end of the bar mirror. His .38 exploded, the lamp chimney shattered apart, and the flame guttered out.

He wheeled in time to catch Ison's right hand blurring up a weapon from holster. He lunged, left his feet headlong in a rolling dive, and hit Ison in the side with the hard drive of one shoulder. They went down, a second explosion from up front burst upon the stillness, and the swing doors up front swung inward as Tom Gault's voice yelled stridently: "Hold it, you high-binders!"

A fraction of a second later, Gault's gun stabbed flame to punctuate the exact instant the second lamp at the bar's far end flew apart in a crash of flying glass. As the gun's deafening racket filled the suddenly darkened room, Ed was rolling clear of Ison. But all at once a grip closed vise-like on his arm. He slashed viciously at Ison's hand and felt his gunsight rip through giving flesh. He caught Ison's choked oath, and then the ramrod's .45 was spitting a four-inch stab of powder flame that scorched the side of his face and completely deafened him. He threw his body into a roll, and this time he was clear.

His roll carried him into the legs of another man. He came to his knees, then stood erect, and took a full blow low on his left side. He struck out wildly, and his left connected full with a face. He heard the man hit the bar and fall heavily to the floor.

Up front, Gault yelled: "Watch it, Ed! They're across there!"

Ed reached out, felt of the bar, raised a booted foot, and put it against the bar's upright face and pushed. The counter gave way under his thrust; it tilted, and a moment later the sound of splitting wood and falling glassware rose above the scuffling sounds toward the front of the room, where Gault's voice momentarily sounded in a throaty cry of obscenity.

Someone slammed into Ed solidly from the right, knocking him from his feet. As he went down, the back of his head struck a second man's shins, and Ison's voice snarled: "Who's that?"

He rolled aside quickly, and the vicious kick of a boot slid harmlessly off his thigh. Clear of those feet, he swung with his six-gun at the legs he'd rolled against a moment ago. The man groaned in pain, and then Ed came to his knees and threw a hard blow at the stomach of the second figure that was momentarily outlined by the scant light shining through one of the saloon's two front windows. His blow connected. He dodged out of the way as Ison, with the hurt shins, and the one with the aching stomach stumbled into each other and started slugging it out.

He ran back along the room and felt at the wall at a point he judged to be a few feet short of the door to

14

Pinto Mundorff's office. His hand closed on an iron clamp and went up to the rope above it. This rope, running through two pulleys to the center of the room, supported a massive and ugly four-lamp iron chandelier the saloon owner used on rare occasions when the room was crowded.

Ed tugged at the end of the rope, felt the clamp come loose. He let go the rope and waited, and a second later the chandelier crashed to the floor in a jarring thud that sounded above the shattering of the glass lamps. A man out there howled in pain. A gun spoke twice, the powder flare lining obliquely upward at the ceiling. Ed stepped backward against a chair. He picked it up, swung it over his head, and let it go straight at the bar mirror. The crash of glass and falling bottles made a prolonged and growing sound that took several seconds in dying out.

A familiar figure was outlined between the bursting inward swing doors, and Sheriff Peers yelled stridently: "Break it up, damn it, break it up!"

The scuffling sounds that had filled the room ceased, and the room gradually quieted.

"Get a light," Peers called. "Ison, where the hell are you?"

There was no answer. The lawman called again: "Pinto, light a lamp!"

Someone growled surlily: "Pinto ain't feelin' so good."

A moment later the feeble light of a match flared up front. Ed saw Peers standing spraddle-legged before the

15

swing doors. His face bore an ugly look, and his hand fisted a six-gun.

Behind him, Ed heard a small sound and wheeled warily in time to see the saloon's back door open. Then Tom Gault's stocky figure was momentarily outlined in the reflected light from the face of a woodshed across the alley as he edged out the door.

Ed followed, closing the door after him and calling softly: "Tom!"

Gault came up out of the shadows and said: "Let's get out of here."

They passed the backs of two stores and took a narrow passageway between two buildings toward the street.

As they made the walk in under the awnings along the street, Gault said dryly: "You'll turn wild once too often, friend."

Ed laughed softly. "Milo Peers has his good points."

"Such as bein' able to give a gent a cell cot for tearin' up a saloon. You'll never be able to slice it that thin again, Ed. And this is only the beginnin'!"

CHAPTER
TWO

Kip Ison stared dully into the match glow from where he stood in the heavy shadows along the room's back wall. The sheriff hadn't seen him yet. His hand was clamped about his left wrist to stem the flow of blood from the jagged gash Ed January's gunsight had ripped in the fatty muscle of his thumb. His side ached throbbingly from the crushing weight where January's shoulder had first taken him.

His glance ran over Pinto Mundorff's wrecked place. The bar mirror was cracked and half fallen out in a huge broken spiderweb. The bar lay on its side, split its entire length, and the floor out from it was sprinkled with broken shards of glass and pooled with spilled whiskey. The room smelled like the inside of a keg.

Pinto's booted feet stuck out from beneath his overturned counter. One of Ison's men was down near Pinto, half sitting against the bar and staring stupidly out of uncertain, winking eyes, blood streaming down off his forehead. A second man's legs were pinned beneath the fallen chandelier, and he now cursed obscenely and made an effort to lift the heavy wrought iron from across his skinned shins. Ison's third man stood near the sheriff, holding the match and looking warily back into the shadows for a sign of someone moving there.

Ison went to the alley door, let himself out soundlessly. He was in time to see January and Gault disappear into a passageway between two buildings below. He followed, not seeing them again until he stood in the deep impenetrable shadow of a cottonwood just short of the loading corrals along the tracks below the station.

January and Gault were riding their horses toward him out of the shadows, along the line of a road that ran past the tree. He lifted the short-barreled Colt he had carried in his right hand all the way down here. He leveled its sights on January's flat wide chest.

Then an instinct for caution steadied him, and he lowered the weapon and watched them draw abreast of him. He heard January, barely twenty feet away now, saying: ". . . out there tonight. I might as well settle this with him for good and all."

"Ain't one scrap a night enough for you?" came Gault's dry query.

"This won't be a scrap. I'll tell Pace he's wasting his time getting that buyer in here. Tonight's as good a time as . . ." January's words trailed off as he rode out of hearing.

Ison stood there under the cottonwood a full minute after they had gone, frowning in thought. He wrapped his bandanna around his bleeding hand and finally walked back up the street to the Gem. Inside, he found Peers and the others working over Pinto Mundorff in the eerie and uncertain light of the miraculously unbroken and chimneyless lamp at the front end of the bar mirror. The bar had been righted, and they had carried Pinto out and laid him on the floor in front of it.

The sheriff got to his feet as Ison strode in. He eyed Uhling's man sourly as he said: "This is the first thing I ever saw you start and not finish, Kip. It's goin' to cost somebody."

Ison asked brusquely: "You preferrin' charges?" There was little respect in his manner of speaking.

Peers shook his head. "No. You're all alive, which is mighty considerate of January." His tones were mild, for Simon Uhling represented the patronage that kept him in office.

"Pinto hurt?" Ison asked.

"Nothin' he won't sleep off."

Ison glanced at his men. "Come on. We'll settle with Pinto tomorrow." He led the way out through the swing doors. His ignoring of the lawman was pointed.

Peers heard their ponies lift into a quick trot and go out the street. He glanced down at the saloonkeeper, and a slow smile wreathed his gaunt features. "Take care of your own mess, Pinto," he mused, half aloud, and blew out the lamp and left the saloon. He curtly ordered away a few curious onlookers out front and went home and to bed.

On the trail two miles west of town, Ison reined in and let his men come even with him.

"Slim, you're runnin' out on us tonight," he announced, speaking to a tall slat of a man who was holding a bandanna to a cut along one cheek. Slim forked a roan horse.

"How come, boss?" he asked.

"You got spooked over the trouble we had with January. You drew your pay and high tailed." Ison's smile was a sly one. "That's what it's supposed to look like." He stopped abruptly, frowned, and asked Slim: "You reckon anyone in this part of the country knows Tombstone Bates's two-fingered hand?"

"He ain't never been this far north, boss," Slim said. "Why?"

"I've got a job for Tombstone. You know where to find him?"

"At Charley's place in Wagon Mound."

"Can you get down there and have him back here again before dark tomorrow night?"

Slim thought a moment. "That's a hell of a ways. But if I had the money for a couple spare horses, I could make it."

Ison reached into his pocket, took out a wallet, and leafed out some paper money, handing it across. "I'm dependin' on this, Slim. If Tombstone asks any questions, tell him he'll be workin' for good pay. Another thing, have him wear his Sunday suit."

Slim nodded and pocketed the money. "Where'll we meet you?"

"At the East Fork line shack. Keep out of sight and be there before dark." Ison turned to the others. "Duke, you and Ben are to be ready to swear in the mornin' that I rode in to the layout with you tonight and went straight to bed. You get it?"

The man whose shins had been skinned said —
"Sure, boss." — and the other grinned and drawled:
"For a hundred and fifty a month, I'd say you walked
out from town on your hands."

"I'll be gone a couple hours," Ison told them. He
wheeled his black gelding and struck out on a line
taking him south from the trail. At a hundred yards'
distance, he glanced back over his shoulder to see Slim
on his way back to town, the two others going on.

In the next forty minutes he crossed the unfenced
and poorly grassed range that extended far to the west
of Sands and all the way to the limits of the Basin.
Clumps of *chamiza* and sage and mesquite along with
a few stunted cedars and ragged bunches of prickly
pear dotted the rolling land, turned a somber gray in
the faint starlight. Ison rode fast, skirting most of the
countless dry washes, crossing a few, always keeping to
his southwesterly direction.

He came to a low rim that cut a crooked line from
north to south across the range. The country beyond
lay at a lower level. He spent two minutes finding a way
down off the rim, and, from there on, his way lay across
richer gramma-grass range. He rode the line of a fence
until he came to a wagon road, which he took south;
and at that point cottonwoods and willow brakes
marked the line of a stream a hundred yards or better
to the west of him.

Once, two miles beyond the place he had turned into
it, he swung wide of the road to circle a small ranch
house that sat near the creekbank. Less than a mile
below that, the trail turned abruptly in toward the

21

stream. Ison followed it, fording the creek and riding in past a corral, a barn, and then up a low knoll to a poplar log cabin that squatted on its crest.

He reined in close enough to the cabin's door to lean out from the saddle and pound on the panel. No answer came from inside. He knocked again, harder, and this time his voice boomed: "Pace!"

The warped sash of the cabin's one window grated up, and the octagonal barrel of a rifle poked through the opening and gleamed faintly in the starlight. A suspicious and sleepy voice growled: "What you want, Ison?"

The ramrod reined out so that he could see the window more directly. "What's the matter, Pace? Spooky?"

Pace snorted angrily: "I asked what the hell you want?"

"Things are shapin' up, Les. January and Frank Tarbe are over with Uhling. They sent me after you. It looks like Uhling's buyin'. He took out a loan at the bank today."

There was a brief silence, until at length Pace said in thinly veiled sarcasm: "Next you'll be tellin' me I've been picked to run for governor."

Ison replied hotly: "What good would it do me to run a sandy on you? I told you from the beginning that, if you'd start a dicker with a sheep outfit, you'd sooner or later get your price from Uhling. Hell, is it my fault it's taken so long to work out? You're gettin' your price now."

"January's sellin'?" There was more conviction in Pace's present tone.

"That's what I said, ain't it?"

"I'd give a nice piece of change to know what you're gettin' out of this, Ison."

"You're gettin' your nice piece of change to keep your mouth shut." Ison's glance all at once narrowed. "Have you told anyone about this? Tarbe or any of the others?"

"When I give my word, I don't break it," came Pace's slow answer. Then, after another pause in which his suspicions were made clear, he said: "All right, I'll come along."

"And bring along that telegram you got today," Ison said quickly. "The boss wants to be sure he isn't layin' out his money for nothing."

The rifle barrel disappeared, the window sash fell heavily, and Ison reined over toward the door. Pace could be heard moving about inside. In less than two minutes the door swung open, and a stooped figure appeared. Pace had a rifle cradled in the crook of his right arm. He stood motionless on the slab step beyond the door, his left hand reaching back and still holding the latch ajar. He eyed Kip Ison sourly, saying: "Damned if I know why I should take your word for this."

"You got the telegram?"

Pace nodded, pulled the door shut. He took two steps out into the yard. Kip Ison's hidden right arm suddenly lifted from his side. His hand fisted his .45. The weapon swung into line and exploded in a burst of sound. The bullet caught Pace with one foot lifted to make the beginning of a frantic lunge back toward his door. It drove him backward, and he bent double. The Winchester slid into the dirt, and his hands clawed at his chest. He fell heavily on one shoulder, rolled onto his back, and his body straightened out, poker stiff. His muscles had relaxed in death before the echoes of the shot died out along the willow brakes upstream.

Ison dropped his weapon back into leather. His glance clung to the dead man for a good ten seconds. Then he turned the black and trotted the animal down out of the yard and into the creek. He rode the stream for three miles north, until he came to the point where the main trail from town, striking west, crossed it. There he reined his horse from the uncertain footing of the gravelly creek bed. Fifty minutes later he was climbing in between his blankets in the end room of Simon Uhling's sprawling L-shaped adobe ranch house.

CHAPTER
THREE

January was barely beyond Frank Tarbe's place, a mile above Pace's, when the racketing echo of the single shot sounded out of the distance. He had been walking his chestnut for the last mile, and now he spurred the animal into a quick trot and swung into the bend of the trail that would take him across the creek.

He saw Pace's outstretched shape when he was halfway up along the face of the knoll toward the cabin. He reined in immediately, and his hand swept aside the flowing tail of his coat and drew the .38 from holster. His eyes scanned the shadows under the low eaves of the cabin and ran on to the unrelieved obscurity around the shape of a stunted cedar twenty feet away; then he glanced below, to the willow brake. A full quarter minute he sat there, his tall body tense, listening. Then he swung aground, and with the weapon still in his hand he walked on up to where Pace lay.

The faint starlight failed to bring out the details clearly. He circled the body and went to the cabin's door, throwing it open, and stepping immediately aside. When he moved in, it was to take a quick step through the opening and lunge to one side of it. In another ten seconds, in which he heard no sound, he was reaching into a pocket for a match. He palmed the match and, using an overhand motion, threw it far out onto the floor. Its impregnated end burst into flame, momentarily lifting each detail of the small room out of darkness. Ed's hasty, but sure, glance brought enough relief so that he holstered the Colt. The room was empty.

He found a lantern hanging on a nail near the door, took it down, and lit it. Outside once more, he made a hasty circuit of the cabin, scanning the ground for sign. Before the door again, he saw the clear hoof marks of Ison's pony outlined in the hard-packed and sandy clay. But farther out there was more hoof sign, a lot of it. So he ignored it, striding over to set the lantern on the ground and kneel beside the body.

Pace's gray shirt was blood matted, one small hole centering the red stain. Ed didn't touch the body, but his glance took in each detail — the Winchester lying almost within reach, the twisted grimace of pain etched on Pace's thin still face. The eyes were open, staring. Ed gently closed them.

As he took his hand away, a voice from near at hand said levelly: "Lookin' for something, January?"

Ed acted purely on instinct in the next split second. He recognized Frank Tarbe's voice. From his crouch beside the body, he gathered his muscles and made a long leap out of the lantern's glare, right hand flashing his six-gun out of holster as he moved. He landed spraddle-legged, facing the direction out of which the voice had come, his .38 cocked and at his hip. But no target was in sight.

Tarbe's laugh came softly to him: "It won't work, January. Drop that hog-leg or I'll let air through you!"

Ed realized then that his lunge hadn't quite carried him beyond the lantern's circle of light. He made a perfect target. And Frank Tarbe, in with Pace on this sheep deal, had no love for him.

So he let down the hammer of the six-gun and dropped it at his feet. A moment later Frank Tarbe stepped out of the deep shadow beyond the bushy cedar thirty feet away, a Winchester .30-30 half raised to his shoulder.

Tarbe said — "Kick that iron across here." — and stood where he was until the Colt came sliding through the dust to within ten feet of him. He picked up the weapon and thrust it through the waistband of his Levi's, and then came to stand beyond the body, opposite Ed.

He glanced briefly down at the dead man, then regarded Ed and asked: "What were you lookin' for?"

"Trying to get an idea who killed him."

Tarbe was a man of Tom Gault's general build, short but of more ample proportions. His face was softer than Gault's, features rounded and loose jowls hiding the line of his jaw, and now, as he smiled wryly, the habitual serenity of his face was wiped out. "Why did you do it?" he queried.

Ed said: "You're short on brains, Frank, but not this short. It doesn't add up."

"It does to me," Tarbe drawled. Then, musing aloud, he went on: "You were inside, lookin' for something. You didn't find it, or you'd have cleared out. Instead, you came out here and had your look at Pace. It must be here, whatever it is." So saying, he knelt alongside the body and went through the pockets of Pace's vest. His hand came out of one pocket fisting the yellow envelope of a telegram.

He held it up, looking across at Ed. "This it?"

"You think it is, don't you?" Ed drawled.

"I don't think, I know. Les promised this sheep buyer he'd have you ready to sell with the rest of us. How in hell he thought he'd swing it is beyond me, but that's what he did. You found out about it in town tonight and rode out here to settle with him. But why kill him for that? Because he wouldn't show you this?"

"I like to keep my hand in, Frank." Ed's tone was thin edged with sarcasm.

Tarbe picked up his rifle, stood up. He walked over to Ed's chestnut, swung clumsily into the saddle. "My mare's down by the creek," he said. "You can ride her in to town. She's old and fat enough to discourage any ideas you might have of gettin' away."

An hour and twenty minutes later, Frank Tarbe was pounding at the door of the sheriff's small white frame house at the edge of town. Ed January stood beyond, near the railing of the porch.

Milo Peers finally opened the door. He had pulled on trousers over his flannel nightgown. His thin head of hair was mussed, his eyes were heavy with sleep, and he was barefooted. But when he saw who it was, his eyes opened wide.

Tarbe said — "Customer for you, Milo." — and motioned Ed in through the door.

Peers lit the lamp on the room's center table before he looked at Ed and allowed himself the comment: "I thought I was rid of you for the night. What's wrong now?"

"Frank can tell it."

Tarbe did the talking. He had heard the shot, had hotfooted it out to the corral for his mare, and then ridden down to Pace's. He'd seen Ed go into the cabin and come out later and make a circle with the lantern and then kneel alongside Pace. It seemed that Ed was looking for something, probably the telegram.

Tarbe handed the telegram to the lawman. "Read what it says. Pace showed it to me this afternoon."

Peers unfolded the yellow sheet of paper, glanced down at it. Then he turned to January. "Well, did you do it?"

"It's supposed to look like I did."

"That ain't what I asked. Did you?"

"No."

Tarbe laughed dryly and put in: "Hell, I caught him, didn't I?"

Peers turned to the Basin rancher and snapped irritably: "I'll handle this, Frank." Then, to January: "Why did you ride down there tonight?"

"To see Pace. To tell him he was wastin' his time tryin' to get me in on the sheep sell-out."

"And he was dead when you got there?"

Ed nodded.

The sheriff tossed the telegram onto the table and queried: "Have you read it?" He caught Ed's slow shake of the head and added: "Maybe you ought to."

Ed glanced down at the yellow sheet and read:

Lester Pace
Sands, Arizona.

Arrive Sands evening train Thursday. Congratulations on bringing January around. Expect to close with you immediately.

E. J. Dunn.

Ed looked across at Tarbe. "So this is what I was lookin' for?"

"That's the only answer. Pace let it get around town today that he was bringin' that buyer in here. Only he didn't say what else the telegram had in it. You heard about it, knew he'd promised something he couldn't deliver. So you went out there to tell him it was no use. He argued with you, maybe tried to throw down on you with that rifle. You let him have it."

"And why was January there ten minutes afterwards, when you rode in?" Peers asked bluntly and with a sense of fairness that surprised Ed as much as it did Tarbe.

Tarbe pointed to the telegram. "Huntin' for that. He wanted to know what else Dunn had to say."

"That's a mighty thin reason for swearin' out a warrant for murder, Frank."

"Enough reason for me, Milo."

The lawman sighed wearily and gave Tarbe a scornful glance. He began — "There's times when even sheep would be a blessin' compared to . . ." — and then broke off and shrugged his stooped shoulders and pulled open a drawer of the table to take out a pair of rusty handcuffs.

30

As he closed them about Ed's wrists, he said: "I've hated your guts about as bad as I can remember ever hatin' any man's, January. But I'll give you credit of the doubt this time. I don't think you'd murder a man."

"Then why hold me for it?"

Peers shrugged, ill humor once more taking possession of his face. "Frank said he'd swear out a warrant, didn't he? And I've taken an oath to a certain duty. This is part of it. We'll let a court decide."

"You're damn' right we will," Tarbe put in.

Peers snorted. "At that, you'll be safer in jail than out when Uhling hears about it."

CHAPTER
FOUR

Milo Peers's deputy rode in at the Flying U before six that morning with the news of Pace's death and Ed January's arrest. He asked for a buckboard and the loan of a man to help take the body into town. When Uhling and Kip Ison rode out the trail, headed for Sands, the deputy was eating a hurried breakfast in the bunkhouse with the rest of the crew.

Simon Uhling didn't make it a habit to air his thoughts, and for long minutes he rode in stolid silence alongside his foreman, their ponies at a reaching, mile-eating trot and both men standing in the saddle. Uhling looked his part, cattle king of this vast range. He was medium tall, white haired, and with a hawkish sun-blackened face that bore a stamp of rugged strength and toughness. His blue eyes for the past half hour had been sharp lighted in anger. He was crowding sixty years, yet he sat in the saddle erectly and without a spare ounce of flesh on his frame.

"Any idea how we can handle January?" Kip Ison ventured to ask finally. He laughed and added: "I'm not a hell of a lot of help, am I? That ruckus last night ain't much to my credit."

"We'll go at it a different way today," Uhling said. "I've spent thirty years building up a name in this country. Maybe I can use it to some advantage."

He said nothing further until they had covered another mile and ridden through the low line of hills that formed the western rampart to the Basin. As the trail took them down the slope and opened out a wide view of this four-mile-wide stretch of good grass, Uhling growled: "Damned if I'll stand the stink of sheep in the wind every time I ride through here. I'll buy January out if it takes my last dollar. It'll crowd me to borrow more from the bank, but I'll do it if I have to."

Ison frowned, obviously framing in words a thought occurring to him. "Why not wait and let January stand trial and hang for murder? His spread will be up for auction after that. You can buy it at your price."

Uhling shook his head. "He's no murderer, Kip. He'll never hang for this, much as I'd like to see it."

"Then why not take that thousand I offered you a month ago? Use it along with what you've got to buy his place. You don't need his layout. Fill out the deed in my name and I'll take the spread over, sign a note, and pay you back your money with interest. A man has to make a start sometime. This is my chance to own my own brand. You'd be doin' me a favor."

"You seem to really want that spread, Kip."

"Sure I want it. I ain't got any complaint on what you're payin' me, and no man was ever better treated in roddin' an outfit. But it's time I took out on my own."

Uhling thought a moment, finally nodded. "You're right, Kip, I don't need it. And you'd make me a good neighbor." He wasn't looking at his ramrod, and didn't see the mixture of relief and cunning in Ison's eyes.

CHAPTER
FIVE

At eight o'clock that morning, Milo Peers led Tom Gault down the corridor between the jail's two pair of cells. He stopped at the end one on the street side, Ed January's, unlocked the door and handed in a bundle wrapped in newspaper, announcing gruffly: "Here's your things." He locked the cell door, asked Gault — "You want to talk to him?" — and, when Gault nodded, he turned and left them, going back into his office and locking the jail door.

The bundle contained Ed's everyday work clothes. He began removing his white shirt and hard collar, the broadcloth suit, looking out at Gault to say: "Any man who'll wear one of these outfits is out of his head. They're just cousin to a straight-jacket."

Gault looked in at him for a long moment in silence, the expression on his freckled face one of faint anger. Finally he said dryly: "You don't *have* to tell me about it."

Ed explained briefly what had happened the night before. When he had finished, Gault said: "I warned you. You laid yourself open to it."

"I wouldn't have missed it, Tom. Now they're playin' a tune I can dance to."

"They? Who's *they?*"

Ed shrugged his wide shoulders as he pulled on a faded blue cotton shirt.

Gault apparently saw that his questions weren't netting him much, for he said warily: "Anything else you need? Tobacco, papers, cards?"

"You could hunt up a hacksaw and a file. Peers hasn't been as sour as usual. Maybe he'd let you pass 'em in to me."

Gault ignored this banter. "I can break you out of here," he said seriously. "But it'll have to be damned quick, before Uhling and Ison hit town. And we'll both have to hightail out of the country."

Ed shook his head, for the moment serious. "I'll stick around. Whoever framed me with this wants me in here. I aim to find out why."

"Damn Peers!" Gault said explosively. "He's got a head on his shoulders. He knows damned well you didn't do it. Is he in with the rest against you? Why would he take Tarbe's word for a thing like this?"

"He's in the middle, like I am. He has to serve any reasonable warrant, and he has to think of his votes."

"Which means Uhling."

Ed nodded.

Gault reached to a shirt pocket for a sack of tobacco dust. He sifted the making's from it, passed it in through the bars to Ed. As he rolled the paper into a tight cylinder and tongued the edge, he announced: "Helen Atwood's on her way over here to see you." He caught Ed's puzzled frown and explained: "The redhead you spotted in the restaurant last night. Only her hair's brown, not red."

"To see me? Why?"

Gault shrugged. "She wouldn't say. So I ordered a breakfast and told her to bring it on over. Maybe Peers will let her in."

As though in answer to his words, the jail door swung open and the girl of the restaurant, carrying a tray covered with a clean napkin, came down the corridor ahead of Milo Peers. The sheriff had a half-belligerent, half-respectful look on his face as he unlocked the cell door and handed the tray to Ed.

"This here's Bill Atwood's daughter," he told Ed. "Says she wants a talk with you." He locked the cell door again and then stood there waiting, obviously wanting to know more about this.

Ed's glance was on the girl, who seemed slightly embarrassed at having intruded. Her blue and yellow printed gingham dress revealed subtly the lines of a tall and graceful figure. Reddish-brown hair framed an oval face that seemed at first very pretty and then as being hauntingly beautiful. Her eyes were a deep blue, and their expression was now touched with a measure of confusion.

She said haltingly: "I wanted to talk with Mister January. You see, my father wrote me about him, Sheriff . . . he was . . . well, he was one of Dad's best friends."

It was the lawman's turn to be confused. He said: "Go right ahead. Call when you're through, and I'll let you out." He turned to Gault. "You stayin'?"

Ed said — "Yes." — for Gault and waited until Peers had gone out before he told the girl — "Tom and I are partners." — making it clear to her that Gault shared his confidence.

She nodded to indicate the tray of food and told him: "You'd better eat while it's hot, Mister January."

Ed set the tray on the cot and came back to the cell door. "Bill called me Ed. I'm hopin' it was a family custom. We'll forget the food. I can eat any time."

She laughed pleasantly, her voice richly musical. "Ed it is, then." She seemed to sense that he was waiting for her to explain further, and went on: "Dad mentioned you in his last letter. You saw a lot of him, didn't you?"

Ed glanced quickly toward Gault, then back to the girl. "Bill didn't see a lot of anyone. He liked his own company. But he'd stop in at the layout maybe once a month or so. Tom and I usually packed out his grub from town. We brought some stuff out for him a day or so before I went on my trip. He was prospecting the hills in back of my place."

The girl nodded. "I know. He wasn't very sociable. But he did regard you as one of his best friends." She paused, seeming to consider something before she added: "You'll have to take my word for this. I burned the letter before I knew what had happened."

Tom Gault shifted nervously, scraping his boots along the stone floor. Ed asked: "What was in the letter?"

"Several things I couldn't understand. He seemed excited. He wrote about coming to Saint Louis and taking me out of school. I was in college there, you know. He said we'd go East for a long vacation, that at the end of another year he'd be able to give up prospecting. He spoke of having a surprise for me."

Ed let the silence following her words drag out for several seconds. Then: "You think Bill had run onto something?"

She nodded, her glance grateful. "I'm sure he had. Dad was a pessimist. He'd been at this game too long to build hopes on something that wasn't pretty real. Yet he left only six hundred dollars. I . . ."

"It shouldn't be hard for a good man to go up there and find out where he'd been working," Ed interrupted. "Of course, we'd see that you had claim to anything he uncovered. We knew he was lookin' for gold."

"It's not that," she put in hastily. "It's that . . . it's that I don't believe he died accidentally." Ed's glance sharpened. Before he had the chance to speak, she went on: "I've been up into that cañon. I've looked the spot over on the hunch that both Dad and his mule wouldn't trust a weak trail. That ledge isn't broken. Whatever . . ."

Her words ceased as the hinges of the jail door squeaked, and the panel swung open. Peers stood in the doorway. Beyond him January could see Simon Uhling and Kip Ison in the office. The sheriff said: "Time's up, miss."

Ed told the girl, low voiced: "Keep in touch with Tom. We'll go into this." Then louder: "You can leave the tray here and pick it up at noon."

Helen Atwood went along the corridor and out the door. Gault shot Ed a significant glance before he turned to follow her, and said loudly enough for the lawman to hear: "I'll be on the walk out front in case they gang up on you."

Peers stepped aside to let Gault pass, and then Uhling and Ison were following him back along the corridor.

As he stopped before the barred door of Ed's cell, Uhling's voice intoned flatly: "Milo, you're to witness this."

He turned to look at Ed then, and the expression on his face was granite hard. Ison stood before him, half a head taller, heavier, and with a complacent smile on his rugged face. Ison wore a six-gun in plain sight in a holster at his thigh. Uhling's coat bulged at the armpit where it covered a shoulder holster. Peers, his gaunt face paler than usual, leaned against the door of the cell opposite, his manner plainly nervous and uncertain.

Uhling said: "I'm here to settle this thing once and for all, January. Either sell me your layout, today, or hang for murder!"

Ed drawled: "You'll have me bawlin' in a minute, Uhling."

"Sell to me and I'll have you out of this jail tonight," Uhling went on, ignoring the sarcasm. "I'll buy you out by paying Peers to tear up that warrant. He'll keep his mouth shut and give you time to get clear of the country. If you don't sell, I'll see you stretching a rope if I have to plant evidence and bribe a judge and jury to bring it about."

Ed said: "I hope you're takin' all this in, Milo."

The sheriff made no comment. His manner betrayed no emotion.

In a sudden burst of what seemed cold anger, Ed said: "Uhling, use your brains. You know me better than this. You may have me where you want me, out of the way. But so long as I'm in jail, there's not one damned thing you can do to make me sign over my layout. Let me out of here, sit down with me, and talk this over like a white man, and maybe we'll get some place."

Uhling frowned, trying to follow Ed's reasoning. At length, he said: "You mean if we turn you loose, you'll sell?"

"Try it and see."

Uhling shrugged, turned to Peers. "Let him out, Milo. We'll go into the office and talk this over."

Peers's look clung sharply to Ed a moment. Then he came across the corridor and got out his keys and swung the door open. Ison stepped out of the way and over next to Uhling.

Ed said — "This is more like it." — and thrust his hands in his pockets and sauntered out the door.

He stepped around it, close in to Ison. All at once he threw himself to the side, ramming Ison hard with his shoulder. His hands came out of pockets, and, as Ison's gun side turned toward him, he snatched the weapon from the ramrod's holster.

He slashed downward with the heavy .45, and the savage blow caught Ison on the side of the head. Ison slumped to the floor. Ed swung the weapon on Uhling and Peers. "Reach! Both of you!" he said. Uhling

41

ignored the warning, stabbing his hand in under his coat lapel. Ed whirled in behind him, pinned his arms, and lifted him bodily as a shield against Milo Peers's upswinging Colt.

His left held Uhling's two arms locked behind him. His right fist was low at the rancher's side, holding Ison's bluntnosed .45 on the sheriff. Uhling tried to kick back with his spurs and catch Ed in the shins, but Ed's feet were spread wide apart and his hold had Uhling helpless.

Ed said: "Drop it, Milo!"

The lawman studied his chances, saw that he had none, and let his weapon clatter to the stone floor. There was no fear in his eyes, but a faint excitement showed there. It was as though he inwardly felt a grudging admiration for Ed. He said tonelessly: "You sure pick the hard way, January. I wasn't sure about you before. Maybe I am now."

Ed ignored him, reaching over Uhling's shoulder with one hand to get the rancher's gun from below his armpit. He saw that Ison was moving, trying to push himself up to a sitting position, and shaking his head to steady his reeling senses. "Drag Ison into the cell, Milo," he told the sheriff.

Uhling said in a voice hushed by his impotent rage: "Don't, Milo."

His words were barely out before Ed let go his arms, put a hand at the middle of his back, and pushed him headlong in through the cell's door. Uhling stumbled and went to his knees, rising quickly and whirling around and taking one step back toward the cell door. But Ed's weapon was lined at him.

"You next, Milo!" Ed said. Then, when Peers hesitated, he added hotly: "Are you goin' to make me belt you one, too?"

Peers breathed — "Damned if you wouldn't." — and sullenly stepped in through the door.

Ed backed over until he stood behind Ison. He glanced down at the ramrod, saw that Ison was having all he could do to hold himself up with his arms, and said to Uhling: "You ought to get a new understrapper, Uhling. This is twice he's fumbled it." He came across to swing the cell door shut and lock it. He threw the keys in the cell across the corridor.

Uhling said in a voice he was barely able to control: "You're makin' it easy for me, January. Now I can run you out of the country and keep you out. I'm puttin' a price on your head."

Ed laughed. "Not before I've had my fun, Uhling. Right now, I'm headed out to your place. If you break loose in time, you may sight the smoke on your way home."

Uhling breathed a choked: "You wouldn't . . ."

"The hell I wouldn't! I'll ruin you as sudden as you thought you would me. I'll burn your barn and touch off your haystacks. I'll fire your house. If there's time left, I'll butcher a steer or two and drag 'em into your waterholes. You'll have bought my place twice over by the time I pull up stakes and drift."

He wheeled, stepped around Ison, and walked out the jail door and swung it shut after him. A five-second search in the office located his own .38 and holster in the bottom drawer of the sheriff's desk. He threw Ison's and Uhling's weapons into the wastebasket at the wall and belted on his own. Then he heard glass fall from the cell's one window and Simon Uhling's shout go out along the street.

Pushing open the screen door, he saw Tom Gault hurrying along the walk toward him. Behind Tom the walk was clear for a distance of forty feet. Crossing the walk toward Uhling's palomino horse tied at the hitch rail, he told Tom in a low voice: "Beat it! Meet me in the loft of the livery stable tonight."

He vaulted the rail, jerked loose the reins, and swung into the palomino's saddle. As he turned out into the street, ramming his spurless boots into the palomino's flanks to lift the animal into a hard run, a six-gun exploded in a staccato bark behind him. One bullet whipped the air along one cheek; the others were wide, for Ed reined the pony from side to side as he flashed out past the stores and in under the overhanging cottonwoods. He put the horse across the dirt walk, ran the depth of a vacant lot, and made the alley. Beyond the last house he swung back onto the west trail and let the palomino run.

Twenty-five minutes later he was thanking Simon Uhling for his love of fine horseflesh and reining in a badly blown animal for the twisting in the trail that would take him down off the rim and into the Basin. Far behind, barely in sight, the horses of the pursuing posse laid a smoky line of dust across the horizon.

He trotted the horse the mile to the banks of Brush Creek. A hundred rods beyond the stream he rounded the high shoulder of a hill and abruptly left the trail. His last glance behind, to the rim, showed him that the trail was clear. A quarter mile to the south, still hidden from the rim trail by the hill, he put the horse down the steep bank of a deep wash and came out of the saddle. He threw the reins around a thick finger of sandstone rock that jutted from the bed of the wash and climbed back up the bank, taking off his Stetson and sitting so that he could see the line of the trail where it cut straight into the west beyond the hill.

In the next ten minutes he built and smoked a cigarette. The morning glare of the sun was making it uncomfortably hot. When he had flicked the butt of his smoke into the sand behind him, he could hear the muffled hoof pound of the oncoming posse. In another half minute they suddenly appeared from behind the shoulder of the hill. Simon Uhling and Kip Ison led the fourteen riders, with Milo Peers trailing a good hundred yards behind the last man, well out of the boil of dust the others kicked up.

Ed smiled at that sight of Sands' sheriff. He wondered how much Milo had guessed, for he saw the lawman looking to right and left, paying scant attention to his posse up ahead. Perhaps the sheriff knew that his threat of burning out Uhling was all bluff.

Finally they were out of sight beyond a far rise, Peers's spare figure the last to disappear. Ed slid down the bank and spent five minutes unlacing the rawhide thongs that held the stirrups and letting them down a notch to suit his long leg reach. Then, in the saddle once more, he climbed the palomino up the far bank of the wash and made a wide circle back toward Brush Creek, fording the stream a full mile below the point where the main trail crossed it. Two hundred yards east of the stream he rode into the wagon road he had traveled last night and turned down it toward the lower end of the valley.

He swung wide of Frank Tarbe's place, and at the turning the road made to head in toward Pace's layout he stopped at the sight of a buckboard and two men working in the yard before the cabin. He quickly reined into the concealment of a low-growing clump of cedar, and from there watched Milo Peers's deputy and Uhling's borrowed crewman load Pace's tarpaulin-wrapped body into the bed of the buckboard. Later, as the team of bays trotted past pulling the buckboard, Ed was behind the crest of a knoll less than fifty yards above the road.

With the buckboard finally out of sight, he crossed the creek and rode up to the cabin and spent ten minutes in futile search for some telltale sign that would give him anything to work on in guessing who had done the killing. Even the hoof prints he had noticed near the door by the light of the lantern last night were now obliterated by fresher hoof and boot prints.

Without having found anything to help him, he at length struck south from the cabin, keeping to the west bank of the creek. He followed the willow brakes of the stream some five miles and there rode in between climbing rock walls that formed the beginnings of a cañon. Twenty miles to the south, beyond a tangle of uptilted barren hills and rocky buttes, lay a broad expanse of desert, backed in the far distance by a heat-shimmering and purple line of high mountains. This cañon into which the thin trickle of Brush Creek emptied made a twisting line down through the badlands all the way to the desert.

At midday Ed was halfway the length of the cañon. In ten miles its walls had taken on a sheer height of some two hundred feet, and here, around a sharp turning, he came abruptly within sight of a high railroad trestle spanning the cañon, the timbers crisscrossing the chasm to look like the web of some giant spider. On the east side, high above, the twin lines of steel entered the black maw of a tunnel.

He came out of the saddle at the mouth of a narrow brush-filled offshoot of the cañon fifty yards short of the trestle footings. He tied the palomino in the shade of a mesquite thicket. Nearby, he scooped a hollow in the sand and stretched out in the heat-relieving shade of a juniper. In two minutes he was asleep.

CHAPTER
SIX

Ed was awake an hour before sundown. He looped the palomino's reins over the saddle horn, slapped the animal across the rump, and watched while he trotted off upcañon. It took Ed ten minutes to climb to the high built-up right of way that led from the trestle to the tunnel. He saw immediately that its steep sides and the narrow roadbed wouldn't suit his purpose. He looked beyond and through the hundred-yard-long tunnel that cut through the high pinnacle hill of solid rock, deciding he might find a better place at the other end. He walked through the tunnel and met the same obstacle there, a narrow and high roadbed that left no room to either side so that a man might find secure footing alongside a moving train. Another trestle spanned a shallower gorge on this side of the hill. Beyond, the rails cut through a steep-sided V-wedge cut out of the shoulder of a low and rounded rise.

In the end, he climbed up the side of the steep and rocky slope to a point directly over the tunnel, where he worked down low enough so that he judged the drop to be no more than eight feet. He waited there.

Dusk was thickening the shadows in the gorge below when he finally caught the labored panting of the locomotive coming into the upgrade on the other side of the hill behind him. He heard the rumble of the heavy trucks as the train crossed the long span of the trestle, then the muffled pound of the exhaust as it entered the short tunnel.

In another quarter minute the locomotive emerged suddenly below him, engulfing him in a blinding cloud of sooty black smoke. When the smoke had cleared enough for him to see what lay below again, the second coach of the train was slipping halfway out of the tunnel. He jammed his Stetson down on his head and jumped.

He landed hard, and with his momentum against that of the train his feet were swept from under him, and he fell backward. For one interminable moment he thought he would roll off, but then his reaching hands closed over the rounded ventilator ridge of the coach roof and held on. He rode that way across the hundred-foot drop of the trestle. When the train finally slid through the notch in the hill beyond, gathering speed, he got to his feet and walked gingerly to the front end of the car and climbed down onto the platform between the cars.

He met the surprised conductor immediately inside the door of the coach and paid him eighty cents, his fare in to Sands, explaining: "Never trust a horse not to run away on you while your back's turned." He had an amused chuckle as his answer and then went down the aisle between the two rows of green plush seats, studying the faces of the passengers in the swaying light of the kerosene lamps.

The faces were mostly weather burned, those of men and women and children of this country. Some were gazing out the dust-grimed windows, others were asleep, heads rolling gently to the swaying of the car's motion as the train held its scant speed on a second long upgrade out of the badlands.

He lifted the newspaper off the face of one man in a dark suit and said — "My mistake." — as the passenger opened his eyes and glared balefully up at him. He went on, didn't find the face he was looking for in that car, and crossed the platform at the rear and went into the next coach. In the third seat to the left he saw a man outfitted in an expensive suit of blue serge and a clean white shirt. The man's face was pallid compared to those of the other passengers. Ed approached the seat, said — "Mister Dunn?" — and sat down when he received an answering nod.

"I'm Ed January," he announced as he faced Dunn, the sheep company buyer. "Thought I might be able to save you some trouble. It's about that wire you sent Pace. I wanted to talk to you about it. Town's a bad place for me lately, so I decided to meet you on the way in."

Dunn seemed all at once to place him. He smiled and said pleasantly: "Glad to meet you, January. Not that I should be. You've held us up from the beginning."

"That's just it, Dunn. Pace lied to get you in here. I'm not selling."

Dunn straightened against the cushion, a flush of anger riding into his face. "You're not!" he blustered.

"Then why did Pace promise me? I've spent good time and money to make this trip."

Ed shrugged his shoulders. "I understand all that. You can fight it out with the rest of them . . . Frank Tarbe and the others. But Pace is dead. He was murdered last night."

Dunn's look changed to one of incredulity. "Pace dead?" he echoed.

Ed lifted his long frame out of the seat and stood in the aisle to say: "That's only the beginning. You'd have a war on your hands if you brought sheep in here. But the main thing is, my spread isn't for sale. So get yourself a ticket back to Tucson and forget the whole thing."

Dunn said feebly: "But why wasn't I informed about this? Why . . . ?"

"I'm sorry about that," Ed said, and turned to go. Then a thought made him hesitate, and he told the sheepman: "In case anyone meets you, I'd consider it a favor if you didn't mention seein' me."

Dunn made no answer, seeming too bewildered to find one. Ed went on down the aisle and out the car's rear door. This coach was the end one of the train, and Ed stood braced against the railing on the platform. The rhythm of the iron wheels over the rail gaps clicked shorter spaced as the train made the top of the grade and left the badlands behind to cut a straight line across the level stretch of prairie toward Sands. In the next few minutes the light along the jagged horizon to the west faded in a dying blaze of bright orange, and soon it was night with the myriad stars winking down out of the heavens. The air had a brisk chill in it now.

Forty minutes later, Ed swung down off the train as it rattled past the loading pens below Sands' station. He skirted the corrals and crossed the road beyond them and walked in through a vacant lot and to the alley that backed the stores. Once he froze into the shadow of a woodshed as the back door to a store opened and a man came out to dip a pail of water from a barrel that sat less than ten feet out from where he stood. Farther along he had to stand motionless in a narrow aisle between two buildings as a pair of riders walked their horses down the alley. Finally he let himself in through the gate of the horse corral behind the livery barn and walked soundlessly toward the dark rectangle of the barn's huge rear door.

A light buggy halfway along the center runway hid him from sight of the hostler, who sat back tilted in a chair against the wall of his office close to the doors up front, a lantern hanging from a peg above his head. Ed climbed the ladder to the loft. Loose-piled hay stood knee deep above the ladder. Ed whistled softly.

Immediately he heard a rustle of sound farther toward the front, and Tom Gault's voice spoke in a hoarse whisper from up there: "It's about time."

A match flared alight, and Ed walked over to where his friend stood near a mound of baled alfalfa, the expression on his face one of mixed relief and tension. The match's flame died out, and Tom said: "Where'd you go?"

Ed told him, and Tom listened in silence, saying when Ed had finished: "You believe in goin' to a lot of trouble to have a five-hundred-dollar reward posted on you?"

"Uhling?"

"Who else would it be? Him and Ison and Milo Peers had me on the carpet for a whole hour late this afternoon. Wantin' to know where you'd gone, what Helen Atwood was talkin' to you about this mornin'."

"Who wanted to know that?" Ed asked sharply.

"They all did."

"But who thought of it first?"

Tom took a long moment to give his answer. "Damned if I remember." Then, more irritably: "What does it matter who thought of it first? You'd better be thinkin' about gettin' a fast horse under you and makin' it across the desert tomorrow."

"This is important, Tom. Try and remember. Who asked about Helen Atwood?"

A longer silence fell this time. "It was either Uhling or Ison, I don't know which," Tom mused. "All I know is that after they finished with me, Ison went across to the restaurant and talked to the girl."

"Did she tell him anything?"

Tom said: "Uhn-uh. I asked her about it when I went there for supper. You think one of them framed you?"

"I'm too hungry to think," Ed answered after a moment. "Any chance of your bringin' me a meal?"

"I can try," Tom said. Then, more urgently: "Ed, pull out of this. Let me sell the layout and you get across a state line until I've wound this up. Hell, there's a dozen places you could get a new start with the money Uhling will lay on the line."

"Back at it again?" Ed drawled. "You ought to know me well enough to quit that talk, Tom."

Gault swore under his breath and came down off his perch. Ed said: "Take your time about bringing the food across. First, go to the hotel and see if Dunn's registered. Find out if Frank Tarbe and his bunch are in town to meet him. When you go to the restaurant, ask the girl if she can turn her place over to her cook and take the day off tomorrow. I'd like to take a sashay up that cañon where old Bill died. If she wants to come, tell her to be across here about five in the morning. I'll borrow a couple of horses for the day."

Tom said angrily: "You'll fool around until you slip your head in a noose. Who cares how Bill Atwood cashed in? You tend to your own knittin'."

"Ever follow a hunch, Tom?"

"Not your hunches. They're good for too much trouble. If you hadn't met Ison last night, you wouldn't have had Uhling in the open against you. If you hadn't gone to Pace's, they'd be making someone else the goat. I'd say your hunches stink."

"There's two ways of looking at it, Tom," Ed drawled, and added: "Try and be back in an hour."

Tom was gone better than an hour. During that interval, Ed heard the high double doors of the stable roll shut below, and later the muted creak of the hostler's cot from the office. He climbed over the high mound of baled alfalfa and looked out the dusty front window and down onto the street, seeing that the walks were practically deserted; the town had turned in for the night, with only an occasional straggler homeward bound along the street. While he stood there, he saw the lights go out in the windows of the Gem and knew the time to be eleven, for Pinto Mundorff was punctual in closing at that hour. A few minutes later, he caught Tom's low whistle far back along the loft and went back there to take the pail of food his friend had brought him.

While he ate the tasty hot stew with the spoon he found inside the pail, Tom told him: "She'll be over at five, earlier if you want. She's stubborn as you are. Says she knows her old man was murdered. She's even made a guess as to why. If Bill Atwood found all the gold she thinks he did, he could have bought this range out twice over."

"She might be right, at that."

Gault snorted in derision. "But why worry yourself with her troubles?"

"Here's why. Old Bill died in one of the cañons north of the layout, you say, which means it was on my land. Besides that, someone wants my place, *who* we don't know. Couldn't the . . . ?"

"The hell we don't. Uhling wants it. The sheep outfit wants it."

"All right, answer this. Why would an honest bunch of cattle raisers, Pace and Tarbe and the others, ever get the idea of sellin' out to sheep? Who gave 'em the idea? No one of 'em would have got it by themselves, and no sheep company is goin' to pay more than their places are worth . . . more than they could get from anyone else."

"Then what's the answer?"

"Whoever started this . . . and I don't know who it is . . . wants to either crowd up the price on the Basin to more than Uhling's got or he wants me out of the way. Why I'm not sure. But if Bill Atwood was killed and didn't die a natural death, then we can be damned sure he knew something he shouldn't. Whoever killed him wants my place. The same gent framed me with Pace's murder to drive me out."

"It may be Dunn who wants it."

"Dunn's never been in this country," Ed said. "This is his first trip here."

"Well, at least he's decided to stay," Tom said. "He's registered at the hotel, and he sent a man down here to hire a rig to drive him out to the Basin tomorrow. It'll have to be an ore wagon, from what they say about his size. He must be the biggest thing that ever walked on two legs."

"Big?" Ed echoed. "He's about your size, not so heavy."

"Uhn-uh. You're talkin' about the wrong gent. They say . . ." Abruptly Tom broke off, then asked quickly: "Who the hell was it you saw on the train?"

"Dunn."

"You talked to the wrong man."

"No. He knew all about Pace, about me. He was Dunn, all right."

"Then who's the fat gent at the hotel that says he's Dunn?"

"You guess. I'm tryin' to."

Tom was silent for a moment. Then: "You sure about this, Ed?"

"Plenty sure."

"Then what does it all add up to?"

"It's a cinch no man would claim he was Dunn unless he was getting something out of it. We've got to find out what that something is. Tom," Ed went on with excitement edging his tones, "this may be the break we've needed. A man that isn't what he claims to be settles down at the hotel and gets ready to do business on buying the Basin. You've got your job cut out."

"What?"

"Get a room at the hotel. Watch this fat gent. See if he's got any credentials of any kind. Let him know who you are. You say he's hired a rig to take him out to the Basin tomorrow. All right, offer to drive him out there, to show him around. Get real friendly with him. Tell him you know how to get in touch with me. See how much he'll offer for my layout."

"Then what?"

"Maybe I'll see him and use a little persuadin' to make him talk. I'll be back here tomorrow night to see what you've found out."

"You mean you *may* get back. I wouldn't bet either way."

Ed ignored Tom's skepticism, and said after a moment: "Wonder what happened to the real Dunn?"

"What's your guess?"

"That he's playin' a two-handed stud game with Les Pace about now . . . unless he stayed on the train and went on through."

CHAPTER
SEVEN

E. J. Dunn, vice president of the Middle Arizona Sheep Company, got off the train with three other passengers. After his brief but potent talk with Ed January, he was still undecided about what to do. The first thing, of course, was to wire Tucson and explain the circumstances. By noon tomorrow he'd have an answer and know what the others thought about his staying and making any further effort to buy out the Basin.

He was halfway across the platform, headed for the telegrapher's office, when a deep-toned voice behind him said: "You Mister Dunn?"

The sheepman turned and faced a short individual of ponderous proportions. The fat man wore a neatly-trimmed Van Dyke beard, his dark serge suit was shiny at the seams, and the trousers showed no sign of a crease. His flowing black tie hung down over a shirt that had once been white but was now slightly grayed and dirty where it sloped out across his expansive paunch.

But the loose-jowled face wore a genial smile that was reflected in an amused pair of dark brown eyes, and Dunn answered politely enough: "That's the name."

The fat man extended his hand, saying: "Allow me to present myself. Horace J. Appleby, attorney-at-law. I represent Lester Pace."

Dunn took the outstretched hand and was surprised, on grasping it, to feel that the two middle fingers were missing. But the fat man's grip was hearty, and he didn't seem annoyed at Dunn's obvious and sudden embarrassment over his maimed hand, so Dunn said: "Glad to meet you." He frowned then, went on: "You mean you represent Pace? I understand he's dead."

The fat man nodded. "Unfortunate, most unfortunate," he said a trifle pompously. "But that needn't interfere with your purchase of his property. I hold full power of attorney."

"And what about January?" Dunn asked.

The fat man seemed startled, but said easily enough: "I can help you with that, too. Here, sir," — he reached out and took Dunn's cowhide suitcase — "let me carry this for you. We'll have to walk to the hotel."

His manner was so affable and disarming that Dunn forgot his understandable misgivings and followed him around the far corner of the station and along a cinder path that led through a vacant lot to the street. Dunn remembered his intention of sending a telegram but decided finally that he would wait until morning and act on what information the lawyer could give him.

They were halfway between the station and the line of shadowy trees that marked the street when Dunn caught a whisper of sound behind him that might have been a man's boots slurring against the cinders. He looked back over his shoulder. He had a quick vision of a man's tall shape almost close enough to reach out and touch. Then the down-whipping blow of a six-gun handle crushed in the top of his skull, and his hands made a feeble attempt to rise, and he slumped backward into his assailant's arms, dead before he could cry out.

"Take his legs," said the man who had struck the blow. The fat man shifted Dunn's cowhide suitcase to his good hand, wrapped his arms about the dead sheepman's legs, and they carried him out across the vacant lot and along the road skirting the siding and finally into the end pen of the long line of cattle corrals.

Two saddled horses stood hip shot and tied to the top bar of the corral. The fat man said: "Hurry it, Slim! Get his papers."

Slim went through Dunn's pockets, handing up a sheaf of papers, some small change, a gold watch, and finally a fat wallet. The fat man pocketed everything. They worked in silence, lifting the dead man and throwing him across the saddle of one of the horses as though this had all been prearranged.

"Go ahead and get up the street," Slim said, and started lashing the body to the saddle with a length of rope.

The fat man picked up the suitcase and left the corral, hurrying out across the vacant lot and then down the dirt walk of the street. He stopped in front of the first lighted store window he came to and took Dunn's papers from his pocket and hastily examined them. He put the watch in his vest pocket and then went on, slowing his waddling stride as he came in sight of the hotel. He smiled a little at hearing the coughing pound of the train as it pulled out of the station.

He was climbing the hotel steps, when Kip Ison, sitting in a chair alongside Milo Peers on the verandah, said: "That must be him, Sheriff. Better tell him."

Peers got up out of his chair and came over to the head of the steps, asking: "Are you Dunn, from Tucson?"

The fat man nodded, smiled, held out a hand. "E. J. Dunn, Sheriff." He looked down at the five-pointed star on Peers's vest.

The lawman took the hand reluctantly, receiving the same uncomfortable shock Dunn had had on noticing the two missing fingers on the fat man's hand. "We've got a disappointment for you," he said. "Your friend, Pace, died yesterday."

"You don't say! Sorry to hear it," the fat man said, his face showing the proper amount of surprise. "Who's managing his affairs?"

"No one, yet," Peers said. "But there's more bad news. Ed January isn't sellin' his place. That is, it's doubtful if you'll be able to see him. We had him in jail under suspicion of murderin' Pace. He broke out. He's gone."

The fat man's face reddened. "Then I've had this trip for nothing?" he flared. "Why wasn't I informed?"

"There ain't been time," Peers said mildly. "This all happened in pretty short order."

Ison, who had sauntered over to stand behind Peers, said: "There's a train back to Tucson in the mornin'."

The fat man's angry glance whipped over to Ison. "I'll remember that," he said curtly. Then, to Peers: "I'll want your help, Sheriff. I'm going ahead with this, buying whatever land is for sale in the Basin. If necessary, we'll lease a driveway through January's place to get to our summer graze."

Ison laughed softly. "You think you will."

The fat man glared at Ison a moment, then ignored him and picked up his suitcase and went in through the door. He registered, and the clerk took him upstairs to a room at the front end of the hall.

Two minutes later the fat man had his vest and coat off, collar unbuttoned, and was sitting in a rocker with his feet on the room's center table, examining the papers he'd taken from Dunn's pockets and several more that came out of the suitcase.

One interested him particularly. It was a letter of credit on a Tucson bank, to the amount of ten thousand dollars, and was signed by Dunn. After examining it a long moment, and staring vacantly at the wall beyond the table for a longer one, the fat man abruptly took his feet down and crossed to the door and locked it.

Back at the table again, he found a rusty pen and a nearly empty bottle of pale blue ink in the drawer. He sat down, uncorked the ink, and started writing **E. J. Dunn** over and over again on the back of an envelope, comparing his efforts with the signature on the letter of credit. As he worked, a beady perspiration came to his broad forehead.

His penmanship at first bore no similarity to the signature he was trying to copy. But when both sides of the envelope were filled with his tightening scrawl, after he'd filled one side of a blank sheet of paper he found among Dunn's possessions, his writing bore a fair resemblance to Dunn's. Finally it bore a close one; at the end of a forty-minute interval it was nearly perfect.

He was hunched over the table, paunch folding out over the edge and hard at work when a knock sounded at the door. A trace of panic came to the fat man's beady eyes. He hastily folded the scrap paper and the letter of credit. He got up out of the chair, thrust the papers into his pocket, put the ink and pen back into the drawer, and went over to unlock the door.

When Kip Ison edged into the room, the fat man was smiling blandly.

Ison closed the door behind him. "Nice work, Tombstone," he said, laughing softly. "The sheriff took it whole hog." He crossed casually to the table, saw Dunn's papers, and picked them up. "Find anything interestin' on Dunn?"

Tombstone produced the wallet, handed it across. "Just this. There's enough there to get started on."

Ison counted the money, and, when he looked across at Tombstone, his dark brows were gathered in a frown. "No letter to the bank?"

Tombstone shook his head. He took his coat from the back of the rocker beside the bed, fished a few more papers from the inside pocket, and tossed them to the table. "Nothing to the bank here."

Ison's inspection of the papers didn't ease his frown. When he had finished, he counted the money in the wallet. "This'll have to do us, then. There's only a little over a thousand here. Go to a lawyer in the morning, get him to make you out some sixty-day option forms, and then get on out to the Basin. See Frank Tarbe first and get him to take you to the others. Pay a hundred for each option, no more."

"What about this Ed January?"

Ison thought a long moment. "Gault will be around town. Get acquainted with him and make him an offer. He'll see that it gets to January sooner or later. If we make it hot for January, he'll have to let his spread go. And by now he hates Uhling's guts bad enough to sell out this range to sheep. Uhling's offered him five thousand. You're to offer six for a quick sale. We'll use Dunn's money for a down payment. I'll arrange the rest through the bank."

"And what comes then?"

"He'll make the deed over to you. You're to practice on Dunn's signature and be able to write it well enough to pass it off at the recording office, when you sign it over to me. You'll get your pay and get out after that. Disappear. We'll let those other options go."

Tombstone smiled and said: "Damned if you haven't thought of everything, Kip. What's behind it all?"

"You're not drawin' your money to ask questions," Ison drawled, regarding the fat man pointedly as he crossed to the door. "But if we pull this off without any slips, I'll put you wise to something that'll make every dollar you can lay your hands on grow one hell of a big family." He started to open the door, but paused to add: "I won't be in until noon tomorrow. See you then."

Ison used the alley door in leaving the hotel. His black gelding was tied to a cottonwood two hundred yards out in a pasture that ran back from the outbuildings beyond the alley. He made a wide circle to the west trail and an hour and a quarter later was riding down on the grove of poplars and an orchard that marked Uhling's ranch headquarters. It lay at the foot of a grass-blanketed hill several miles beyond the western edge of the Basin. He walked the last hundred yards into the layout, circled the wagon shed, and went certainly through the darkness to what appeared to be a mound of earth near the orchard fence. It was a root cellar, and he pulled open the stubborn heap to the sunken door as soundlessly as he could and went inside. He used one match to locate a small keg in one corner.

He tossed the match aside and lifted the keg and hefted it. Then he went out of the cellar, closed the door, and walked back the way he had come. On the ride back to town, the keg made an awkward and unsteady weight balanced across his thighs. But he was in no hurry and took his time, finally riding in under the same cottonwood in the pasture behind the alley. He tied the black there and took the keg and walked with it in toward the alley. He turned down the alley in the direction of Helen Atwood's restaurant.

CHAPTER
EIGHT

Ed was awake at four-thirty the next morning, seeing the first faint gray light of dawn through the murky window at the front of the stable loft. He stood up in his makeshift bed of hay, stretched, and stepped over to the window to look out onto the street. Faintly visible blue smoke was coming from the chimney at the rear of Helen Atwood's restaurant. There was a light behind the drawn shade of the window of her second-floor room. Ed was all at once impatient to be started, realizing that the hostler in the livery office below would be awake before long.

He climbed across the mound of baled alfalfa, went down the ladder, and felt his way through the darkness to the saddle rail halfway along the runway toward the front of the barn. As quietly as he could, he carried first one saddle, and then another, to the small door set in the closed larger one that opened onto the corral out back. Once a cinch ring striking a bare steel stirrup made a sharp sound in the stillness to bring the hackles rising up along his neck. He stood motionless a full minute, breathing shallowly, listening for a sound from the office. None came, and only when he had the saddles on the ground beside him in the corral, did he breathe easily once more.

He picked two good horses, a bay and a claybank, and had them saddled and hidden in a deserted barn behind a vacant house far out toward the edge of town before it was light enough for him clearly to distinguish objects more than fifty yards away. That done, he went back along the alley and started along the passageway between the feed barn and the neighboring building, heading toward the street to watch for Helen.

He was halfway the length of the passageway when a sudden concussion beat the still air. A fraction of a second later the muffled thud of an earth-jarring explosion ripped away the early morning silence. He broke into a run and came onto the street in time to see a pluming fog of smoke and dust dotted with falling débris above the rear of Helen Atwood's restaurant. A woman's shrill scream turned his blood to ice as he raced on across the street and along the side of the restaurant toward the alley in back.

The main building of the restaurant was a two-story affair, a room on each floor, the lower one serving as the lunchroom, the upper as Helen Atwood's living quarters. Adjoining the rear was the thin-walled frame kitchen directly flanking the alley. Running toward it, Ed saw that the side wall of the kitchen was now a mass of outthrust and splintered boards, most of them torn in two. He had to push aside two boards to edge through the narrow space and into the alley. And from there he could see the gaping hole in the kitchen's rear wall, the litter of dented pots and pans inside, pieces of jagged iron that had once been the stove, the sagging and broken tarpaper roof and the zinc sink twisted out of shape and lying in a far corner. But the thing that held his attention the longest was what appeared to be a bundle of bloody rags lying in the open doorway to the lunchroom, that and the downthrust and jagged ends of broken planks that had once formed a stairway leading up out of the kitchen to the girl's room above.

He stood there for long seconds, in a paralysis of stark fear, when all at once he heard Helen Atwood's voice call frantically from above: "Ling! Ling, where are you? Are you all right?"

Then two things happened so quickly that Ed acted on instinct alone. First, the kitchen roof, unsupported now, gave way and crashed into the wreckage in a smother of dust to give him a fleeting glimpse of Helen Atwood, alive, drawing back out of the doorway of her upstairs room. Next, at the limits of his vision, he saw a shadowy figure come through the gate of the picket fence behind the hotel. He turned and ran back along the alley and in behind a lean-to in time to keep from being seen.

He worked his way back behind the outbuildings and into sight of the restaurant again to see George Clevenger, night clerk of the Plains House, lean a ladder against the rear wall and call up to Helen Atwood: "Ling's dead. Thank God it wasn't you, miss!"

Before the girl had climbed down the ladder, the sound of men running along the street and alley warned Ed to move away. Satisfied that Helen hadn't been hurt and relieved to think that he hadn't given away his presence here, he went back to the loft of the stable to wait. On his way in through the rear door he noticed that the front ones were open now, that the office door stood open. The hostler had evidently joined the crowd gathering across the street in the alley. From the window of the loft, he saw men cross and recross the street, going in through the front of the restaurant.

An hour passed. As the first full light of the morning sun slanted down the street, a group of people moved out of the restaurant door and formed two lines out across the walk. Four bareheaded men emerged from the restaurant doorway, carrying a large oblong box between them. In the box, Ed decided, was the crushed and torn body of Ling, the Chinese cook who had served the last three owners of the eating establishment.

The next two hours dragged endlessly. Ed remembered the two horses tied in the deserted barn at the edge of town and decided he'd let the hostler make his own guesses on where they were. He might need one of them later on, and the barn was as good a place for them as the livery corral. He stood at the window, trying to get a glimpse of Tom Gault. Dozens of men he knew came and went from the restaurant; he saw Milo Peers and Helen Atwood several times. Then, as the glare of the sun was making the heat in the loft close to unbearable, he had a momentary glimpse of Tom Gault hurrying down the opposite walk.

Half a minute later, Tom's head was appearing through the ladder opening to the loft. His friend was out of breath and had a worried look on his face.

Before Ed could put the question uppermost in his mind, Tom was saying: "I got here as quick as I could. Get set for a jolt, Ed."

"I saw part of it. It was supposed to be the girl instead of the Chinaman, wasn't it?"

"That's the only thing it could be. She gets up every morning and has the fire built by the time Ling gets to work. Only this morning she'd asked him to come early. He built the fire. Something in the stove blew it clean to hell, him along with it. I couldn't eat my breakfast, thinkin' about it."

"Has Peers any ideas?"

"He don't say much . . . except that you might have been mixed up in it."

Ed said: "For a while there it looked like Milo was part human. Now I'm not so sure. When this is all over, I'll have a few things to say to him."

"All over!" Tom said bitterly. "Hell, it'll never be over, not for us, anyway. First it's Tarbe and Pace against us. Then Uhling and his understrapper. Now the sheriff's put in his oar. And there's Dunn."

"The fat man? What about him?"

"You tell me. That's why I took so long gettin' here." He rubbed his bandanna over his perspiring face and let out a sigh. "I can't get next to what he's doin'. I watched him like you said. He was in the crowd over there at the restaurant for a while. Then he went across to the bank when it opened. He went straight to old man Jessup's office and was in there a half hour. I asked a few questions and found out he was cashin' a letter of credit or some such thing from a Tucson bank. He left the place with ten thousand dollars that Jessup gave him. From there, he headed for the station. He's down there now."

"On his way out?" Ed's look had become sharper.

Tom shrugged his shoulders. "He didn't check out at the hotel. His grip's still in his room, as far as I know. Maybe he's down there waitin' for the morning papers to come in. There's a train due in twenty minutes."

"We know he isn't Dunn. If you'd just cashed a letter of credit that wasn't yours, for ten thousand dollars, what would you do?"

Tom said: "I'd get the hell out of here."

"And with every man, woman, and child in town across the street looking over the restaurant, it wouldn't be hard to leave without being seen, would it?"

Tom's blunt face took on a frown. "What're you drivin' at?"

"That we'd better get down there and have a talk with our fat friend."

"And get caught doin' it?" Tom laughed dryly. "Can't you get it through your thick head that there's about three hundred people around here who'd jump at the chance of collectin' the reward on you? You're done here, Ed. You don't dare show yourself."

"We're not licked if we can make this gent talk, are we? All I know is he's not what he claims to be. If we can throw a scare into him and make him talk, we'll . . ."

"And how're you goin' to make that barrel o' guts give up what he knows?"

"We'll see," Ed said. "Get down there to the station and tell him who you are. Tell him you've found me and that I'm ready to sell. So long as he says he's Dunn, he's got to act interested. I'll be waiting down below the station by the water tank." Ed started toward the loft opening. "I'm not takin' much of a chance."

Tom let out a gusty sigh and grunted: "If you wasn't runnin' a chance, you wouldn't be doin' it. But go ahead. I've done all I could to stop you."

CHAPTER
NINE

Tombstone paced restlessly along the station platform, trying to hide his uneasiness and getting more nervous every minute. Each time he came to the end of the platform, he'd look out along the cinder path that led to the street to see if anyone was coming. He lit a cigar, and he was fond of good tobacco; but right now the taste was flat and bitter, and he threw the cigar away after only two drags on it.

He was hot but didn't dare remove his coat because of the spring-holster he was wearing at his armpit. Time and again he took off his flat-crowned hat and wiped the perspiration from his face and head. In five minutes' time he had looked at his watch — actually E. J. Dunn's watch — twice, and each time shook it and put it to his ear to make sure it was running.

Finally he went to the open window of the ticket agent's office and asked: "Where the hell's that train?"

"I told you she was late, mister. Be here in ten minutes."

Tombstone resumed his pacing. From time to time his maimed hand, the two middle fingers missing, would edge up to feel a bulge along his coat front made by an object in the inside coat pocket; this gesture seemed to reassure him each time, but only momentarily.

Tombstone saw Tom Gault turn from the street into the station path and come along it. He stopped his pacing and waited for Tom's approach with his eyes taking on the hard flintiness of mixed suspicion and wariness. Then, when Tom came straight up to him, every muscle in his ponderous frame was tense and cocked, and his face set in a bleak scowl.

"You're Dunn, ain't you?" Tom queried.

Tombstone nodded.

"I'm Gault. I hear you're lookin' for January."

Over his relief, Tombstone said: "I was. Why?"

"I located him for you. He's waitin' up the tracks a ways."

Tombstone's eyes mirrored a momentary indecision. Then he said hurriedly: "I'm through here, giving the whole thing up. I shouldn't have made this trip. And I won't have any dealings with a wanted man."

"But if January'd sell, it'd square things, wouldn't it?"

Tombstone saw it coming and said angrily: "I tell you I'm through. I don't want anything more to do with this."

"But Ed's ready to pull out, Dunn. He's got his deed. He'll let the layout go for eight thousand."

Tombstone shook his head. "It's too risky."

"Why?"

Tombstone had to hesitate a moment to think of an answer. "Because we can't use the Basin. There's too much trouble connected with it!"

"You're singin' a different tune than you were to Pace. What's a little trouble to a big outfit like yours?

The Basin's the best sheep range you'll ever lay eyes on. Now that January's comin' around, you got a chance you'll never see again. Better take it."

Tombstone half turned to look out along the sun-glinting ribbons of steel that cut a straight long line toward the far horizon. He felt an immediate relief in seeing the train, an inch-long black worm, crawling with painful slowness through the distance.

Into the short silence, Tom said: "Hell, it won't hurt to talk to Ed, even if you ain't doin' business with him."

Tombstone took out his watch and looked at it. "All right," he said gruffly. "I'll give him two minutes."

"It'll only take one." Tom started down the platform. "He's out here by the water tank."

Tombstone followed, scowling darkly and eyeing Tom's back with a harried glance. They left the platform, skirted a tool shed, and followed the line of a siding in past a string of boxcars and flatcars and abruptly came to the weathered red water tank.

Ed stood leaning against one of the tank's thick timber legs. His thumbs were hooked in his belt; his lean face was hard chiseled beneath its two-day crop of beard. His eyes were fixed stonily on the fat man as he approached.

"Here he is, Ed."

Tombstone stopped a few feet short of Ed and began — "I told Gault I didn't want . . ." — when Ed's slow drawl cut him short.

"Easy, fat man. Save your wind. I want to know who you are, who brought you in here. And I want to know damned quick!"

In a fraction of a second, Tombstone understood what he faced. He took a quick backward step, and his hand started up under his coat.

Ed pushed out from the tank timber and swung his right hand from the back of his knees. His fist caught Tombstone on the neck below his ear. The fat man stumbled, caught himself, and stayed on his feet. Ed stepped in and flicked a Smith and Wesson .44 from the holster beneath Tombstone's coat. In trying to snatch at Ed's hand, Tombstone lost his balance and sprawled heavily onto his side, his senses still reeling from the blow.

Ed tossed the six-gun in under the tank, where it splashed into the drippings that made a black pool of water in the sooty mud. "Get up," he said flatly.

Tombstone got slowly to his knees and then dove headlong at Ed's legs. Ed sidestepped, drove both fists in to rock the fat man's head from side to side. Tombstone fell sprawling, face down.

"Get him onto his feet," Ed told Tom.

Gault stepped over to Tombstone, took a hold beneath his armpits, and heaved him to his feet. Tombstone whirled with surprising speed and locked his arms about Tom's waist and bent him backward. Tom tried to jerk his arms free, couldn't. Ed drew his six-gun from holster, stepped in close, and struck a blow so that the weapon's barrel caught the fat man fully on one cheek.

Tombstone groaned, let go his hold on Tom, and snatched at the gun. Ed hit him with a hard left to the jaw. Tombstone's outreaching hand missed the gun, and he lurched sideways. Ed struck again, and his knuckles wiped Tombstone's broad nose sideways. Blood spurted from Tombstone's nostrils. He backed away and hung his head and let his nose drip onto the ground. He swore softly and reached for a bandanna in his hip pocket and put it to his nose.

Ed asked: "Ready to talk?"

"You can go to . . ."

Ed's fists knocked Tombstone's jaw shut and cut off the words. Tombstone staggered backward under the force of the blow, failed to get his feet under him, and sat down, sliding a few inches across the gravel.

The train's whistle howled out of the distance. Tombstone heard it vaguely as he struggled to his feet again. He looked up to see Ed's back-drawn arm, cocked for another blow. "Hold on!" he gasped.

Ed's hand came down.

"What is it you want of me?" Tombstone asked in a muffled sullen voice, speaking through the bloody bandanna he held pressed to his bleeding nose.

"Who brought you here?"

Tombstone sneered, thought better of it, and said: "What do I get if I tell?"

"You get to hop the train and go as far as you like."

Tombstone considered a moment. "All right," he said. "It was Ison."

Ed's look narrowed, and after a brief glance he said: "You've made a fair start. Now tell me what happened to Dunn."

Tombstone shook his head. "I wasn't in on that. All I know is he was slugged and loaded into a saddle. Ison

78

and Slim managed that, something about cavin' in a cutbank on him." The train whistle sounded again, much louder, and Tombstone glanced apprehensively toward the station. He said tonelessly: "I'm not missin' that train, January."

"You'll make it if you talk fast," Ed said. "What's Ison's game? What makes him so damned anxious to get my place?"

Tombstone smiled wryly. "Brother, when you find out, you tell me."

"Don't you know?"

"I don't know nothin'. I was brought in here to work a few days and get two hundred out of it. All Ison's told me is that, if I have any spare cash when this is over, he'll see to makin' it grow a hell of a big family."

Ed caught his breath. "He said that?"

"That's straight."

Ed breathed in suppressed excitement. "This is it, Tom!" Then he took a step toward Tombstone, held out a hand. "Where's the money?"

"What money?" Tombstone asked blandly, backing away a step.

"The ten thousand you got at the bank."

Suddenly Tombstone wheeled about and started running. Ed stuck out a boot and tripped him, and he went down, hitting the gravel. Ed stepped up to him and was reaching in under his coat when Tombstone clamped a hold on his wrist and yelled stridently — "Help! Help!" — in a voice loud enough to have carried to the center of town.

Ed hit him alongside the ear with his free hand. Tombstone ducked his head in between his shoulders but held on and bellowed once more — "Help!" — with his voice carrying loudly across to the houses that backed the railway yards.

Tom was close now and said urgently: "Beat it, Ed! There'll be a mob down here."

But Ed, pulled to his knees now, was reaching back to his holster. He spun out the six-gun so that he held it by the barrel, and tapped the fat man, not hard, above his ear. Tombstone's grip went loose. Ed's hand snaked in under his coat and drew the bulging wallet from the inside pocket.

As Ed came to his feet, Tom said: "Run for it. There's people comin'!"

"See you at the feed barn," Ed said, stuffing the wallet into his hip pocket and running in behind a flatcar. He was barely out of sight when two women appeared at the rear door of a house whose back yard flanked the tracks. Ed heard a man running toward him along the cinders and crawled under the car and out of sight as the station agent came running in answer to Tombstone's cries. He crawled to the other side of the siding, found himself between two lines of freight cars, and ran in toward the station. He hid behind the tool shed while another man ran past toward the water tank, and then sauntered casually along the platform and around the far end of the deserted station and past it as the train rumbled in. Once beyond the station he angled off obliquely behind a line of trees and through the back yard of a house and in toward the far end of the street. His last glimpse back toward the water tower showed him a group of people gathering there.

Once Ed was out of sight, Tom looked down at Tombstone and drawled: "By God, you sure wanted that money!"

Tombstone struggled to his feet, called once more loudly — "Help!" — and took a menacing step toward Tom.

Tom said: "I ain't got it, mister. You lay a hand on me and you won't be able to climb onto that train."

Tombstone heard the train. It was close, brakes squealing as it slowed past the station. He looked frantically around him as the station agent and then another man ran out from behind the string of cars and in toward him. Three women and two children were coming through the gate leading out of a neighboring back yard. Two other women and an old man were watching from beyond a fence close by.

The station agent came up, breathless, and asked curtly: "What's goin' on here?"

Tombstone, his face purple with rage, pointed at Tom. He had to yell to make himself heard over the noise of the train. "Him . . . him and his partner robbed me! Go look for him, damn it! He ran in along that siding!"

The locomotive came out from behind the line of cars on the siding with a roar of escaping steam and pounding drive wheels. The agent shouted above the riot of sound: "I just come from there. Didn't see no one." He glanced at Tom, shouted belligerently: "You know anything about this?"

Tom shrugged his shoulders and made a circular motion of his hand alongside his ear. "Drunk maybe," he said loudly. He stepped back and leaned against one of the tank supports. The locomotive ground to a stop, and the roar of the steam suddenly broke off. Tom added: "Found him flat on his face with a bloody nose."

"You been drinkin', mister?" The station agent eyed Tombstone coldly.

Tombstone looked helplessly around him. One of the youngsters who had come to look on was giggling, hand over his mouth. "Do something!" the fat man sputtered. His glance moved from one onlooker to the next. They were all smiling now.

Tom drawled: "You've got a train to catch, fat man."

"And I got things to do," the agent growled. He turned and walked back toward the station, in a hurry.

Tombstone's hostile glance whipped around and fixed on Tom. Tom reminded him: "These through trains never wait long at these tank towns. I'd hate to have you miss it and run into Ison. There ain't another till late this afternoon."

The locomotive's bell suddenly started its clanging. Sheer panic came into Tombstone's glance. He turned and started running up along the tracks toward the station. Tom stepped over alongside the tender and watched him. With a cough of smoke from its stack, the locomotive jerked at the train, started it slowly rolling. Tom saw Tombstone grab the hand rail of the first coach and swing with an awkward lurch up onto the step. The train rolled faster. As the platform between baggage car and passenger coach came even with him, Tom raised his hand. But Tombstone had his back turned.

In the loft of the feed barn twenty minutes later, Tom was saying in a low voice to Ed: "Hell, I just can't do it! It ain't fair to the girl."

"But I'll be there waiting. Nothing can happen to her. It's the only sure way."

Tom made one final protest. "Can't just the two of us do it alone?"

"You know how we could?"

Tom reluctantly shook his head. "All right," he said. "As soon as Ison rides in, I'll get started. But, damn it, how can you be so sure of this?"

"You heard what the fat man said, that Ison had promised to put him in the way of making some big money."

"That could mean anything."

"Not on top of what we know. Ison wants my place, wants it bad enough so that he murdered old Bill Atwood and then Dunn and probably Pace. We aren't guessin' from here on. Bill ran into something, and Ison caught him at it. The girl knew, even if everyone else was wearin' blinders. What Bill found must be on my land, or Ison wouldn't want it. He can file on anything north of my fence."

"And you think we have to go up there?"

"It's the only way we can get proof."

Tom shrugged his sloping shoulders and went over to the loft ladder. "Don't fumble anything," he said. "We'd be in a hell of a fix if you weren't there in time."

"I will be," Ed said, and added: "Remember, don't tell her about it before Ison hits town. She might give it away."

CHAPTER
TEN

Milo Peers and Helen Atwood came down the walk and turned in at the jail office at two that afternoon. As soon as the screen door banged shut, Peers said in a harried voice: "Now, Helen, for the love of God tell me what this is all about! I can't even get a start on it until you talk. You wouldn't this morning, and maybe you won't now. But I can try. Sit down."

She took the chair near the door, and he the swivel chair at his desk. He pushed his Stetson far back on his head and let out a weary sigh: "First, how come Ling built that fire this mornin', instead of you? Why was he there early?"

He saw Helen's glance go beyond him, saw sudden surprise come into her eyes, and then a widening strip of light fell out across the floor from the back of the room. He wheeled around in his chair, dropping his right hand to the holster at his thigh.

His move brought him face to face with the small bore of Ed January's .38 Colt. Ed kicked the alley door shut behind him. "Take it easy, Milo," he drawled. His eyes didn't stray from Peers as he said: "Helen, get on across the street and find Tom Gault. He's lookin' for you. He'll tell you what's up."

Helen came up out of the chair. She started to say something, thought better of it, and went out the door onto the walk.

The gladness that was in her made her obey Ed without questioning his motives. She had been worried about him and twice this morning had started across to the livery barn only to turn back on seeing that she was watched. Since then, she hadn't tried again, thinking he would be gone. Just now she had a moment of panic as she saw Kip Ison and two of his men ride their ponies up to the hitch rail in front of the hotel. She waited until Ison had sauntered on down to join the sprinkling of curious onlookers in front of the restaurant before she went on.

In the jail office, Ed was saying: "Shed the hardware and we'll be on our way, Milo. I'll feel better if you're de-horned before we start."

Peers said bluntly: "We ain't goin' any place that I know of."

Ed lifted a booted foot and kicked the swivel chair hard. The sheriff was caught by surprise, with his feet off the floor. The chair spun halfway around before he could stop it. Ed's hand dipped in under the chair arm and snatched the lawman's six-gun from holster.

Peers swung about savagely. Ed rocked open the loading gate of the Colt and punched the loads out of the cylinder as the sheriff glared up at him. Finished, he tossed the gun into Peers's lap and said: "You comin' along peaceable, or do I have to give you the same medicine Pinto Mundorff got the other night?"

"Comin' where?" Peers growled.

"You'll find that out. Better bring along a pair of handcuffs."

"Who says I'm goin' anywhere?"

Ed hefted his Colt in his palm. "Milo, you're thickheaded as hell this mornin'. Do you want to find out who killed Pace, who killed Bill Atwood?"

"Bill Atwood fell sixty feet onto some damned hard rock. That's what killed him. You know damned well who killed Pace!"

Ed smiled thinly. "You're wastin' my time. Are you comin' under your own power, or do I have to carry you?"

Peers saw that this wasn't a bluff. He jerked the brim of his Stetson lower over his eyes and got up out of the chair. Ed leathered his weapon, took down a rifle and a handful of shells from the rack over the desk, and indicated the alley door. As they went along the alley and out behind the bare yards of the first few houses, Peers said with only a trace of his customary rancor: "This had better be good, January."

"It's goin' to be."

Five minutes later they were in the saddle and riding the two livery horses west from town on a line parallel with the road that cut a straight line to the hazy flat horizon. January rode alongside Peers with the rifle cradled across his knees.

Kip Ison's first glimpse of Helen Atwood, from where he stood with the group of loungers on the walk before the restaurant, gave him a feeling of uneasiness mixed with an indefinable relief. Last night, after half filling the ash drawer of the restaurant stove with black powder, he'd once or twice been tempted to go back and remove it. But yesterday, when he was questioning the girl about her talk with January at the jail, she had asked him a question that added a new complication to his plans: "It was one of your men that found my father up that cañon, wasn't it? Did he say anything about that ledge . . . ?"

She had stopped there, and all his indirect urging had failed to draw out what she had been about to say. But it had been enough to plant a seed of suspicion in his mind, the thought that she knew more about her father's death than she was telling anyone . . . that is, anyone but Ed January.

Ison had made a shrewd guess that her conversation with January concerned the subject of Bill Atwood's death. And from there his reasoning had gone on to show him how dangerous the girl could be if she ever voiced her suspicions to anyone else — Peers, for instance. He had taken a direct method of removing this threat to the so far perfect operation of his plan and had planted the powder in the stove.

Now, seeing the girl alive, his relief was immediately put from his mind by the desire to see her, and this time to find out exactly what she knew. He left the fringes of the crowd and started out across the street to meet her. He saw her turn all at once off the opposite walk and come on across the street and go up the hotel steps. Tom Gault leaned against one of the roof pillars at the top of the steps. She stopped and talked with Gault.

Ison sauntered on down the dusty street and over to where his horse stood at the hotel tie rail. He took a clasp knife from his pocket and began fiddling with the rawhide lacing of a latigo. He heard Gault say to the girl: "You go change your clothes and I'll be here in about three minutes with the horses." Then Gault and the girl came down off the steps and went along the walk, and Gault crossed over it to the livery barn as the girl disappeared inside her restaurant.

When Helen reappeared five minutes later, having changed from her dress to a plain blue blouse, high-heeled boots, and a pair of men's denim trousers, Ison was once more loafing in front of the restaurant. The girl crossed the street and went into the feed barn. She and Gault mounted horses in the barn's runway and rode off a few moments later.

Ison stood watching them go along the street and finally out of sight beneath the low-spreading cottonwoods. He was asking himself where they could be going that would take them out the west trail. Could it be to January's place to meet January, who might have had the gall to hide out and not leave the country? Or had the girl talked to Gault, and was she taking him up into the cañon where Bill Atwood had died?

A sudden impatience took its hold on Ison. He hurried along the walk to where his gelding was tied. Slim, coming out of the hotel lobby, hailed him as he swung up into the saddle. Ison waited impatiently.

Slim came out across the walk with his thin face set bleakly. "Better get a good grip on that horn, boss," he said. "Tombstone's hightailed."

Ison stiffened, barked: "He's what?"

"Frank Tarbe was in this mornin', lookin' for him. Tarbe told the clerk inside he'd heard Tombstone had cashed a letter of credit at the bank for ten thousand. Tarbe was ready to make the deal on his place, but couldn't find him."

"Who said he was gone?" Ison rasped, his face turning livid at the mention of the letter of credit.

"No one," Slim drawled. "But if I had ten thousand in my jeans, I know damn' well where I'd be now. On that train that come through this mornin'."

Ison swore time and again, viciously, his anger impressing even Slim. As soon as he could get in a word, Slim said: "This is no place for me. I'm takin' the shortest way out, boss."

The tall man's words sobered Ison. He laughed harshly, shook his head, and said: "Don't worry! Tombstone'd never give the rest of us away." Then, more soberly, he added: "We didn't need him, anyway. Come along with me. I have a hunch we'll see this thing finished before the day's out. Where's Duke and Ben?"

"Over at Pinto's place."

"Get 'em and meet me out the trail a ways." Ison saw the lurking doubt in Slim's glance. "There's an extra hundred in it for you if we pull this off."

"Pull what?"

"I know where to find January. This time we'll bring him in . . . in a box. You three can split the reward."

A recognizable greed crept into Slim's glance. "Now you're talkin'," he drawled as he started across the street toward the saloon.

Twenty minutes later Ison met the trio beyond town. He didn't wait for them to come alongside but motioned them to follow and spurred his black gelding into an easy lope as they fell in behind. He ran the black for two miles, until far ahead he saw two crawling dots along the line of the trail that were Gault and the girl. Only then did he pull in.

When the others were alongside, he motioned up ahead. "They're takin' us to January," he explained, and for the next hour and a quarter he kept his distance without losing sight of the pair ahead.

That interval took them far north, past January's layout with its small adobe house and weathered outbuildings, deep into the broken land directly below a line of high mountains. Finally they came to the mouth of a cañon that twisted upward through a long reach of barren and rocky land that ran clear to the green of the higher foothills that bounded the uneven line of the peaks.

Ison reined in after they had ridden a hundred yards into the mouth of the cañon. Something had been worrying him these past few minutes. He wanted Slim and the others close at hand yet didn't want them to know what lay ahead. He said finally: "One man can do better at this than four. Give me a five-minute start and then come along slow."

He rode on ahead without giving them time to ask him questions. The cañon deepened abruptly, the rocky floor rising with the walls climbing even more stiffly. He nudged the long leather scabbard under his right knee, at once thankful that a premonition of trouble had prompted him to bring along his saddle gun. Now he drew the Winchester from its sheath and rode with it across his thighs. Scarcely a hundred rods after he'd left the others, he passed the beginnings of the ledge trail Bill Atwood had been travelling the day he had met his death. The cañon twisted crazily along most of its length, so that, by riding cautiously and examining the short reaches beyond each turning, he could be fairly certain of riding ahead without being surprised.

Off to his left, along the sheer west wall of the narrow gorge, the ledge trail climbed gradually upward until it hung seventy feet above the cañon bottom. The going became rougher, with uneven outcroppings of rock flanking the snaking dry bed of a wash that centered the cañon floor.

Finally Ison reined in and got out of the saddle, winding the black's reins about the gray branches of a dead and twisted cedar. He left the black there, going on toward a high shoulder of the wall that hid what lay beyond a turning.

As he approached the turning, he took off his wide Stetson and held it in his right hand, the Winchester ready to swing to his shoulder and gripped along the barrel. He edged cautiously in toward the wall and then looked around it at what lay beyond, sure that he'd see Tom Gault and Helen Atwood.

But the narrow reach of climbing rough ground ahead showed no sign of life. The east wall was sheer, unbroken. At the foot of the west wall lay a slanting mound of rock rubble and heaped earth directly below the ledge trail. Here was the spot where Bill Atwood's body had been found. He had expected to find Tom Gault and the girl examining the spot. Yet they weren't there. They had gone on.

A look of cruel cunning set Ison's face in a down-lipped grimace. He tossed his Stetson aside, ran around the turning, and out across the broken floor to the next bend above. If they had gone on, it could mean but one thing. They knew about what it was that had taken Bill Atwood up toward the head of the cañon, the thing Ison himself had stumbled on one day while riding through a break in January's north fence looking for strays. And if Gault and the girl knew about it, others might.

He covered the next quarter mile quickly, cautiously, studying the ground that lay ahead before he openly crossed it. The ledge trail climbed up and over the rim of the cañon, cutting across a high mesa this cañon bordered. Finally Ison reached a right angle, turning where he used more than ordinary caution. When he stepped around it, he lifted the Winchester to his shoulder and said in a voice that boomed hollowly between the walls: "Need some help, Gault?"

Tom Gault stood twenty yards away, his back to Ison and his glance directed upward toward a narrow ledge fronting a cave-like opening thirty feet up on the sheer face of the wall. Directly below this opening was a slanting mound of tailings. Fresh earth and shards of granite rock made a conical heap against the wall. Helen Atwood, beyond Gault, was still in the saddle. She was looking above, too.

Ison's voice brought Gault wheeling around, right hand stabbing toward his waist. But the threatening bore of the leveled Winchester stayed Gault's swift gesture, and his two hands came up slowly to the level of his ears. The girl gave a low cry of alarm and stiffened in the saddle, and her face lost color.

Ison said — "Take the weight off your belt and be careful about it!" — and came three steps nearer so that less than ten feet separated him from Gault.

Tom's right hand came down slowly and lifted the six-gun from his belt and dropped it at his feet. He said: "Looks like Bill had been doin' some diggin' up there. That why you killed him, Ison?"

Uhling's ramrod let his face relax in a broad smile, yet his black eyes were as hard and bright as glare ice. He nodded his head slowly. "Now I'll have to arrange another accident," he drawled.

At that instant, something at the limits of his vision made him whip his glance off to the right. The late afternoon sun was throwing the west rim of the cañon in clear outline half the way up along the eastern face. Ison had seen the regular line of that rim shadow move, and now it moved again and took on a man's outline.

In the split second he tried to think, Ed January's voice whipped down at him from the west rim behind: "Drop it, Ison! I've got my sights on you"

Ison knew then that he had lost, for the telltale moving shadow had made him turn his back to the west wall. In turning, his Winchester had fallen out of line with Gault.

And yet, sheer desperation made him lunge backward toward the vertical shoulder of rock that formed the bend in the cañon. He had taken two steps when a hard blow wrenched the Winchester from his grasp and the sharp *crack* of January's rifle racketed down.

As he froze into inaction, his glance went above, and he saw January finish levering another shell into his weapon and line it down at him. January called: "You take him, Tom."

Gault had already snatched his six-gun from the ground at his feet and now stepped in behind Ison and rammed the blunt nose of the weapon in at his spine.

Ison saw a thing then that drove home his feeling of helplessness at this quick turn of his luck. Above, behind Ed January, another figure had come to stand, looking down. Even across the hundred-foot interval of distance, Ison recognized Sheriff Milo Peers's thin shape.

As Gault pushed Ison on across to the foot of the west wall, Ed said from above: "We'll need both ropes, Milo. Leave the horses where they are."

Gault said nothing during the next three minutes. Helen Atwood stared at Ison with a mixture of wonder and bright hatred in her blue eyes. She had dismounted and now stood apart from them.

High above, Ed January was tying together the two coiled reatas the sheriff had taken from the saddles of the two livery horses. Ed made the lawman go down into the cañon first, looping a noose under Peers's armpits and lowering him gingerly. Peers brought along

95

the rifle. When the lawman stood with the others below, Ed tied the rope end securely about a firm outcropping and came down hand over hand.

Where they now stood, directly below the cave-like opening, was a good thirty yards up the long shank of an L-shaped turning in the cañon. The heap of tailings that lay below the opening was on the same side as the sheer wall's right-angle bend.

Once Ed was alongside him, Peers looked sourly across at Ison and said: "I've seen some things this past hour I'm needin' answers to, Kip. Who rolled them big boulders down off the rim over the ledge where Bill Atwood died?"

Ison made no answer, and Peers snorted and muttered: "I'll apologize for a few opinions I've had of you, January."

Tom touched Ed's arm and pointed upward with his Colt toward the round opening in the wall: "There's your answer, Ed. Bill Atwood's test hole, if my guess is correct. I don't know much about it, but, when Ison come up on us, I'd just finished lookin' at something I'd say was a piece of good picture rock. There's a lot of it here in this muck Bill threw down." He indicated the upslanting heap of tailings against the wall, plainly the result of someone having worked to enlarge the opening behind the ledge above.

Ed wasn't listening. His tall frame had gone rigid and his head was cocked to one side, and he was listening intently. All at once his glance swung down to the turning in the cañon forty yards below. He whipped his .38 from leather and snapped — "Watch it, Peers!" —

and lunged squarely across and into Helen, who was standing a few feet away.

The drive of his move surprised the girl, and they both went down at the exact instant a gun's flat explosion came from beyond the turning.

Slim and Duke and Ben Meade reined their horses out from behind the protecting shoulder of wall that made the bend. It was Slim who had fired, and now he threw his weapon into line once more. As he fired again, Ed was rolling clear of the girl and onto his feet. Slim's bullet ricocheted in a high whine from where he had been sprawled a moment ago.

Ed's answering shot, thrown from the hip, drove Slim sideways in the saddle. The gunman dropped his weapon, made a reach to steady himself on the saddle horn, missed his grip, and slid awkwardly to the ground, hitting hard on one shoulder. But he was on his feet and behind the protection of his horse before Ed could fire again. An instant later he had run in behind the protecting wall and out of sight.

Kip Ison whirled and ran a zigzag line for the bend. Tom, ten feet away from Ed, had jerked his six-gun up and was firing at the uncertain target Duke made on his rearing horse. Ed's gun once more added to the inferno of sound bound in by the two high walls. Ben Meade's horse went down, reared to its feet again, and plunged back out of sight around the turning.

Peers was the first to be aware of what Kip Ison was doing. He hurried his shot with the Winchester, and his bullet only speeded the ramrod's frantic dive in behind the protection of the right angle of the wall. That rifle shot of the lawman's was the last, for both Duke and Ben Meade had gone out of sight. The whole thing had been only a matter of a few short seconds.

Ed was the first to size things up, and it sent him running on down to hug the wall a few feet short of the turning. He threw two warning shots across to the opposite wall, then called back to the others — "Get up into the cave!" — and the urgency in his voice made Tom run up to Helen and take her arm and start her climbing along the insecure footing of the pile of tailings.

As Tom and the girl worked their way upward, Ed hugged the wall and swiftly punched the empties from the .38 and reloaded. His glance whipped around from the narrow neck of exposed ground directly ahead to Tom and Helen. He was relieved only when they had climbed slowly up over the narrow small ledges that afforded hand and footholds and were on the broader ledge fronting the mine opening. Peers was a few feet below them.

Helen had disappeared inside the opening in the wall, and Peers had handed the Winchester up to Tom and was reaching for a hold on the main ledge when, suddenly, a rifle's exploding *crack* sounded from the turning. Ed wheeled around in time to catch a momentary glimpse of Kip Ison, darting back to cover, too late to throw a shot at the ramrod. Then, from around the bend, two guns opened up and threw lead close in to the turning. Ison's men were making certain that no one came around after Ison.

Tom had been reaching down to give Peers a hand up onto the ledge when the rifle spoke from below. He heard the *whup* of the bullet as it took the sheriff. Peers choked out a groan; his body went slack; his hand fell. Tom's hand shot down and caught the falling arm, and he held on. Then, with Peers's suddenly slack weight almost pulling him off the ledge, Tom dragged the lawman up beside him.

He laid the sheriff on the shelf, seeing the spreading stain of red across the shirt and vest. A hasty examination showed him that the bullet had entered the fatty muscle along the left side of Peers's back. The sheriff's face was a sickly yellow, and his teeth were clenched against the pain.

"This is goin' to hurt, Milo," he said, and lifted the lawman's slight body and carried him back to the tunnel mouth.

Helen had crawled back out onto the ledge again. Tom told her curtly — "Get inside." — and stooped and half dragged Peers through the opening after the girl. He could see vaguely that a low tunnel ran on back from the opening. He carried the sheriff back as far as the feeble light lasted, then laid him down, and told Helen: "Do what you can for him. I've got to get Ed up here." He crawled back and out onto the edge of the ledge. He picked up the rifle Peers had dropped and called down: "Make it fast, Ed! I'll cover you."

Ed saw that Tom had the Winchester lined down at the turning behind which Ison and his men were hidden. He sheathed his .38 and ran back the forty yards to the foot of the tailings heap below Tom. Then something stopped him, and a moment later he was running up the cañon to where Tom's and the girl's horses stood. He picked up their reins, led them farther on up and in behind a broad outcropping of rock near the west wall, and tied them as well as he could, out of line with the bend below.

As he came back, Duke, the short and frail-bodied crewman of Ison's, stepped out momentarily to throw two shots at him. But Tom's hair-close answer with the Winchester sent Duke dodging back to cover.

In less than half a minute Ed stood beside Tom on the ledge before the cave mouth. He looked below. Slim's horse was across the cañon, reins dragging, and walking uncertainly up to where Ed had tied the other pair. Beyond that, nothing in sight moved.

Ed asked — "Did they get Milo?" — and caught Tom's answering nod of the head.

But one more thing was worrying Ed. He stepped out and took a hasty look upward, frowning when he joined Gault once more. "I don't like it," he drawled. "No way out now but to go down past 'em."

He stooped and crawled in through the opening, Tom coming immediately behind. From the darkness farther in, Helen called: "Can I have some light? He's bleeding."

Ed wiped alight a match along his thigh, and in the fitful flickering light he saw Helen kneeling beside Peers's outstretched form a few feet away. The lawman's face looked drawn and pale. The tunnel was narrow, too low for January to stand erect. Beyond the match's feeble circle of light, the tunnel ran darkly on back and out of sight.

Behind Ed, Tom said: "Here's a lantern. And . . . hell, it's a rifle . . . Bill's!"

Ed struck another match and turned. There, close against the wall, stood a lantern with a cracked chimney, a Marlin .32 rifle, a pick, two shovels, and a mattock.

Ed shook the lantern, heard coal oil slosh around in it, levered up the chimney, and lit it. Then he took the rifle, a slow smile coming to his face. He levered it open and in the lantern's light saw that it was loaded.

He turned to the girl, was about to say something, and then laid the weapon aside and bent over Peers. The lawman's wound was painful but not serious, for the bullet had gone cleanly through the fatty muscle on the left side, midway between hipbone and ribcage. As he tore the tails of the sheriff's shirt into strips for bandages, Ed said: "You must be packin' a rabbit's foot, Milo. Two inches to the other side, and we'd be holdin' a wake over you."

"All I care about is gettin' down there and corrallin' that sidewinder!" Peers said. "Ed, you must have guessed this pretty close."

Ed finished the bandaging and leaned back, sitting hunkered down on his heels. He took out a sack of tobacco and made a smoke for Peers and one for himself, then handed the makings across to Tom, who had just come back from another look out the opening.

He reached out and picked up Bill Atwood's Marlin rifle and hefted it in his two hands again. "We can use this," he said. "Now we're about even with 'em on guns."

Peers pushed up onto his elbows, wincing in pain as he moved. "When do we start? I can help."

Ed reached over and pushed the lawman down again. "Not yet, Milo," he said. Then, glancing at Helen, he went on more soberly: "I didn't know what I was letting you in for when I had Tom bring you up here. I thought Ison would be alone."

"You couldn't have known how it would turn out," the girl said. Then a worried look came to her eyes. "What was Dad doing, working on your land?"

Ed said quickly: "We knew he was up here somewhere. I told him a long time ago he was welcome to what he found inside my fence. Now don't let that get to worryin' you." He hid his misgivings nicely, for in reality Bill Atwood had never asked permission to prospect these badlands to the north of his place. This had been as much of a surprise to him as to any of the others.

There was a momentary gratefulness in the glance Helen gave him. Then she was saying haltingly: "Can we . . . is there a way out?"

Tom replied dryly: "Maybe if we could grow wings."

Peers looked up at Ed, a question in his eyes. "Is it that bad?"

Ed admitted: "Pretty bad, Milo. There's no way out except downcañon. It's a box above, with the walls straight up like they are here!" He frowned a moment in thought, added soberly: "And in Ison's place, I'd send a man up onto the rim. One man could start enough rock down off the rim to fill over this tunnel."

"He'll think of it," put in Tom. "Four dead people aren't goin' to be able to do much talkin' against him."

They sat in silence for a long moment, each experiencing the closing down of a common feeling of helplessness. Finally Ed said: "It's a long way down and up onto the rim. A man couldn't make it before dark. It'll give us a chance to get out of here and up the cañon before anything happens."

"And what comes after that?" Tom asked.

Ed had been inspecting Bill Atwood's rifle that lay across his knees. He raised his glance and looked at Tom with a light of warning in his eyes. "You talk too much," he drawled, and Tom, understanding that Ed wanted to keep the girl from realizing fully the gravity of the situation they faced, turned and crawled back to the opening to keep a watch below.

CHAPTER
ELEVEN

Full darkness found Ison and Ben Meade and Slim standing in the shadows below the circle of light cast by the fire they had started immediately below the cañon's turning. Better than two hours ago Ison had sent Duke downcañon. Duke's orders were to go down as far as the ledge trail and take it to the rim above, then to come along the rim to a point above the opening to Bill Atwood's mine that Ison had explained was a natural cave. The rim all the way along the cañon was topped by eroded and rotten rock, boulders balanced precariously enough so that a man's weight could push them over and into the cañon.

Duke's job was to start a slide of rock above the tunnel. Once started, Ison was working on the hunch that a section of the rim would give way and choke the tunnel opening with tons of earth and rock. The purpose of the fire was to make it light enough so that neither January nor Gault would try so foolish a thing as shooting their way out. Ison's confidence was running high.

Ben Meade had been nervous as a cat since Ison's shot had caught the sheriff. Slim, with his shoulder broken by Ed's bullet, didn't seem to mind anything but the pain that kept his face set in deep lines of tension. They had bandaged his shoulder as well as they could and made a sling for it. Ison had even offered to let Slim ride into town to have the shoulder cared for. But Slim had chosen to stay, for Ben Meade was his friend, and he could read the signs of Ben's nervousness clearly enough to want to be there.

Just now Ben's strangely trembling hands were trying to shape a cigarette. Slim saw this and said caustically: "First time I ever knew you to turn gun shy, Ben."

Ben threw the paper and tobacco savagely to the ground. "Gun shy, hell," he muttered. He wheeled around on Ison, his temper for the moment outriding his good judgment. "I'll stand for most anything, Kip. But I wasn't hired to fight women! Let the girl go!"

"She knows too much," Ison said. His right hand hung within finger spread of one of his pair of .45s.

Ben was too blind angry to see this warning signal. "Knows what?" he gritted. "None of us know a damned thing . . . why we're up here or why you want January out of the way! This whole play's forked, Ison!"

Slim drawled: "Kickin' about the pay you're drawin', Ben? It's more than you ever earned before."

"I've no kick," admitted Ben, steadied by Slim's words. "But if this thing goes through, I don't want to be here to see it. That girl never hurt me, nor any of you. Either let her go or I pull out. It's a two day ride to the border!" He had blurted it out before he quite realized what he was saying.

Ison's hand came up in a smooth gesture that planted his Colt in line with Ben's belt buckle. "Not for you, Ben," he said tonelessly. "Maybe you ought to get over there behind that shelf now. Duke ought to be comin' along any minute." Ison was watching them both, not because he distrusted Slim, but because Slim liked Ben and the thin man's actions were sometimes unpredictable. He flicked the weapon in his hand. "Get on over there, Ben."

They had arranged a few minutes ago to take to cover when Duke was ready above, so as to block the bend effectively in case January and Gault should try and break out at the last moment. Ben's spot was the most dangerous, a waist-high outcropping close to the bend on the east side and fully in the light cast by the fire. Slim was to wait in the shadows below the fire, where they now stood. Ison was to be waiting deep around the turning, behind the screening of a low-growing clump of *chamiza* halfway toward the dark shadow along the west wall.

When Ison spoke over the threat of his six-gun, Ben didn't move for a few seconds. Only when Ison's thumb drew back the weapon's hammer in an audible click did it penetrate Ben's mind that he had gone too far. Realization drained the color from his face. He backed away, hands clear of holsters. Then he turned and walked quickly across to the outcropping, looking back over his shoulder and held by stark terror at expecting to see Ison's weapon explode at him.

Once he was crouched down behind the outcropping, he realized he was no better off here than he'd been before. He was fully in the light, and somewhere across there stood Ison. Even when he heard the ramrod moving over to his position toward the west wall a minute or two later, he knew that Ison could do what he pleased with him. For the clump of *chamiza* was in shadow and directly in line with the exposed side of the outcropping.

Twenty minutes later, when Duke's low whistle sounded down off the rim to let them know he was ready, Ben was vainly trying to think of a way out.

The first few boulders fell from the rim in racketing explosions that filled the cañon's narrow corridor with deafening sound. One of them sheered off a solid ledge, and it was the earth-jarring fall of the ledge's weight that shook loose a whole section of the rim. Tons of earth and rock slid downward in a mounting roar and a cloud of dust and flying small rocks. The mass built outward across the cañon floor in a wave of deep-toned and ominous rumbling. Then, gradually, the sound died out and all that remained was the slurring of small pebbles down the conical high mound of rubble. The tunnel mouth was buried ten feet below the top of the mound.

A full hundred yards above the turning, Helen and Ed and Tom stood watching the settling gray fog of dust that dimmed the light of Ison's blaze far below.

Helen said in an awed, hushed voice: "I didn't believe he'd do it." Her voice was on the verge of breaking with emotion, and abruptly she turned and left them, walking back to where Milo Peers sat on the saddle blankets they'd taken from the horses. The lawman was weak from loss of blood, glad to be leaning back against a low outcropping.

They had moved down from the tunnel opening barely in time, Ed carrying Peers across his shoulders, and Tom with a rifle lined at the turning below, where the light of the fire glowed against the far wall. They had just finished making the saddle-blanket bed for Peers when Duke's signal from the rim had sounded down to them. The falling of the rim section had held them all mute and awed, realizing how narrowly they had escaped being buried alive.

Ed now held Bill Atwood's rifle cradled under his arm. A long moment after Helen had left them, he said to Tom: "We'd better get down there. Ison will come in to look things over. We'll take him." He started down the cañon, skirting the foot of the slide that filled the level floor to leave only a narrow clear strip along the east wall. Tom followed him, carrying the Winchester.

"We'll have to make it stick this time," Ed said in a low voice when they were halfway along the foot of the slide. "Once we have Ison, the others will head out. Nothin' tucks tail and runs quicker'n a hired gun when things go against . . ."

The sharp explosion of a rifle from the rim above cut in on his words. Behind them, they heard the girl's voice sound in a low, startled cry. Ed whirled about and had run back two strides when a second shot racketed down to them. He faced the west rim, raised Bill Atwood's rifle. A moment later, when the powder flash of the next shot came, he swung the rifle's sights in line with it and squeezed the trigger.

The hammer clicked down with a metallic sound, and the shell didn't explode. Frantically, Ed levered in a fresh shell, lined the rifle once more, triggered it. Again it missed fire. He threw the weapon savagely away and reached for his six-gun.

Behind him, Tom's Winchester spoke in a sharp, cracking report. From up on the rim a hoarse scream rose against the silence. It held on, seeming to travel down the cliff face. Then there sounded the sickening thud of a body. Small rocks rattled down the face of the slide, and against the firelight they saw a shapeless body roll down to within ten feet of them.

Tom stepped down there and was back in a moment. "Busted every bone in him," he said. "It was that kid they called Duke."

Ed led the way back upcañon at a fast walk, all at once impatient to be near Helen, yet dreading to discover what might have happened.

From behind them a six-gun exploded in a staccato riot of sound that went booming up between the walls.

"We ain't goin' to toll Ison out of there now," Tom muttered

Helen was standing alongside the sheriff as they came to the outcropping. She started to say something, but Peers cut in: "Someone ought to brain me! I got hungry for a smoke and lit a match. Forgot about the man up there."

Helen said lifelessly: "I did it. I thought his side was bleeding again." Her voice broke in a sob, and she said helplessly: "Now we'll never get out. Ed . . . Ed, it's just as though I'd shot you both, all of us, with my own hand!"

Ed reached out and tilted her chin up so that he was looking down into her face. "Don't," he said quietly, in a tone that checked her sobs. "Haven't I put things pretty plain to you so far?"

She nodded, and in the faint starlight her face was touched with a tenderness that made it beautiful.

"And will you believe what I say now?" he asked.

"I'll try, Ed."

"Then wait here. I know a way out. Tom and I will be gone a while. Don't worry. If there's shooting, neither of you move out from here. We'll be back."

She smiled, a smile that eased the tension in her face. "You say it as though you meant it." Her voice was no longer trembling.

"I *do* mean it."

"Then I believe you. But, Ed . . . please . . . if anything should happen . . ." Something within her held in check the thought she would have uttered, and with a last grateful glance up at him she turned and knelt beside Peers.

Ed said gruffly to Tom: "Get the ropes from the saddles. We'll need 'em."

Tom walked off toward the spot where they had tied the horses. He was back in less than a quarter minute, handing across the two coils of rope. They walked away from the outcropping, in toward the slide again. Tom said: "That sounded pretty straight. But I don't see how in hell you figure to get us out."

Ed didn't answer but kept on downcañon, toward the turning. They picked their way carefully and sound-lessly along the foot of the slide and almost to the

110

cañon's bend. Tom still carried the Winchester, but Ed was armed only with the .38. Close in to the turning, Ed crouched down and let Tom come up to him. Then he pointed upward along the sheer climbing face of the jutting wall.

"I remembered it while I was talkin' to her," he said. "See that rock that sticks out up near the rim?"

Tom saw what he meant. The reflected light of the fire around the turning outlined faintly a jutting small finger of rock high on the face of the wall that formed the bend.

Ed went on in a voice barely above a whisper. "If a man could climb high enough along this slide, he could throw a rope up there."

Tom's glance measured the distance from the nearest point along the slide to the finger of rock. He shook his head. "There ain't a man alive who could make that throw in the dark. It's a good fifty feet."

Ed nodded toward the turning. "There'll be a man forted up behind that near shelf. You're to open up on him when I'm ready. I'll toss a rock down."

He stood up and was about to turn away when Tom said: "Hold on! What about the drop on the other side?"

"I'll see when I get there." Ed didn't wait this time, but walked away, back along the slide. He smiled a little as Tom let out an angrily whispered oath behind him. As he walked along, he tied the ends of the two reatas together.

He picked the upcañon side of the slide for his climb, hoping the greater distance would help smother any sound he made. Climbing up over the loose rock would have been difficult in the full light of day. In the dark, it was close to impossible. But Ed used a long-trained patience, not putting his weight on a boot until he was certain that the footing was solid. One hint of sound would warn Ison and his men down the cañon, and he moved as silently as a cat.

He made it at last, to the topmost crest of the slide nearest the turning in the wall. He stood thirty feet above the cañon bottom. A full forty feet overhead, barely in sight in the reflected light of the fire, he could dimly make out the slender finger of rock that he had picked as his target. He shook out the loop in the rope.

He had one chance, and only one, and knew it for a certainty. If the snaking rope should miss the rock and fall below to start a sifting of pebbles or earth, Ison and his men would be on the alert and waiting. Tom's chance of staging the surprise would be gone.

He swung the broad loop carefully, his glance fixed above. Every muscle along his flat body was taut, ready for the flawless timing that called for the throwing of the rope fifty feet almost straight upward at a slender horizontal target less than two feet in length.

On one upward surge of his arm, he released the whirling noose. The coils snaked swiftly from his left hand. He moved his left once in a quick flick that sent a ripple along the slender line and seemed to give it added speed. The noose slowed, stopped, and fell slowly. It struck the very edge of the rock finger and swung there.

112

Ed caught his breath, held it, and a beady perspiration moistened his forehead. He reached for the rope gingerly with his right hand and snapped it. The noose jumped, settled well in on the rock. Ed pulled the rope taut and tested it. It held his weight.

He took his .38 by the trigger guard and held it by the forefinger of his right hand, gripping the rope with his other fingers. Then he thought of warning Tom. He stooped, caught up a pebble, and threw it far out and into the turning. Before it had started its arcing fall, he gripped the rope with both hands and jumped out into emptiness.

CHAPTER
TWELVE

He had swung even with the apex of the turning around the point of the L before the falling rock struck below him with a racketing report. Thirty feet of empty air was below him. He swung beyond the face of the bend, around it, into the upper limits of the fire's light.

Behind him, Tom's rifle opened up in a burst of sound to be immediately answered by the deeper-toned explosions of Ben Meade's six-gun from behind the outcropping. Ed could see Ben, crouching behind the protecting ledge of rock. He ignored him, letting go the rope with his right hand and flipping the .38 into his palm. As his swing carried him on, he went beyond the fire's spread of light and in toward the wall. Small trees and shrubs swept past far below. Then, in keen relief, he saw a talus slope break the floor's even monotony and sweep up toward him.

When he had to let go his hold on the rope, the talus slope was fifteen feet under him. He dropped fast, struck the slanting surface boots first, and fell, sprawling, backward in a smother of dust. Then, as he rolled onto his feet, he saw Kip Ison's shape rise up from behind a clump of *chamiza* between him and the fire. Ison was swinging a pair of six-guns into line with him.

He swiveled up the .38, hip high, and thumbed the hammer. He was about to squeeze the trigger when Ison fired. At almost the exact instant of Ison's shot, another came from downcañon, beyond the fire. Ison's bullet tore a shred of denim from Ed's trousers. The other, Slim's, crashed hard into his left thigh and knocked him off balance, and his own shot went wild.

He fell, and, as he went down, he was staring into the winking powder flashes of both of Ison's guns. One leaden slug kicked up the dust beneath his falling body. The second grazed his upper right arm. Before he struck the ground, he had thumbed one shot at Ison. He saw the ramrod lurch backward, catch himself, and bring his guns to bear again.

Ed threw his long body into a roll, his left leg going numb from the shock of the bullet in his thigh. Ison fired once again. Then Ed was sheltered momentarily by a low-growing and scrubby cedar. He came to his knees behind it, looking toward the fire. At that instant Slim fired again, laying his bullet close enough so that Ed could feel its air whip along his neck. He targeted the powder flash of Slim's gun and threw two shots over there, and then lunged to his feet. He ran, dodging from side to side, deeper into the shadow beyond the fire, Ison's gun speaking once off to his left.

At last the darkness hid him completely. As he reloaded the .38, he looked around. Far across there, Ben Meade lay sprawled face down, his body half exposed from behind the outcropping. Tom stood in the turning, barely out of line with Ison's guns, his Winchester held ready.

Ed called stridently — "Back, Tom!" — and moved to one side immediately, looking toward Ison's hiding place behind the *chamiza*. But Ison didn't make himself a target by firing again.

The .38 reloaded, Ed walked stealthily back and in toward the wall. He knew where Ison had been a moment ago. Yet with the clump of *chamiza* between him and the fire, he could look in between its slender branches and see that it hid no one.

He stood still, breathing shallowly, trying to catch a hint of sound. His thigh was pulsing in pain, and each move of his left leg sent a knife-like pain up into his hip. He ignored it, waiting for Ison's next move which he knew wouldn't be long in coming.

It came suddenly, the rattle of a dry cedar stick striking the wall almost immediately behind him. Ed stood motionless, waiting. Then, almost within reach to his left, Ison's solid bulk loomed out of the darkness, back toward him.

As deeply as he hated this man, Ed couldn't bring himself to squeeze his trigger at that exposed back. He took one step in, rammed the snout of his .38 hard against Ison's spine, and drawled: "Drop 'em, Kip!"

Ison stiffened for a fraction of a second. Then he kicked out with his left boot in a vicious swing that carried him away from Ed's gun and sent his sharp spur ripping up along Ed's shin in a red-hot lance of pain. Ed swung vainly, in an attempt to club the ramrod over the head. He missed, and the force of his blow carried him forward off balance.

Ison fired both weapons, in his frantic haste hurrying his shots. One bullet took Ed in the thick neck muscle above his left collarbone. The other ripped the cloth of his loose-hanging vest at his right side. Then, only four feet separating them, Ed squeezed the trigger of the .38 with the weapon centering Ison's wide chest.

Ison staggered back, his two thumbs working back the hammers of his .45s. He coughed blood, yet his feet were spread wide and held him erect. His guns swung down. Ed's Colt exploded once again. A hole suddenly centered Kip Ison's broad forehead. His head tilted back, his hands clawed open, and his guns fell to the ground. His wide, high frame went loose, and he fell forward inertly, his right shoulder striking Ed's arm and pushing him aside.

Ed let his gun arm fall to his side. A fuzziness was blurring his sight. He shook his head to clear it, and that motion brought up a pain in his shoulder that weakened him and nearly blotted out his senses. He sat heavily, alongside Ison, head down. It took the strength of both arms to fight off the weakness and keep from falling on his face.

He was dimly aware of Tom striding up and lifting him to his feet. He heard Tom say in mock cheerfulness: "Hang on, Ed. It's all over."

Ed couldn't summon the voice to answer, and, when Tom threw him over his shoulder, he gritted his teeth against the pain of his shoulder.

The next hours passed in a haze of semi-consciousness and unreality. Ed halfway knew that he was lying close to a fire, and once he tried to focus his eyes on a moving shape near him he thought he recognized as Helen's.

In the grayness of the full dawn, iodine stinging in the open wound of his shoulder finally cleared his head. Old Doc Milford, a Sands institution, was kneeling alongside and staring down at him, saying: "Thought that might turn the trick."

"It'd feel better if you cut it off, Doc," Ed said, wincing at the pain.

He looked beyond the medico to see Helen and Tom and Simon Uhling standing close by. Helen and Tom were smiling down at him. An expression of bewilderment was all he could catch on Uhling's narrow face.

He lay quietly while Milford finished bandaging his shoulder. When the doctor got to his feet and said — "He's too tough to hurt much." — and walked away, Ed asked Tom: "How's Milo?"

Tom nodded his head toward the other side of the fire. "Haven't you heard him? He's riled because we didn't let him in on it there at the last." He smiled broadly and looked in some embarrassment at Helen, and said to her: "Hadn't you ought to tell him?"

She nodded, her bright glance not leaving Ed. Tom turned and took Uhling by the arm and led him away.

Helen came over and knelt beside Ed. For a moment she sat silently, looking down at him with a smile of tenderness on her face. Then she asked in a soft voice: "Do you feel like talking, Ed?"

"Sure. But first, how did Uhling and the doctor get here?"

"Tom rode in after the doctor when we saw how bad that shoulder was. They must have sent the word out to Uhling from town. He's already asking how he can make it up to you, and he hasn't been here two minutes."

"And Ison?"

"They're burying him here in the cañon . . . along with the others." A bleak look touched her oval face for an instant and was gone. "But there's something else, Ed. Tom remembered how that rifle of Dad's missed fire when you tried to use it. While the doctor was bandaging your leg, Tom and I went up and got it and had a look at it. We found this poked down the barrel." She held up a tight cylinder of grimy paper. "The firing pin was filed down to keep it from firing."

"What is it?"

"You remember that I said it was queer Dad was working inside your fence? And you lied to me and said you'd told him he could?"

Ed insisted: "That wasn't a lie. I . . ."

"Let me read it," Helen interrupted. "It says . . . 'Whoever gets this, tell Ed January I'm sorry it had to be this way. I knew I was on his land, but I wanted to make sure before I told him about it. Ison's had me cornered in here two days. I'm taking my best rifle and trying to make it back to Ed January's. So long, Helen.'"

Ed took a long moment to get the full implications of old Bill Atwood's message. He said finally: "I knew I couldn't be wrong about Bill. That's like him . . . not wantin' to bank on anything he wasn't sure of."

Helen nodded. There was a moistness in her eyes she fought against. Yet he saw that a tiredness that had been in them a moment ago was gone now.

"Sort of makes us partners, doesn't it, Helen?" Ed went on, a little confused as he looked up at her. The light was stronger now and laid a copper mist on the fine-spun hair about her face to remind him once more of the beauty he'd seen in her that first night through the restaurant window.

A startled look crept into her eyes at his words. She echoed softly: "Partners?"

"It's yours, most of it," he said. "I reckon I couldn't lay claim to it." His glance held hers, and then in utter confusion he blurted out: "I don't quite know how to say it, Helen. My place isn't much, but you could fix it up. I'm a cattleman and wouldn't know the first thing about runnin' a mine . . . I . . . well . . ." He could get no further.

A gladness was in her eyes. "Ed," she said in a low voice, "is this a proposal?"

"It's meant to be." He smiled in sudden relief.

All at once she leaned down and kissed him. His two arms went about her, and even the stab of pain in his shoulder went unheeded.

SAGEROCK SHERIFF

This story was completed in February, 1938. It was submitted by Jonathan Glidden to his agent on March 10, 1938, but it was not published for some time, first appearing under the title "Paroled to Purgatory" in the May, 1941 issue of *Best Western*, a Red Circle pulp magazine. In the meantime the author's first book-length novel, *The Crimson Horseshoe*, had won the Dodd, Mead Prize for 1941 which carried with it an award of $2,000, and Street & Smith's *Western Story Magazine*, having co-sponsored the contest, serialized this first novel in seven installments (11/16/40–12/28/40). "Paroled to Purgatory" was subsequently reprinted in *Western Novel and Short Stories* (4/56). The author was paid $94.50 for the original publication of this story and $25.00 when it was reprinted. For its first appearance in book form, the author's original title has been restored, and the text is derived from Jonathan Glidden's original typescript.

CHAPTER
ONE

Outside his jail office, Tom Platt heard the mutterings of the mob mount to a roar. As though it were a signal he'd been waiting for, he unbolted the door, picked up a sawed-off shot-gun leaning against the wall nearby, and stepped out onto the walk.

His appearance was timed nicely. The leaders had already swung to the margin of the street and were on the edge of the walk now. Sight of the sheriff brought them to an abrupt halt. The high-pitched crescendo of voices gradually faded to a restless hush as the crowd fell in behind, packing the width of the street.

There was a ten-second silence in which the fog of dust, lighted orange by the glow of the lamps in the store windows, settled a little. Then Tom Platt let the shotgun rock down into the bend of his elbow and drawled quietly: "Either clear out or cut me down before you take Taichert! Make your choice, gents!"

The silence hung on for a short, tense moment that was in a way a tribute to the lawman. It was a token of respect these people held for him — this lessening of the mob spirit that had made them lose all reason. At length, one of those nearest said: "Hell, Tom, we didn't come here after you!"

"You didn't?" Platt laughed harshly. "Did you think you elected me to stand here and see a mob make its own law in Sagerock, Curly? Remember twenty years ago? There was a lynching here, then. And because we got the name of a wild town, the railroad laid its steel twenty miles south."

"Twenty years ago ain't now!" someone shouted in a brash, hard voice. "Get out of the way, Platt!"

A wave of approval rippled back through the crowd in a low undertone of sound.

The lawman's eyes singled out the speaker, another of those directly in front. He swung his shotgun up quickly, trained it on the man. And once more the restless mutterings across the street died out, this time more abruptly. Into that silence Platt drawled: "I'm an old man and won't mind this. But before you can cut me down, I'll blow the guts loose in half a dozen of you! Owens, I see you've got your crew here with you. I'll give you the first barrel! Curly, you get the second!"

In the face of that sober threat a quick panic took hold of those immediately behind the two leaders. A broad lane opened the width of the street as men cursed and pushed to get out of the way. Curly, a short, squat-framed man, glanced quickly back over his shoulder. When his head whipped around front again, he held up a hand: "Hold on, Tom!" he called. Then, braving the threat of that buckshot charge, he took a forward step that put him onto the plank walk. He turned his back on the gun and threw up his hands. "Get back!" he shouted. "The whole damned bunch of you, move back! We're goin' at this thing the wrong

124

way! Clear the street! Me and a few others'll stay and have our talk with the sheriff. The rest of you clear out!"

The long-drawn silence that followed his words was ominous. The crowd didn't give ground. Curly, his back still turned to the lawman's weapon, abruptly reached down and lifted the six-gun from the holster at his thigh, snarling: "What Tom Platt says goes with me! I'll back him! Anyone want to try and make this walk?"

"You're backin' down, Curly," Owens called out. He was a huge, hulking giant of a man, his unshaven, black-bearded face now twisted in an ugly grimace of disdain.

Curly didn't answer, only moved his weapon through a two-inch arc that lined it at the bigger man's broad chest. Then, hesitantly, the outward fringes of the throng melted across onto the far walk. Someone back there lifted a gun high over his head and thumbed two thunderous shots into the air. A man alongside brought up another gun and whipped it down onto the other's skull. As his neighbor went down, this second man swung his six-gun in a half circle, his voice sharp edged as he barked: "You heard what Curly and Tom said! Clear the street!"

It was a tense half minute. The crowd divided, those who had whipped the mob to a killing lust staying the longest, crowding around Owens who had now moved out from the walk. A few of the others, these level-headed ones who had hoped for something like this to happen, lined up alongside the sheriff and Curly, guns out. They were a sober, hard-faced group, and their will carried.

When the last sullen knot of men had backed off the thoroughfare, following Owens, Platt turned to Curly and drawled bitingly: "Thanks for the help, but for a gent with half a brain, you played a poor hand tonight!"

Curly ignored the pointed implication. He said: "Taichert crawled out of this with a life sentence, Tom. He deserves hangin'. If the law won't take care of him, we will."

"Will you?" Tom Platt took one backward step that put him in his office doorway. A moment ago he had leaned the shotgun against the wall alongside, but the others had leathered their guns to offset this. All Platt did to emphasize his words was to let his right hand settle within finger spread of the holster riding at his thigh.

That stubborn gesture, plus the knowledge that this friend of theirs would back the authority his badge gave him, wiped out the last trace of insanity that had been swaying these men.

One of them muttered: "Lay off, Curly! Tom knows what he's doin'."

Curly's rugged countenance broke into a half smile as he said: "I believe you'd do it, Tom. You're as mule headed as any man I know."

"I'm mule headed enough not to let a crowd boss me. Remember one thing, all of you. Taichert is young. Spendin' the rest of his natural life in prison is goin' to be a damn' sight harder than hangin' for five minutes at the end of a rope with a busted neck." He turned, picked up the shotgun, and went into his office, slamming the door behind him.

A few seconds later they saw the glow of his lamp through the drawn shade at his single window. It was then that Curly jerked himself abruptly from his indecision and growled: "He's right. What we'd better do is get on up to the saloons and stop anyone from shootin' off at the mouth. Otherwise, we may have this all over again."

Inside, Tom Platt heard Curly's words and breathed a long sigh of relief. He sat down in his swivel chair behind the rolltop desk and reached for his bandanna and wiped his moist forehead. Five minutes ago his stomach muscles had been corded like rock in anticipation of the chopping blow of a lead slug from one of those guns out front. Those muscles still ached, and his hands were trembling with the sudden let-down.

In an hour, the town was quiet. Tom Platt was himself once more, half ashamed of the things he'd said out there — some of them things he didn't believe.

He was wondering what he really did believe when he heard the door to his office open. He pushed back out of the glare of the lamp for a better look at his visitor. His brown eyes lost a little of their customary warmth, yet he said, affably enough: " 'Evenin', Grove. You're a bit late for the fun. Have a chair."

Grove Dines, tall, white haired even though he hadn't yet turned forty, and with a lean, aquiline face set severely, ignored the invitation and drawled flatly: "I heard about it. You were lucky . . . as usual. Ben said you wanted to see me, Sheriff."

"So it's *sheriff*, eh, not Tom?" Platt felt a faint irritation at the other's smug arrogance; he also knew he was at a disadvantage, thinking that, when Dines was on his dignity, he was a hard man to deal with. But there was something he wanted to say: "Owens was one of the leaders of that mob. Grove, you could find a better man to rod your outfit."

"You had friends of your own out there tonight. Owens is a good man. What he and the crew do on their time off isn't any concern of mine. As for the *sheriff*, you don't expect me to be overly friendly, do you . . . after what's happened?"

"No, I reckon not." Platt sighed wearily. "Here we are, on opposite sides of the fence again. Before this, we've been able to talk things out like reasonable men. Maybe we can do it again."

"Maybe. I'll know better when I find out why you sent your deputy out to bring me here and miss half a night's sleep."

Sensing the other's hostility, Tom Platt had an old man's foreboding of failure. He'd had hopes for this interview with Dines — until a minute ago. Now he knew what was coming as well as he knew the look of his littered, untidy desk. But he was a stubborn man, willing to try, so he said: "It's about Taichert again."

Dines reached back and laid a hand on the knob of the door, ready to leave. His thin-lipped smile bore out the sudden granite-like quality of his gray eyes. "Then I'll be on my way home."

"No, you'll hear what I have to say." Platt was stubborn now. He took a blackened, chewed-stemmed briar out of his pocket and sifted tobacco into it. Dines didn't move during the interval of silence. After the lawman had touched a match to the weed and thumbed the freshly burning ash, he looked across at the rancher and intoned abruptly: "Bob Taichert isn't guilty! I'd bet my last dollar on it."

Dines's hand fell to his side, his impulse of a moment ago forgotten. He laughed, mirthlessly, softly. "And you call yourself a law officer!" His drawl was edged with scorn. "We proved Taichert guilty beyond a trace of doubt, yet you have the guts to sit there and say he isn't guilty. Someone ought to start lookin' for a good man to run against you this fall."

"Taichert couldn't be prodded into killin' a man," Platt insisted. "He's too straight, too honest. Besides that, the last man he'd ever cut down would be Tad Silvers. He thinks too much of the girl."

"We'll leave Fran Silvers out of this." Dines's words were slow paced, harsh.

"How can we? I'm after things that didn't come out at the trial. One of them is this. She's your main reason for turnin' against Taichert, one of your own men. Grove, you know damned well Fran loves Taichert, even if you're marryin' her."

"Then she can be glad she found out what kind of a man he is."

"I wonder," the lawman mused. "I wonder if she believes he did it." He fixed his glance uncompromisingly on Dines. "Any other man would have stuck by one of his crew, especially since all the evidence was circumstantial. When you turned against Bob, it was plain you were afraid of him. Afraid because of the girl."

"That's a lie, Tom!"

Platt's grizzled face went a little gray. He said levelly: "That's the first time any man ever called me a liar, Dines. Most men credit me with tellin' the truth, as I see it. Maybe it's just as well we've got things clear between us." He got up out of his chair, motioning toward the door. "You can go now. I thought you might help. I was wrong. And I'll remember that about your tryin' to run another man for sheriff this fall. Thanks for the warnin'."

Dines looked as though he was about to say something. But all at once his jaw muscles corded in stubborn resolve, and he turned on his heel and went out, slamming the door behind him. It wasn't his habit to give any show of emotion, and the slamming of that door strangely enough brought a wry smile to Tom Platt's face.

He sat back in his swivel chair once more, sucking at his pipe, faced with a task that galled him. Tomorrow night, on the eleven-thirty freight, he and Bob Taichert would start the six-hundred-mile journey that would end at the gates of Yuma prison. Just now, Platt felt as though he, not Taichert, had been sentenced to life for the killing of Tad Silvers.

Platt had long ago learned patience, and not so long ago the true difference between right and wrong. One of the things that had kept the sheriff's badge pinned to his shirt front these eleven years was his blunt insistence on fairness, his honesty. Many times that honesty had lost him votes. If he followed his hunch in this case, it would cost him more votes.

But he had discovered that it is sheer hell for a man not to be able to answer to his own conscience, and tonight he couldn't look at himself squarely without squirming. So now, with sudden resolution, he opened the drawer of his desk and took out a bunch of keys and went to the jail door, a solid rectangle of steel set in the back wall of his office. He took down a lantern hanging beside the door, lit it, opened the lock, and went into the cell block.

He heard the jail's single prisoner stir in his bunk, and, when the cell door was open, Taichert was sitting up. Platt went on in, leaving the grating open behind him, and growled: "Move your feet over a bit." Taichert moved, and the sheriff sat down on the bunk and put the lantern at his feet.

Taichert had a clean look. He was a medium-size man, with a square, rugged face burned to the color of saddle leather. His eyes were pale blue, openly honest, and now regarded the lawman with faint surprise. His glance traveled first to the open door, then to the lawman's gun, which was within easy reach. Abruptly he smiled, yet he said nothing. It was obvious that Platt was giving him a chance to escape — the keys, the open door, the gun, the town and street quiet for the night.

"I came here to listen," Platt said finally.

Taichert thought the lawman breathed a long sigh of disappointment. "Listen to what?"

"What we all should have listened to this week at the trial . . . your story of what happened that day."

Taichert smiled, ran his thin fingers through his sandy hair. "So you're at it again? Tom, get this through your head. There's nothin' I can say that'll help."

"So it's all right with you that you spend the rest of your life at Yuma."

Taichert shrugged. "Maybe there's a way out of the place. If not, there's always parole."

"Hell, Bob!" Platt exploded. "Where's your guts! All you do is sit here and take it! I've known you five years, and damned if I didn't think you were more man than this."

Taichert made no reply, although the expression in his eyes was now one of suppressed anger.

Finally Tom Platt put it squarely: "Bob, I want to know about Fran Silvers."

Taichert's head whipped around; his eyes were staring coldly now. "You want to know what about Fran?"

"What she had to do with this . . . with your not talkin'."

"Nothing. Forget her."

"I won't. Either you'll talk or I'll ride out there in the mornin' and see her. I'm not blind. Every time you looked at her during the trial, your eyes gave you away. Bob, you love that girl."

Strangely enough, Taichert nodded. He said simply: "I do."

Platt waited, knocking the dottle from his pipe and repacking it, his attention on his job. He had long ago learned that it takes a man time to break down inward reserve, especially a strong man — and Taichert was strong. So he took his time, packing the tobacco into the bowl carefully, lighting it even more carefully.

And as he flicked out the match, Taichert began: "You'll want the whole story, won't you? Where I was that day, and why. At the trial I didn't bother to say, knowin' how it would have looked. Tom, the afternoon Tad was killed I was over near Dines's east fence, in that draw a mile north of the Fort Chester road. I was waitin' for Fran."

Platt looked up sharply, letting the smoke and air sough out of his lungs in what was meant to be a gasp of surprise. But he wasn't surprised; nothing could surprise him after what had already happened. "You were waitin' for Fran? Why?"

"To get the answer 'most every man waits for at least once in his life. Fran was choosin' between me and Grove Dines. She was to meet me there to give me that answer. She didn't come."

Platt said slowly: "I see. You were there alone, within two miles of where they found Tad's body, waitin' for an answer from the girl Dines is goin' to marry. That would have made it worse for you at the trial."

"Worse for me, worse for Fran. It would have started the town talkin'. They wouldn't soon forget."

"Who the hell cares what the town thinks?" Platt snorted.

"I do. Fran made her choice. She took Grove. How would it look to her if I give away that she'd been thinking of not taking Dines? How would it look if I branded her with a scandal she'd never live down? Uhn-uh, Tom." Taichert shook his head slowly. "It wouldn't have helped me one bit to tell all this, and I think too much of her to spoil things. She wants it this way, and I'll see that she gets what she wants."

"So I'm to take an innocent man to Yuma?"

Taichert shrugged. "Like I say. Nothing I've told you tonight would have helped."

"Aren't you goin' to do anything about it?" Platt flared, staring pointedly toward the open cell door, the open door to his office beyond.

"And have a reward put on my head?" Taichert laughed coldly. "Not me! I wouldn't last long on a high lonesome. I drew a poor hand, and the only thing to do is play it out."

For a moment Tom Platt wondered at the calmness of the man, and he felt a momentary lessening in the respect he'd had for Taichert. But then he saw the old truth of how bull-headed the male can be where the female of the species is concerned, remembering a time, long ago, when he had himself been almost as foolish over a woman.

"You don't know a thing that'll help?" he queried, unwilling to give up.

Taichert's answer was surprising. "There's one thing I do know that might give you something to work on," he said. "It's something I haven't been able to understand. I heard the shot that killed Tad . . . or rather, two shots."

"Say that again, Bob," the lawman breathed, sitting more erect and staring hard at his prisoner.

134

"Two shots," Taichert went on. "And they were close. I'd swear that the first was from a shotgun. The second came two or three minutes later. It was a Forty-Five. It must have been the one that killed him."

"One a shotgun?" Platt's thoughts were racing now. "But how could you hear them when Tad was found lyin' two miles east of the fence . . . in the road?"

"That's what I don't understand. But I did hear those shots . . . and they weren't far away."

Vainly, Tom Platt tried to see how Taichert's story would fit the facts. Tad had been found two miles from that stretch of fence with a .45 slug in his chest. He had been shot in the back, and the ground nearby had been scarred and gouged and pounded by boots, plain evidence that he had fought before he died. His face had been bruised, his shirt and vest torn. A spur, one of a pair long ago discarded by Bob Taichert, was found underneath a low-growing bush close to the body. That was the bit of evidence that caused Taichert's arrest. Then old Boyd Silvers had testified to the fact that his son had set out that afternoon to see Bob Taichert, expecting an argument. He wouldn't say what their differences were.

"You're sure about this?" Platt asked. "You're sure you heard a shotgun?"

"Dead sure. I know guns well enough to tell."

Platt said: "Then I'll ride out there tomorrow. Maybe I'll find something."

"You'll keep this other quiet . . . about Fran and me?" Taichert was intent as he put his question.

"You can trust me," Platt answered.

He was a little hurried as he went out of the cell and locked it. He knew as much as necessary now to prove his hunch on Taichert's innocence. And in the office again he worked with a feverish haste, taking a sheet of paper from a drawer of the desk and half covering it with his precise, even handwriting. He took down his Stetson and blew out the lamp a minute later, locking the office door behind him.

CHAPTER
TWO

It was past midnight. Even the lights in the saloons were out, and the street was deserted. Platt walked a good two hundred yards along the street, out beyond the end of the walk, before he turned into the yard of a small, low adobe house. He knocked softly at the door, waited, and, when no reply came, knocked again, louder.

This time there came the sounds of someone moving about inside. Suddenly the door swung open on the figure of a square-built, bulldog-faced man in Levi's and underwear who held a blunt-nosed .45 leveled in his hand.

"Lay off the Wild Bill stuff, Ben," Platt growled. "I want to talk with you."

Ben Healy was Platt's deputy. As the lawman stepped in the door, Ben said: "I'm sure sorry I wasn't there to help out tonight."

"Good thing you weren't." Platt closed the door as Ben lit a lamp.

Healy was young, slow of mind, filled with the importance of his job. He was also something of an institution in Sagerock. The 'punchers from the outfits in Sagerock Basin had their fun with him, enjoying such harmless sports as the time they'd shot the heels off his boots, or getting him drunk and locking him in his own jail. Ben's more placid weekdays had become a nightmare, for Saturdays sometimes brought him so much trouble that he spent the intervals between getting over it. He took quite seriously the threats of lynching, shooting, or tar-and-feathering that were often made when he became too officious. Opening the door with the weapon in his hand was, therefore, quite natural and to be expected.

"You'll let that thing off at the wrong man some day," Platt said as Ben laid his weapon on the table at the room's center.

"Hell, Tom, I didn't know it was you!"

Platt said tersely: "Get into your clothes. I'll talk while you're dressin'."

Ben's eyes, still heavy lidded with sleep, opened a trifle wider. "Trouble?"

Platt shook his head. "No. But you're leavin' town tonight for a week's vacation. Tomorrow's the first of the month, payday for the Line H. It's too risky, lettin' you be on hand when they hit town tomorrow mornin'."

Two weeks ago, on the last payday for the Line H, Ben had tried to break up a rough-and-tumble in a saloon, only to have the participants forget they were fighting each other and suddenly turn on him. The affair had ended with Ben tossed into the watering trough out front, some of the Line H's 'punchers threatening him as they went back into the saloon. Of course, they had framed Ben. But Platt chose to ignore this and use the incident as his means to an end.

"You think they'd start anything?" Ben queried. Then his face lighted up in a broad smile. "Say . . . a week's vacation? That won't go down bad!" He was putting on his boots and now looked up at Platt with a spaniel-like quality of devotion in his glance. "Thanks, Tom. I wondered what'd happen between me and that bunch. It ain't my fault . . ."

"Who said it was?" Platt cut in gruffly.

Ben made a good deputy even with his shortcomings. He wasn't equaled at following sign; he was loyal; he could keep his mouth closed when necessary; and in rare cases of bad trouble, the few times Platt had really needed him, he had showed a rare good judgment and a cool head that seemed bred of danger.

Remembering these things, the lawman took the folded paper from his pocket and handed it across. "You're to leave as soon as you can throw a hull onto your pony. It's fifty-seven miles to Prairie City. I want you to be there by sunup. Go to the Black Bull Bar and ask for Humphrey Slade. They'll tell you he isn't there. Buy a drink anyway and sit down and wait. It may take 'em all day to find him, but he'll come."

Ben's eyes were now round as two silver dollars. "Hump Slade," he breathed, his voice barely above a whisper. "He'd shoot any Sagerock lawman on sight, Tom. You don't know what you're sayin'. We got a thousand dollars on his head. It was you that sent his kid to jail."

"The reward's to keep him clear of this county," Platt said. "Hump knows why we jailed his boy. He's also a friend of mine." He saw Ben's glance grow even more astonished. "Give Hump this letter. That's all. Answer any questions he might ask. Then you can go any place you like, take a good rest. A week from Sunday, I want you back here again."

Awed, Ben folded the paper and had started to put it in his pocket, when Platt said: "You'd better read it."

Ben read it, not once but three times. When he'd finished, his jaw was hanging open in sheer amazement. "You can't mean this?" he muttered. "Taichert wasn't the one?"

"That's what it says. Now you get a move on. If you don't find Hump by sundown tomorrow, you needn't bother ever comin' back."

The next day was an unusually quiet one for Sagerock. It was a Thursday, the middle of the week, and except for the Line H crew in to spend their two weeks' pay the town was peopled only by its own citizens. It was the lull that always came after a big trial such as Taichert's had been.

The Line H was an orderly bunch. They usually took over the Cowman's Bar and had their fun without trying to tear the town apart. Different, Platt was thinking, from the Anchor outfit on paydays. Thought of the Anchor made the lawman remember Dines's haughty manner of last night in the office. He had many times speculated on what would happen after Dines and Fran Silvers were married. Old Boyd Silvers wouldn't live long — he was aging fast, and everyone knew he had a bad heart — and, when he died and his Dollar range and the Anchor were eventually thrown together under one brand, there was likely to be real trouble.

Grove Dines had already had run-ins with the smaller outfits, chiefly over the use of free range which Dines didn't need but claimed only for the reason of asserting his rights. He had come here a newcomer five years ago, with plenty of money and ambition. In these five years he'd built up the biggest outfit in Sagerock Basin. And along with that had come prestige through an interest in politics. Last year he'd swung his influence to elect a senator.

And maybe this year he'll use it to kick me out of office, Platt mused. *When he's elected his own sheriff and thrown ten thousand more acres under his brand, he'll be hard to hold.*

At mid-afternoon he saw Fran Silvers drive her father's buckboard down the street. She turned in at the hitch rail out front. As she stepped down to the wheel hub and then to the ground, Tom Platt couldn't help but admire her looks, her sure, easy grace. She was tall, chestnut haired, and today her deep brown eyes set wide spaced in a tanned, oval face didn't have that sunken look he'd noticed at the trial. She had color today, too, and Platt decided she was the pick of all the Silvers he had known in three generations.

She came in with a brief, serious: "Hello, Tom. I came to say good bye to Bob."

Platt answered — "I wondered if you would." — and got his keys from the desk and unlocked the doors. He left them alone, the cell door open, the other shut but unlocked.

She was with Bob Taichert less than five minutes. When she finally came into his office, Tom saw that her eyes were glistening with tears. He went in to lock the cell grating, saying — "Wait'll I get back." — as he stepped past her.

In his office again, he made her take his swivel chair, while he sat on the broad ledge of the window. He waited for her to speak until the silence lengthened awkwardly, then said explosively: "If there was only something a man could do!"

She smiled, her eyes suddenly mirroring a deep thankfulness. "Then you don't believe he did it."

"What kind of a sidewinder do you think I am? Of course, I don't."

"I'm glad, Tom. It helps." She paused, made a visible effort to suppress her emotion, then went on more evenly: "It's hard at home . . . with Dad."

"Boyd always was a headstrong cuss," he said mildly. "I reckon if he hadn't been, he wouldn't have done so well. But there are times when a man should go soft. Now's one of 'em. I suppose he's wantin' to send the crew in to lynch Taichert?"

"Not as bad as that. He's got his own theory on how it happened. He seems to think that Bob and Tad met that afternoon to talk about me . . . you see, I'd told them both about Bob, how I felt . . ."

Words failing her, Platt put in: "Sure, I know. Bob told me all about it. I'm stubborn enough to wish you'd chosen him."

"I did, Tom. I had it out with Dad that morning . . . the morning it happened. I told him I was to give Bob my answer that afternoon. Dad was mad clear through, wouldn't let me ride out to see Bob. That's why I wasn't there . . . wasn't there to prove his innocence." She buried her face in her hands, and her body swayed slightly as she gave way to her silent grief.

"So you really did choose Bob?"

Fran Silvers's head came up. She held it high, proudly, her eyes flashing now. "Of course, I did," she said heatedly. "Grove knows it . . . knows if I marry him I'll never, never love him. But he wants it anyway. So does Dad. I can't turn against my own flesh and blood."

Her words were so unexpected, so surprising, that Platt sat wordless for long seconds. Suddenly he was thankful for having sent Ben Healy on his errand to Prairie City. Once or twice today his doubts had assailed him. He'd even thought of seeing Judge Connors and demanding a retrial. Now he was glad he hadn't, and suddenly he was impatient to set about a task he had been looking forward to all day. He was finally convinced that he owed Bob Taichert and Fran any help he could give them. Perhaps the thought of Grove Dines's smug belief in Taichert's guilt made him a little firmer in his resolve.

"Sit tight and maybe something will change all this, Fran," he told the girl.

For an instant the light of hope shone in her eyes, but then it dulled. These past few days had taken a measure of her spirit away, and now she thought that Platt was merely making an effort to be casual about the whole matter, hiding his true feelings. It hurt Platt to hear her say, as she went out the door: "Nothing will ever change it."

He had decided not to tell her where he'd sent Ben Healy, and why — not that he didn't trust her, but he was wise enough to see that a word, or even a look, might later give it away that she had known what was to happen. And he didn't want her needlessly involved.

A minute after she had gone, he hurried to the livery stable, saddled his dun, and rode west from town on the Fort Chester road. It was five miles before he reached the cattle guard that marked Dines's boundary. He turned north without going through the gate alongside the guard and rode along the line of the three-strand fence. This side of the wire was Dollar range, Boyd Silvers's land. And it was from over here that Bob Taichert claimed he'd heard the shots the day Tad was killed.

Soon he was on the rim of the draw where Taichert had waited for Fran that day. It slanted down, a broad, shallow bowl hemmed in by low hills on both sides of the fence.

Tom Platt picked out the spot to the north, the crest of the low hill where he imagined Taichert had waited that day for Fran. He rode on, until he was parallel with the line of that hill top. Then he looked off toward the east, toward town, studying his surroundings carefully.

What finally took his eye was the deep slash of an arroyo that cut a twisting line between two high shoulders of rock to curve out of sight beyond. His glance swept above and below the arroyo, but to either side the range rolled smoothly in shallow domes dotted with sage and a poor growth of gramma grass, bare-rock outcroppings breaking the lines of the slopes. It was poor range a mile to either side of the fence.

With sudden decision, the sheriff put his dun down the slanting side of the shallow part of the arroyo and followed its twisting course between walls that climbed higher as he went on. Soon he was between two towering hills, the arroyo deepening.

Rounding the bend that had hidden what lay beyond from his sight, he saw that this wash was in reality the beginning of a broad cañon. Its floor was studded with dry grass, boulders, an occasional bushy cedar. A quarter of a mile farther on he remembered the spot ahead. He knew that this shallow cañon grew broader, until finally the walls disappeared and became a part of the rich-grass plain nearer town.

The lawman's reason for remembering it was that years ago, when he had ridden one summer for Boyd Silvers, the rancher had mined out a pocket of coal up this cañon. Curiosity now took Pratt part way up a narrow offshoot until he could look up and see the mouth of the shallow tunnel of the mine ten feet above him. Below it, spreading fan-wise down the slope, was the scar of the muck dump.

Wonder what it's like inside? he mused. But his curiosity wasn't quite strong enough to make him want to use the effort to go up there and find out.

He had wheeled the dun around and was about to ride out into the main cañon again when he saw something that made him draw rein. Twenty feet ahead, in the shallow sand washed over a ledge of rock, he saw the prints of a horse's shod hoofs.

Someone had been up here, recently too, from the freshness of the sign. Realizing this, Platt was all at once struck with the annoying thought that the man whose horse had made that sign was the man who had fired the shots Bob Taichert heard.

The idea brought him down out of the saddle, sent him climbing up the face of the muck heap to the mouth of the tunnel, following that clear sign. He stooped down and had taken one full stride into the tunnel mouth when his right foot caught on an exposed tree root. Bent forward so awkwardly, he lost his balance and fell full length. He put out his hands to break his fall, and felt his right hand touch something that yielded as his weight hit it.

Suddenly a deafening explosion cut loose. There was a flash of flame above his head, the impounded air beat deafeningly at his ears, and a split second later he felt a shower of dirt and pebbles sift down onto his back.

For two long seconds he lay there, paralyzed with a numbing fear. That fear changed to a quick wariness that made him roll onto his back and draw his Colt from the holster at his thigh. He sat up, looking out of the tunnel mouth, across the narrow chasm, down at

146

his horse. The dun was nervously tossing his head, obviously frightened by what he had heard.

To get a better look below, the lawman shifted to one side. And as he moved, his Stetson struck something solid and unyielding that jutted out from the wall. Still scared, Platt reached a hand up to straighten his hat, and his fist touched rounded, warm steel.

He felt of it gingerly, felt the two smooth, round barrels of a shotgun, still warm with the blast that had seconds ago deafened him.

"Then it was a shotgun, after all," he said aloud.

His forehead was damp with a fine, beady perspiration, and the sound of his own voice boomed hollowly back along the tunnel corridor behind. Platt laughed at the tingling expectancy that ran along his nerves. He was a reasonable man and now put down the fear that rose within him. Sitting there, he struck a match.

In the flickering light of that match flame he saw the killing machine that had been rigged to cut down any man who might enter the tunnel mouth. The shotgun's stock was wedged firmly in a cleft of the soft rock, a string looped around trigger, trigger guard, and then down to the floor where it once more curved under a rounded shard of rock before it stretched taut across the floor to the wall opposite. The exposed root in the mouth of the tunnel had saved Tom Platt's life.

And it must have saved Tad Silvers's, too, he reasoned.

Tad had been killed, but not by a shotgun. This close, it'd have blown a hole clean through him. Tad

147

had stopped a slug from a .45, from the gun whose hollow blast Bob Taichert had heard a minute or two after this shotgun had cut loose. Which means that the jasper who had drygulched Tad had been waiting outside.

The sheriff thumbed back the hammer of his weapon, got up from where he sat, and edged forward until he stood barely inside the mouth of the tunnel. His wary glance studied the rock wall opposite, the slope above. Nothing there. He wouldn't trust himself to step any farther into the open so that he could see what lay to either side. But he did glance down at the shadows below, seeing that they had lengthened considerably in the short minutes he'd been in here.

"We'll wait'll it's dark to leave," he said, speaking to the horse that stood hip shot below.

But then he had a better thought. Gun still in hand, he groped back along the tunnel, lighting an occasional match that showed him the damp, glistening black walls. This had once been Boyd Silvers's coal mine. What secret did it hold that had made the killer plant a gun in the tunnel mouth to guard it? That question was uppermost in the lawman's mind as he groped his way deeper into the side of the hill.

Finally, when the light from the opening was a dim shadow far behind, he found what he had halfway expected. At the end of the tunnel, where the walls took on a grayish color instead of the blackness of the coal vein, was a pile of freshly loosened rock rubble. A pick and shovel lay against the slanting heap.

It wouldn't be like Boyd Silvers to leave tools lying about, he reasoned. *Someone else has been doing a little digging.*

He stooped and picked up a piece of the crumbling limestone, then a harder piece of quartz below the thin tracing of a yellowish vein that climbed the gray limestone at the end of the tunnel. Tom Platt had never been even faintly interested in prospecting or mining. By the light of a match he examined that piece of quartz, and regretted his ignorance.

Finally he dropped it in his pocket and made his way back to the mouth of the shaft. It was dark outside. He climbed down the slope with his gun in hand, the hammer cocked. But no shot welled out of the darkness. A mile after he'd turned into the main cañon, the walls fell away and he was once more in the open. Only then did he holster his weapon, heading for the far-off, winking lights of Sagerock.

CHAPTER
THREE

It was past eleven that night, and Platt was beginning to wonder if Ben Healy had failed to find Humphrey Slade. Then he heard the sound of trotting horses in the street and listened intently. They swung in at the hitch rail out front.

When the door opened, Platt's feet were on the desk and his head was resting on his chest, eyes closed. Humphrey Slade stepped into the room, called softly to someone outside — "I won't need help." — and closed the door.

The lawman stirred at the sound. He rubbed his eyes, took his feet off the desk, and only then glanced toward the door. His grizzled brows arched in mock surprise. "Been waitin' long, Hump?" he queried.

Slade shook his head. He was a short man, wide of shoulder, thick framed. He wore two guns, and now his overly long arms let his hands hang close to the handles of that matched pair of .45s. He asked warily: "What you got on your mind, Tom?"

"What the letter said."

"That all?"

"That's the main thing."

150

"Then you can go straight to hell, Tin Star! Why should I do you a good turn?"

Platt smiled. "No special reason. Only I thought you'd like to know I'm askin' the board to parole your boy."

Slade's gray eyes momentarily lost their agate-like quality of hardness. "Parole . . . for Jim?" he breathed, and stepped closer to the desk to ask warily: "What's the catch?"

"There isn't any. Jim's only eighteen. If he gets out, he can either go straight or throw in with your bunch. If he goes straight, the parole will have done him good. If he doesn't" — the lawman shrugged — "then he'll keep long enough to go back to prison again, unless someone cuts him down before the law gets him."

"Jim'll go straight," Slade muttered savagely. "Tom, you let him come back here to Sagerock. Help him to get a job, any job. If he rides north to my country, I'll give him the worst gun whippin' a man ever got. Damned if I'll see a kid of mine live the way I do."

"You're talkin' like a parson, Hump."

"I'm talkin' sense." All at once Slade's glance narrowed. He drawled: "I see. You'll get Jim out if I do what the letter said."

"That's about it."

"I hear this Bob Taichert's guilty. Remember, Tom, I knew Tad Silvers."

"Taichert isn't guilty. I'm goin' to prove it."

The outlaw was silent a moment, obviously considering. Then he said abruptly: "Let's get on with it."

Platt took his keys out of the drawer, opened the door to the cell block. Taichert was sitting up in his bunk, shading his eyes against the glare of the lantern the lawman was carrying. His eyes lost their sleepy look when he saw who stood behind Platt.

"Slade," he gasped. "What're you doin' here?"

Humphrey Slade grinned. "Breakin' you out of jail."

Taichert didn't have time to recover from his bewilderment before Platt said: "Bob, you're to go with Slade. Tonight you'll ride north, into those brakes beyond the Anchor fence." He was speaking to Slade as well as to his prisoner. "You'll have to ride hard, because you're goin' to raise hell leavin' here . . . to make it look like the real thing. You'll have a posse on your tail all the way. Lose your sign on that stretch of rock down in the brakes, Slade. Then take your bunch and head north into your own country. Bob, you'll swing south again. By sunup I want you holed up near that old coal mine Boyd Silvers was usin' years back. Remember it?"

Taichert nodded.

"You'll find something up there that'll tell you a few things," Platt went on. "But be sure of one thing. If you go into the tunnel, crawl on your belly for eight or ten feet. There's a set gun rigged in the opening . . . a shotgun." He turned to Slade. "Get that rope off the rack in the office, and we'll get to work."

Bob Taichert had many questions to ask. Platt answered them tersely, telling what he had found that afternoon, working as he talked. Once he took a firm hold on his shirt and pulled at the front of it until it tore raggedly. He did the same with his vest. Then, kicking at one of the cell bars, he knocked the heel off his left boot and kicked it out into the corridor. Next, he rubbed the knuckles of his left hand raw on the stone wall, wiping the blood on his shirt and face. He mussed his hair, smeared dirt across his forehead, and finally turned with a smile to face Slade, who stood nearby watching, a coil of rope in his hand.

"How do I look, Hump?"

"Like you'd tangled with a grizzly."

Platt chuckled soberly. He went into the cell and sat on the floor and motioned to the outlaw to come in. "Do a good job. Stuff a rag into my mouth and gag me. And on the way out muss up the office a bit. Turn out the lamp and bust it on the floor. Last thing, throw that extra chair through the window. That'll wake up the town." He glanced once more at Taichert, saying: "Bob, you be careful. Take my gun with you . . . it's lyin' on the desk. There's a handful of shells in that top drawer. Remember to hide your pony when you hole up at the mine. Better yet, turn him loose. He'll be Slade's, and he'll head for home, which is north." He was glad to see that Taichert was willing to go, having heard his story. At first he had thought his prisoner would balk.

Ten minutes later, Tom Platt lay gagged and bound on the cold rock floor of the cell. The rope bound him so tightly that his right arm was already numb. Finished with his task, Humphrey Slade got to his feet and stood a moment, looking down at the lawman.

"This had better be straight, Tom," he breathed grimly. "Otherwise, I'll be back."

Platt tried to nod, couldn't. Slade picked up the lantern, closed the cell door, and went out of the jail, locking the steel door to the office.

Platt listened, heard sounds in the office as they moved about. At last came the crash of the lamp, followed five seconds later by another, louder, as the chair went through the window. Then came the muffled thud of hoofs as horses pounded away fast down the street.

The sheriff let out his breath in a long, slow sigh. What would happen now was completely out of his hands. He thought of one more thing and pushed himself toward the front of the cell. And, as the first shouts of alarm came from the street, he raised his head and snapped it back soundly against the steel grating. The blow was a hard one, made him faint. He felt blood oozing from a wound in his scalp.

Minutes later, after someone had found the jail keys lying in the middle of the street where Slade had thrown them, the excited crowd unlocked the doors and found their sheriff. He lay stiffly against the front wall of the cell where the floor was smeared with blood. They saw his scalp bloody from a wound at the back of his head, his face dirty, and his clothes torn.

One of them, the first in, yelled — "Get Doc Rainey, quick!" — as his shaking hands fumbled at the hard knots of the rope.

When they'd taken the gag from his mouth, Platt growled: "To hell with a sawbones. All of you get your jugheads saddled. Hump Slade did this . . . caught me when I opened the cell to take Taichert out. I was gettin' him out of town on the eleven-thirty freight tonight, headed for Yuma. Instead, he's with Slade now. Shake a leg, you . . ." He swore viciously at the men nearest who stood open mouthed, listening to his story.

It took another ten minutes to get a posse organized. Once they were mounted, an argument started. One man was sure he'd heard Slade and the rest leave town by the east road; another claimed he'd actually seen Taichert and the outlaw turn right at the intersection of the town's two streets, heading south. Others joined in, arguing, until Platt bawled out: "The whole damned lot of you hold your talk!" He waited a moment until they fell silent. "Slade's hideout is north, in Tampala county, where he's bought out the Prairie City sheriff. Why would he be ridin' south, or east, when he's safe up there? My hunch is to cut straight north to the county line and see if we can head him off before he gets there. He'll make it about daylight, which means we've got to be there before."

He wheeled his dun in a half circle that headed him up the street. At the four corners he turned left, and within fifty yards he had spurred the animal to a fast lope. The others trailed out behind in a smother of dust.

The news traveled fast, reaching the Dollar layout soon after breakfast. Fran Silvers listened while Matt Hastings, one of their riders, told the story to her father. Boyd Silvers sat stiffly in a grim silence, gruffly sent Hastings away when he'd finished, and, when the man was out of hearing, turned to Fran and said:

155

"There's your proof! There's the man you'd have married! First he killed, now he makes himself an outlaw. Maybe he was in with Hump Slade before any of this happened. We've all lost a few head of beef this past year."

The girl took it all in wordless bewilderment, numbed by the thought of the thing Bob Taichert had done. Silvers lacked the power of observation, and, when Fran turned and left him, he was furious with her.

The girl stayed in her room until after the noon meal. She was numbed by grief, her faith in Bob Taichert shaken, but she stubbornly refused to believe that his breaking out of jail proved him guilty. She couldn't forget his tenderness the last time she had seen him, in the jail, or the honest look in his eyes, his straightforward story of what had happened the afternoon they'd found Tad.

She was remembering all these things about Bob Taichert, growing gradually calmer, when her father's step sounded in the hallway outside. He knocked at her door and called out gruffly: "Fran! Grove is here to see you. Don't keep him waiting."

She was about to answer that she didn't want to see Grove Dines when she was suddenly struck by the inevitability of what was to come. Now that Bob was gone, gone as completely as though he were dead, she no longer had the strength to fight against Dines. Up until now she had put him off, chiding him as lightheartedly as she could at his insistence on an early marriage, hoping that something would happen to show her father and Tad that Grove wasn't her choice.

But now Tad was dead and her father raging at the insanity of her feeling for Bob. He didn't openly blame her for Tad's death but had intimated that Tad might be alive today had it not been for her choice of Taichert, instead of Dines. Tad had left the ranch the day he died to have a talk with Bob Taichert. Fran, even now, believed that her brother would have given in. Yes, he was fine enough so that he'd even have helped her persuade her father, had he lived. But since the afternoon his son's body was found, nothing could change old Boyd Silvers from the belief that Tad had met Bob, quarreled with him, and been killed.

She went out onto the porch, all the fight gone out of her. Grove Dines, tall and handsome, looking younger than his forty years, rose from his chair and gave her a smile that was intended to be gentle and full of kindness. No, she'd never doubted but what Grove was a good man; he would always treat her with respect.

"I'm sorry about all of this, Fran," he said simply, as she took the chair beside him. Her father was doubtless inside the house somewhere, purposely giving Dines the opening for the plea Fran knew was coming.

It came sooner than she expected. For a moment later, after Dines had lit a cigar, he turned to her and said evenly: "Let's forget what's happened, Fran. Let's be married . . . quietly, without a lot of fuss. Then we can go away. I'd like to take you to the coast, to 'Frisco. We needn't come back until you feel like it."

157

She waited a moment, weighing her answer, then knowing that there was only one. At length, she nodded. "All right, Grove. It can be next week . . . now, if you want."

He frowned, and there was a deceiving quality of hardness in his gray-eyed glance as he covertly studied her. "Don't take it so hard, Fran. Bob was no good. Why not admit it? Platt took a posse north to the county line last night. They found sign up there. Slade and the rest went on into the next county. You'll never see Taichert again . . . unless he comes back to steal Dollar beef, or a payroll."

All at once Fran stood up, her eyes flashing in anger. "One thing you'll promise me here and now, Grove." Her face was drained of all color. "You're not to mention Bob Taichert to me again . . . ever! One thing more. You know I loved Bob . . . I'll always love him. If you can take me, knowing that, then you can name our wedding day."

"You'll forget him," Dines said. "I can give you more . . ." He stopped speaking as she turned and left him, going into the house.

He sat there a moment longer, his lean face taking on the hint of a smile. Then he picked up his Stetson and went down off the porch to his horse, a big gray stallion. He rode from the yard without looking back, deciding he'd follow the trail to the Fort Chester road, seven miles south, and go home the long way around. His visit had turned out nicely, and, as he rode on, he was more than satisfied with himself.

He was three miles from the Silvers' house, crossing an open, gently undulating stretch of good grass range, when he saw a lone horse grazing a hundred yards to the east of the trail. It was a black, and he would scarcely have noticed the animal had it not been for the empty saddle on its back, the stirrups and reins looped up over the horn.

Curious, Dines reined the gray to one side and rode straight for the black. When he was close, the gelding raised its head, nickered its fear of the stallion, and started off at a swinging run. Dines was close enough so that he made out the brand, a Bar X, before he reined in. He watched the black until a low rise ahead hid the animal; during this interval he was trying to place that brand. Finally he remembered it. The Bar X was Joe Strong's outfit, a hundred miles to the north. How would one of Strong's horses get down here?

All at once he was seeing again the black's dust-caked flanks, even the reins that were tied to the horn under the hooked stirrups. Whoever had been riding the black had ridden him hard today — or last night — before he had intentionally turned him loose.

Dines was all at once remembering that Humphrey Slade and his bunch were from up around Strong's country, in Tompala County. And that one thought made him swing the gray off to the left, scanning the ground, until he picked up the black's sign.

He made good time, since the black's hoofs had made a clear sign to follow. Dines rode for three twisting miles that gradually took him farther south toward the Fort Chester road. The sign crossed and recrossed the trail from the Dollar, finally keeping to the west of it. And when he rode close in to the broken ground near the mouth of the only cañon on Dollar range, he suddenly drew rein, letting his glance run on ahead to follow the twisting direction of the sign.

He sat there a full minute, considering, his gray eyes first filled with a grave wonder, then a subtle cunning. He was no longer handsome; instead, his lean face was set in a grimace that had a brutal wickedness about it.

It might be, he conceded, at last. And with that he rode the gray close in to the first low outcropping and climbed out of the saddle. Winding the reins about the branches of a low-growing mesquite, he next reached down to lift his black-handled Colt from the holster at his thigh. He flicked open the weapon's loading gate, spun the cylinder with a quick, sure movement of the thumb. Then, the weapon still in his hand, he came from behind the outcropping and walked the sixty yards to the point where he had last seen the sign.

During the next half hour, Grove Dines became another man, one who possessed no trace of dignity. He followed that angling sign, but from cover. He crossed the open spaces quickly, would often run many yards to one side of the sign to spend a minute or two hidden behind a cedar clump or an outcropping while he carefully studied the ground ahead. Not once did he go on before he made sure that no living soul was within his line of vision. He was working higher along the uptilted slope of the high hill that flanked the cañon to the north.

160

He came upon Bob Taichert suddenly, almost without warning. But his keen, searching glance made out the wispy feather of smoke curling up from Taichert's cigarette, so that, when Dines stepped into the open, thirty feet from the rock ledge behind which Taichert sat, his gun was leveled at his hip.

Taichert heard the scrape of the rancher's boots in the gravel, and turned where he sat. His eyes for a moment held a trace of shocked surprise, then, slowly, he raised his hands to the level of his ears.

Without a word, Dines walked around him until he could glance quickly down over the drop off and into the cañon bottom. Twenty feet below was the top of the cone of the muck heap, slanting out from the tunnel mouth of Boyd Silvers's abandoned coal mine. Dines turned once more to face Taichert.

"So you're usin' it as a hideout?"

Taichert made no answer. He was hard eyed now, the tan of his countenance lightened a shade at the emotion that ran within him. Seeing Dines meant a turn in his luck; the dislike he'd felt for the man now jelled to a rising hatred.

"Platt will be glad to see you," Dines drawled. Then his eyes narrowed shrewdly, and he added softly: "Or will he?"

Still Taichert held his silence, but the expression in his eyes at this last pointed query of Dines was easy to read.

Suddenly Dines half guessed at the truth. And, as he became sure of his reasoning, he stepped around Taichert once more, keeping his distance. Then, behind his prisoner, he suddenly took one step that put him in close, and swung his Colt in a chopping stroke that beat down the rounded crown of Taichert's Stetson.

As Taichert fell sideways in a loose sprawl, hands falling weakly to his sides, Dines holstered the Colt. He lifted Taichert's inert bulk with an ease that was surprising.

By the time he had lowered the unconscious man down the drop off to the tunnel mouth, the rancher's clean white shirt was wet with perspiration, clinging to the flat outline of his wide chest. He stepped carefully into the mouth of the tunnel and felt gingerly along the left-hand wall until he found the shotgun. He broke it open, showed a faint surprise at the two empty shells in the breech.

"Damned queer!" he breathed. "That's the second time."

Later, after he'd walked the full quarter mile back to the gray and ridden him up the cañon to the tunnel mouth, he untied the rawhide saddle strings. Deep in the tunnel, nearly at the end of it, he spent five minutes binding Bob Taichert's wrists and ankles with the leather thongs. Finished, he squatted beside his unconscious prisoner, deep in thought.

I'd better make my peace with Tom Platt was his final thought as he rose to his feet and walked toward the dim blur of light at the tunnel entrance.

CHAPTER
FOUR

Tom Platt caught up a little on his sleep that day. Back with the posse at ten, he went straight to bed and slept soundly until three. Then, after eating a hearty meal, he went to the hardware store.

He waited until Jess Calkins had finished with a customer, then went up to the store owner and said: "Jess, I got something in the mail this mornin' I want you to take a look at. Friend of mine down in Pinnacle sent me an ore sample he wants assayed." He dipped a hand in his coat pocket and brought out the piece of quartz he had last night taken from Boyd Silvers's mine. "You're about the only gent in town that knows about these things." He handed the quartz to Calkins.

The store owner examined it closely, turning it over and over in his hands. Finally his eyes lighted up, and he said: "It looks good. But I can't say without testin' it."

"Looks like what?"

Calkins was a cautious man. "Like most anything. You leave this here with me, and I'll take it home tonight and pound it up and try a little acid on it. Nine chances out o' ten it's worthless."

Platt had had hopes, but now he put down his impatience and played his part. "Sure, take your time. Ollie Bird always was one to get steamed up over nothin'."

"You say this sample's from down near Pinnacle? I didn't know they had quartz like this down there."

"Ollie wanders around a bit," was Platt's casual rejoinder. "Maybe he picked it up on one of his pack trips. I'll be in for it in the mornin'."

Five minutes later, as the lawman entered his office, he stopped dead in his tracks, staring at the man who sat in his swivel chair. Then, viciously, he slammed the door shut and growled: "I thought I gave you a week's vacation."

Ben Healy nodded sheepishly. "Now don't get riled, Tom. How was I goin' to stay away with all that's goin' on?" He leaned forward in the chair, his glance all at once taking on a knowing look. "Where'd you hide Taichert?"

So Platt had to tell his story. Finished, he opened the bottom drawer of his desk and took out two twelve-gauge shotgun shells, saying: "I'm ridin' out to the mine now. Takin' Bob some grub and loadin' that gun again. Maybe the gent that rigged it will be back to have a look. I don't want to scare him off."

"How about me comin' along?"

Platt shook his head. "You'll stay right here, Ben. I've got enough trouble on my hands without havin' you to nurse. Why don't you do like I said, take a vacation?"

Ben was plainly disappointed. "I'll hang around and watch the fun," he said.

164

Later, after Platt had been to the general store to buy a sack of flour, salt, a side of bacon, coffee, beans, and sugar, he saddled his dun and took the road west from town, his provisions slung from the saddle cantle in a flour sack. He was a mile out from town before he noticed that in back of him high, dark thunderheads banked the horizon to the east. He cursed feelingly as he remembered that his poncho hung on the nail behind the door in his office. But it would take too much time to ride back after it; he wanted to get to the mine before dark.

Three miles out along the trail he watched the sun go down, a huge red ball of fire against the far flat western horizon. "We're in for a wettin' tonight," he said, speaking to the dun, and touched the animal lightly with spurs so that he lifted out of his walk into a stiff trot.

Platt rode, deeply in thought, looking neither right nor left, intent on finishing his errand, making sure that Bob Taichert was safe, and getting back to his room at the hotel for a good rest. For that reason, he didn't see the rider on the gray that swung wide of the trail at sight of his approach, nor did he notice that, after he'd passed, the gray came back onto the trail once more and dogged his tracks, nearly out of sight behind.

Bob Taichert wasn't at the mine, or waiting above as Platt had thought he would be. But in the semi-darkness the lawman finally saw the fresh-scarred earth on the steep slope above the tunnel mouth where someone had earlier slid down to the top of the muck

165

heap. He found several boot sole prints at the mouth of the tunnel.

Scanning the darkening, gray sky, Platt chuckled and cursed his own short-sightedness. "And what's strange about a man havin' sense enough to get in out of the rain?" As though to echo his words, he heard the splashing of the first big drops as they pelted down out of the leaden sky. In another half minute, after he'd run down to untie the flour sack full of Taichert's provisions, he was in the tunnel mouth, looking out at the rain swirling down in blinding sheets. With a regretful glance down at the dun, he went on back until he came to the set gun.

Platt was a cautious man. Instead of stepping into the path of the shotgun, even though he was sure Bob Taichert would already have tested it, he broke it open and lifted out the two empties and left it that way. As he went back along the tunnel, he breathed a sigh of relief at this slender proof that the killer hadn't been back since his visit here yesterday.

When he saw the gray light of the tunnel end show against the flickering orange light of his match, he was puzzled. Bob Taichert wasn't here. But an instant before the match flame died, he saw a shadow on the floor that made him reach with trembling fingers for another match. And when he'd wiped it alight on the seat of his Levi's and taken a forward step so that he could see better, he caught his breath and held it.

Bob Taichert's inert bulk lay sprawled against the foot of the pile of rock shards, and the pool of blood under his head glistened brightly in the light. His pulse slowing, the sheriff knelt down, thrust a hand in under Taichert's shirt to feel for a heartbeat. It came, feebly, and Tom Platt felt an overpowering relief.

The next twenty minutes were a feverish, hope-dulling, almost endless stretch of time. The lawman untied the thongs that bound Taichert's wrists and ankles. Twice he went to the tunnel mouth and reached out to catch a hatful of water, going back to bathe the unconscious man's face. At last, impatient at the fruitlessness of his efforts, Platt sloshed a full pint of water directly into Taichert's face and watched by the light of one of his few remaining matches.

Bob stirred, opened his eyes, and stared dully about for a few seconds. When his eyes could focus, he looked fully at Platt; finally recognition came, and with it he was pushing up onto one elbow, asking: "Where's Dines?"

"Dines?"

Platt started violently, snuffing out the match. And into the darkness Bob's voice drawled: "It was him, Tom! I was above, keepin' watch like you said, when Dines came up behind me with a gun in his hand. He slugged me with it. That's all I know."

When there was light again, Tom Platt looked steadily at the other and said in a hard voice: "Try and think what he said, Bob. Maybe he thought he was doin' me a good turn by keepin' you here until he could get help to bring you in."

"Help?" Taichert smiled thinly. "Why would he need help?" He shook his head. "I can't remember what it was, but something he said sounded like he knew."

"Like he knew I'd helped you to break jail?"

Taichert nodded.

Platt swore viciously, catching only the obvious significance of what had happened. "Now we've got him to buck . . . along with this other, the gent that rigged the set gun. It puts me in a tight spot, Bob." He was silent a moment, and in that interval his match burned out again. He didn't bother to light another. At length he said: "There's a surer way of handlin' this . . . the way I should have taken last night. I'll go to the judge, present him with this new evidence, and demand a new trial. As soon as this rain's over, we'll ride back to town and lock you up again. You'll be a free man within a week."

"But what'll you do about Dines? He can make it hard for you if he tells what he knows."

"He'll make it hard, anyway," Platt sighed. "You stay where you are while I go out and have a look around. Hell, it can't rain all night."

He crawled back along the tunnel, until once again the roar of the storm sounded loud along the passageway. He stood up in the tunnel mouth and looked out into the grayish blanket of the rain, barely able to make out the shadow of the high wall opposite. Then, turning about, he thought of another thing. He knelt beside the set gun and took out the two shells he had brought with him and loaded the weapon, muttering: "Stranger, here's my callin' card . . . in case you get back before we leave."

From where he sat hunkered down on a ledge directly across from the tunnel opening, Grove Dines made out

Platt's shadowy form as it stood for a second or two outlined against the cobalt shadow of the tunnel behind. Dines had his six-gun in his hand and now raised and leveled it. But then he hesitated, knowing that the shadows were too deceiving for him to make sure. He wouldn't shoot unless he was sure of killing, and the lawman's form opposite was too indistinct for him to make certain of a shot.

Suddenly he thought of something that sent him climbing down the steep rock wall, unmindful of the rain that drove slanting at his face and soaked him to the skin. Below once more, he walked the hundred yards out into the main cañon where he had left the gray ground haltered.

The saddle was wet as he climbed into it, but, again, he didn't mind and put the animal to a stretching run. There was a poncho laced to the saddle cantle, but he didn't bother to reach around and get it, for the slash of the downpour and the coolness of his wet clothing somehow suited his mood. His thin-lipped face was set in an expression that would have passed for a smile had it not been for the bleakness of his gray eyes.

It was twenty minutes before he raised the lights of the Anchor through the foggy blur of rain. He rode directly to the house and swung out of the saddle. Coming onto the porch, a man standing there called out a courteous: " 'Evenin', boss."

Dines ignored the greeting, answering tersely: "Find Owens and send him to the office."

In the small room that served him as ranch office, he changed to dry clothing, first toweling his flat-muscled

169

body to a glowing warmth that felt good after the cold ride. He took a bottle from a cabinet and had a drink of whiskey, and, when Owens opened the porch door and came in, he was buttoning on a white, freshly laundered shirt.

Owens said: "You pick a poor night to be out late, boss."

Dines pushed the bottle across the desk toward his ramrod. "Have a drink. Drink to Tom Platt." His face was set in a tight smile, one that caused Owens to eye him narrowly in speculation.

"What's on your mind, boss?" The ramrod poured himself a drink.

Dines told it then, all of it, and Owens stood held in a paralysis that was a mingling of fear and amazement. When Dines had finished, Owens said in a hollow voice: "That means I'm leavin'! By mornin' I can be halfway to the border."

"You'll stay."

Owens shook his head. "Platt's too smart. Before this is over, he'll look through every reward dodger in his desk. Sooner or later he'll find out I'm wanted. Uhn-uh, Grove, I'm pullin' out."

Dines seemed not to have heard. His gray eyes were fixed in a thoughtful vacancy that ignored the ramrod. Finally he drawled: "There's that half case of dynamite left over from the quarryin' we did up in the hills last spring."

Owens's manner abruptly changed. The trace of fear disappeared from his glance. He grinned, cunningly, and said: "I get it."

170

"There's the rain," Dines went on. "It'll wash out all sign. Four or five years from now, after we've thrown the two outfits together and Boyd Silvers is in his grave, I'll decide to open up his old mine. We'll run onto a couple of skeletons, one of 'em wearin' a sheriff's badge. We'll make a hero of what's left of Tom Platt. Maybe I'll pay a stonecutter to chip out a statue of him to put in front of the courthouse. We could letter some words below it . . . about the bravery of the badge-toters and how they carry out their sworn duty." Dines laughed softly, the look in his eyes hard and bright, touched with a trace of insanity.

Owens had lost color. "You believe in backin' your bets, don't you, Grove? When Tad Silvers caught us up there that day, you didn't waste any time lettin' him have it."

"Saddle two fresh horses and get three sticks of dynamite out of the well house, Ted," Dines snapped, all at once impatient. "We'll need a cap and a foot of fuse. Hurry it up!"

Ten minutes later they rode away from the Anchor into the dark mistiness of the storm. Owens's extra poncho made a rounded, tight bulk at his saddle cantle.

As they were leaving, headed back to the mine, Ben Healy was cutting west from Sagerock along the Fort Chester road. Fifteen minutes ago he had been worried over Tom Platt's absence. Then he happened to see the lawman's slicker hanging on the hook behind the jail office door, and with sight of it his worry was gone. He had listened to the mutter of the storm outside, grinned, and drawled aloud: "It's him that needs the nurse, not me. He's settin' out there waitin' for this weather to break, not wantin' a wettin'. Hell, I might as well take it out to him."

Ben had a live curiosity. Even though it was a bad night for a man to be out, he was thankful of this excuse for going to Boyd Silvers's mine. Up until now he had been only a small unimportant link in this chain of circumstances surrounding Tad Silvers's death. Platt might still refuse to make use of him, but at least he'd get a look at that mine and the set gun that had come near to killing first Tad Silvers, then Tom Platt.

CHAPTER
FIVE

Grove Dines felt easier when he saw the dun standing down headed there in the shadows at the foot of the muck dump. His hunch had been a good one. Platt was still here. The rain had slacked off a bit and a wind was whipping it in fierce gusts that at times blotted out all but the head and neck of the bay gelding he rode.

As he swung around, he called softly to Owens: "Keep that fuse dry."

They climbed the sifting surface of the dump to the tunnel opening. Dines held his Colt in his right hand now as he edged close in to the opening and let his glance search the deep shadows inside. He waited for Owens, and, when the ramrod knelt beside him, he ordered softly: "Rig the cap and fuse."

Owens worked swiftly, and in two minutes the three sticks of dynamite were ready, wrapped tightly together with a strip of cloth, the foot-long length of fuse a black, snake-like tail swinging from one end and fitting into the copper cylinder of the cap.

"You wait here."

Dines took the dynamite and crawled out of sight into the opening. He felt his way, knowing it well. When he came to the two rocks that had held the end of the trigger string, his hand ran beyond them and felt out a small niche in the rock of the wall. It was what he wanted. He rammed the dynamite into the opening and scraped some dirt off the floor and packed it in tightly around the bundle. Then, laying the six-gun within easy reach, he struck a match and touched it quickly to the end of the fuse. It sputtered alive.

He looked up, beyond the glare of the sudden fitful light, and what he saw made him flatten to the floor and send his hand darting to one side to close on his .45.

Tom Platt stood not twenty feet down the tunnel, stooped over because of the low ceiling, staring directly at him in numbed surprise. Those two were motionless for one brief interval, then Platt's right hand swung up to his holster, and he drawled: "So you're the one, Dines!"

As his words carried clearly across the interval, Platt saw Dines's hand close on the gun. The lawman flattened to the wall barely in time to get out of the way of the two thunderous shots the rancher thumbed from his gun. And before Tom could draw his own weapon, Dines had crawled back out of sight.

Behind him sounded Taichert's steps. Bob called: "Tom! You here, Tom?"

"Here." Platt spoke quietly, for Taichert was already alongside in the darkness. "It's Dines," he added, and mumbled a low oath. "I've been blind, Bob. It was Dines all the time."

174

From the tunnel mouth, the rancher called: "Stay where you are, you two! Make a break for it and we'll cut you down!"

Platt ignored those words, for his glance now took in the flickering light of the fuse that made the shadows jump eerily along the floor and wall. He said quickly: "Stay set, Bob. He's planted some dynamite up front. I'm goin' up after it."

But as he took a forward step, Bob Taichert's hand shot out and closed on his arm, pulling him back. In a split second Tom Platt knew what it was Taichert intended. As he swung around at the pressure on his arm, his right hand rose in a tight, hard arc and struck a blow full on the point of Taichert's chin. It was a blow that hurt Platt's hand, but he had the satisfaction of dimly seeing Taichert go down. Then he turned, drew his gun, and walked quickly toward the opening.

Dines saw him, and called: "Get back, you bull-headed old fool!" And he thumbed a shot down the corridor, not aiming it because of an insane desire that Tom Platt should be alive when that dynamite charge cut loose. He could glimpse the fuse as Platt drew back, out of sight again. The fuse had burned nearly half its length.

Suddenly he heard a sound below, a call that came faintly through the toneless murmur of the rain. Someone down there called Tom Platt's name.

Owens reached out and took a tight hold on his shoulder. "Sounded like Ben Healy," the ramrod breathed.

"Then we'll wait for him inside!" Dines answered. He took a quick look along the tunnel, saw that Platt was out of sight, and crawled into the opening. He moved quickly, hearing Owens directly behind. His right hand caught up a fistful of dirt which he dropped on the short length of fuse. It wouldn't burn out, but the flame would be shadowed. There was yet plenty of time for what was coming.

Ben Healy's voice called again, this time closer. "Platt! Where the hell are you? What's all the shootin'?"

Dines tried to make out the deputy's figure outside but couldn't. He whispered softly to Owens: "Wait'll he gets close!" Then, his back crawling from an expected burst of sound behind, he half faced into the tunnel, his gun leveled to line at any sudden stab of flame he saw back there.

Suddenly Ben Healy's stocky figure loomed before Owens. The ramrod thumbed back the hammer of his six-gun, half crouched and facing the deputy. On the heel of the hammer click, he saw Healy abruptly stumble and fall forward. Owens fired, but a nervousness threw his shot wide. Then, a split second later, Ben's awkwardly falling bulk crashed into him, driving him back.

Owens's back-reaching hand brushed aside the trigger spring of the set gun. The shotgun exploded in an inferno of sound that made the ground tremble. And its harsh echo down the corridor blended with Ted Owens's high-pitched scream. Owens writhed and his left hand came around to claw at his useless right side.

Ben Healy, shocked, surprised, picked himself up and ran out of the tunnel.

That burst of gunflame gave Tom Platt a clear picture from where he stood thirty feet away. As the explosion sent back a rush of impounded air, his hand was already swinging up his Colt .45. He shot blindly, three spaced, staccato blasts that chopped out in a wicked lance of flame at the spot where a moment ago he had seen Grove Dines crouching.

Suddenly the fuse burned clear of the dirt Dines had heaped around it. And at the first hint of light Platt's glance took in the scene before him. Owens lay on his back, his right arm torn and bleeding. Dines was coming to his feet in an uncertain stagger, swinging up his weapon. Frantically, thinking he was already too late, Tom Platt fired again.

He saw Grove Dines's flat body jerk spasmodically at the impact of his slug. Dines staggered, sat down suddenly. And as the rancher's head fell onto his chest, a thin trickle of blood came from his mouth.

It was then that Tom Pratt saw the flame licking up the last three-inch length of fuse.

He threw his gun from him and groped blindly along the floor. The three seconds it took him to reach Bob Taichert were an eternity. He took Taichert by the arms, heaved him bodily to his shoulders. Then, with the unwieldy bulk of the unconscious man making his steps uncertain, he half walked and half ran those forty feet to the tunnel mouth.

As he reached the opening and took a half step to one side a terrific blast beat out at him. He lost his balance and fell forward and down the sloping surface of the muck heap. The loose dirt there broke his fall as he hit the ground on one shoulder. He felt Taichert's body pile onto him as he went down into the mud and slime.

It was all over. Platt sat up weakly, feeling a searing pain in the shoulder that had broken his fall. Bob Taichert lay beside him, stirring faintly. Above, a shadowy figure loomed out of the mushrooming cloud of dust that boiled out of the tunnel mouth. Platt didn't recognize that figure until Ben Healy called down: "You sure believe in cuttin' it fine, Tom!"

Afterward, when Taichert and Platt were on their feet, Ben asked: "Who was it I bumped into when I tripped?"

"That's three times that damned root has saved a man's life," Tom Platt muttered. He looked above, toward the spot where the tunnel opening had been. "I ought to spend a day or two diggin' it out. I could frame it and hang it in the office."

"What root?" Ben asked.

So Platt had to explain, in detail.

Later, when they rode down Sagerock's street to the jail, Platt said: "You two go in and wait."

It was ten minutes before he rode back down the street and swung in at the hitch rail out front. By that time Taichert and the deputy had a fire going and were drying their mudcaked outfits before the stove.

Platt came in, slamming the door behind him, a broad smile on his face. He went to the desk and spilled something out of his hand onto the desk top, fully in the glare of the lamp.

Ben Healy said: "That desk's messy enough without your throwin' a handful of dirt on it."

Platt was looking at Taichert. He said: "You'll be wantin' to head directly for the Silvers' place, Bob. After you've seen Fran" — his smile broadened — "get old Boyd Silvers out of bed and tell him he's got a first-rate silver mine on his place." He sobered for an instant, then added: "With two first-class skeletons keepin' guard on it."

GHOST BRAND OF
THE WISHBONES

Jonathan Glidden's title for this short novel was "Ghost-Brand of the Wishbones." It was sent to his agent on October 12, 1939 and was sold for $135.00 on March 2, 1940. It first appeared under the title "Half-Owner of Hell's Last Herd" by Peter Dawson in *Western Novel and Short Stories* (6/40), a Red Circle pulp magazine edited at the time by Robert O. Erisman. It was showcased in first position on the cover. Because of a fascination with railroading in the Old West, Jon Glidden set several dramatic scenes on trains and in cabooses in his Western fiction, in such novels as *Royal Gorge* (1948) and *Ruler of the Range* (1952), and in this story.

CHAPTER
ONE

The first oncoming chill of the early November evening was freshening the still clear air, and the sun's orange disk was rimming the flat horizon behind the string of twenty-six boxcars as the freight crawled in on the way station at Gody. The jerk of poorly applied air brakes banged back along the line of cars, and the bawling of cattle added its din to the racket. The engine, wheels sliding, coasted forty yards beyond the squat red-painted water tank. When the heavy load behind gave its last stopping jerk, the engineer pushed the train back those forty yards, and his firemen crawled up over the slanting heap of coal behind the cab to swing the tank's trough arm in over the tender's reservoir.

The conductor on the caboose, about to swing aground from the rear platform's bottom step when the train started back, cursed beneath his breath and grumbled: "Hose coupling give out. Damn these new-fangled brakes. Ben, go fix it."

Three men stood above him on the platform, a brakeman and two others outfitted in range clothes. The brakeman carried a red storm lantern. He nodded on back along the right of way and queried: "Who's carryin' this lantern back there?"

183

For twenty miles the right of way embankment drew a string-straight and empty line across the sage-studded flats. The conductor glanced back along it, growled irritably: "Nothin' comin', is there?"

The brakeman swung down off the step. "Anything you say, John." He started up along the cars to look for the disconnected hose coupling. "Only you needn't be so damned proddy. Is it my fault you got cleaned?"

The two 'punchers, alighting now and stretching stiffened legs, looked at one another with mock-serious expressions at the brakeman's last remark. The tallest and leanest, the one with the steel-gray eyes, drawled: "Should we make John another loan, Red? It'd help to pass the time." His aquiline face was shadowed by a smile.

"No, you don't!" the conductor hastily put in. "I'm through with that deck of cards!"

Red, shorter than his companion and his shoulders and upper arms heavy muscled and filling out the sleeves of his blue-checked shirt tautly, looked up toward the station a hundred yards ahead and stated: "We won't need John any longer. Here comes company, Bill."

The tall 'puncher faced about and for a long moment eyed three men striding toward them along the embankment. Two of the trio were an average height and lean, while the third was short and chunky of build. All three carried saddles and blanket rolls, and all three were bowlegged, walking with the choppy stride of saddle-bred men unused to even this walk of little more than a hundred yards.

184

The conductor, eyeing the newcomers, said: "I've a good mind to tell them how your luck's runnin', North!"

"Go ahead," Bill North drawled, busy building a smoke. "They look like they'd take it as a come-on."

But the conductor said nothing about Bill North's unbeatable luck at poker as he sold the three passengers tickets to Apache Wells, half a night's ride east. He was privately hoping to see the sixty-four dollars that had been in his wallet early this morning, and that was now stuffed in the pocket of this Bill North's Levi's, change ownership during the inevitable game of draw that would commence once the freight got under way again. He told his three new passengers that the caboose was crowded and to rope their belongings onto the rear platform, then sauntered on up toward the station to pass the time of day with the agent.

A quarter hour later two sharp blasts from the locomotive's whistle sent the conductor on back to his caboose. Ben, the brakeman, reported finding the loose air-brake hose connection. The conductor gave the engineer the highball with a wave of his hand, and the bank of slackened couplings slowly rode the length of the train. Before it had reached the long freighter's rear, the conductor was stepping into the smoke-fogged caboose.

Bill North and Red Huggins and the three strangers were sitting in chairs around the small table in the center of the narrow room. In one of the pair of bunks on the left wall lay the third man of the crew, a brakeman, asleep. The shaded lamp over the table was

185

lighted against the gathering dusk. Red was shuffling a deck of cards, and one of the newcomers, a dour-faced individual whose right eyelid drooped against the curl of smoke from his cigarette, was drawling: "Two bits is a small limit for a short trip like this."

As Bill North responded disarmingly — "How about fifty cents?" — the conductor, climbing the iron steps that led to the cupola along the right wall, smiled to himself. Today's limit had been only a dime, and he'd lost half a month's pay. If Bill North's luck held, he'd have every nickel on the train inside the next three hours. If it didn't, North was wild enough to bet his half ownership of this trainload of cattle, or the conductor had him figured wrong.

Bill North's luck held. At nine, while the freight crawled up the long grade to cross a southward-flung spur of the Wishbones, the conductor estimated North had won a hundred and ten dollars. Red Huggins was about even. It was the three strangers who had lost.

At nine-thirty the man who'd suggested higher stakes, whose right eyelid drooped even when he wasn't smoking, threw down his cards after failing to raise a bet of Bill North's and turned to the conductor to ask: "Whereabouts are we?"

His question came a few moments after the conductor had felt the train gathering speed. He answered: "Just over the grade."

"How long before we make that spur junction?"

The conductor thought a moment. "Twenty minutes, maybe. Why?"

"Just wonderin'. They fixed that stretch yet?"

Ben, the brakeman, muttered: "Hell, no, they haven't!"

"We always slow for it," the conductor said.

The stranger got up out of his chair. "Count me out this deal. I'm goin' out for some air."

"Me too, Ed," spoke up the man alongside him. He pocketed his chips and followed the other out through the door and onto the platform, walking spraddle-legged against the lurching of the car. The remaining stranger, the one they called Runt, said: "Let's get a hand in while they're gone."

Bill North picked up the cards and shuffled them.

On the platform out back, Ed knelt alongside his blanket roll the instant his companion had closed the door. He loosened the rope wound about one end of it and pulled out a pair of shell belts and .45 Colts, bracing himself against the car's swaying rear wall as he cinched them on. His companion did the same, only that he took a package from his roll in addition to his guns.

Ed leaned close, calling above the roar of the grinding trucks: "Got everything straight, Sid?"

Sid nodded. He was tying his package, a foot long and slender, to the belt of his pants by means of a rawhide thong. He said: "Careful, Ed. See that two-fingered hand of the brakie's in there? Don't let that happen to you." A moment later he was throwing a leg over the platform's railing and climbing the iron-runged ladder to the swaying roof of the car. Ed followed.

The footing on the catwalk atop the caboose was uncertain and dangerous. They both went to hands and knees, crawling forward. When they reached the space between the caboose and the last boxcar, Sid jumped across, and Ed climbed down between the cars, using the ladder. But he followed Sid's jump between the next two cars, and soon they were walking in a half crouch as the cars toward the freight's middle rode more steadily. Far ahead, the rosy glow of the locomotive's opened firing door tinted the obscurity of the night's blackness for better than a minute. It helped them to see to walk. Ed, glancing off across the vague-shadowed distance to the north, thought he could make out the high faint outline of the Wishbone peaks but wasn't certain.

It took them twelve minutes to walk the catwalks of the twenty-six boxcars. In that interval the train's speed had slackened even for the downgrade. Finally, as they crouched at the front end of the car immediately behind the tender and were looking down into the engine cab, Sid could make out, far ahead in the distance, a winking green flicker of light, the switch's lantern. He showed it to Ed, shouting: "There she is! We'll have to work fast."

They climbed down from the ladder until Ed stood straddling the link and pin coupling between boxcar and tender. He moved aside long enough to let Sid edge past him and disappear up the tender's short ladder. Then, crouching, he squinted, trying to see clearly the details of the rattling coupling.

It jerked and swayed, massive iron squealing against the punishment of the thrusting loads pulling against it. Ed's droopy-eyed glance had taken in the brakeman's hand, with the three missing fingers; many times he'd seen train crewmen minus fingers, even hands, and knew the reason for it. Guiding the link of a coupling into its slot was highly dangerous. He knew that. What he didn't know was how dangerous it might be to pull out the pin.

He crouched, holding to a rung of the boxcar ladder with one hand, and reached out for the pin. He could feel it move under his hand. Gingerly, he took a hold on its blunt, rounded top. It moved upward under the pull of his hand. Suddenly it stuck as the locomotive pulled against it. Ed's face was a sickly yellow in the faint light. He didn't have much nerve for a thing like this. But then the pressure slacked off the pin, and he pulled it free and dropped it to the gravelly roadbed racing beneath the cars. He let the hose coupling to the air brakes go. It would break loose easily.

When he climbed up the boxcar ladder and stepped over to the broad wheel of the hand brake, he glanced ahead and saw Sid, both guns drawn and lined, sitting back against the slanting heap of coal in the tender. Fireman and engineer were facing Sid from the cab, hands raised to the level of their ears. Ed smiled, put thumb and third finger between his thin lips, and whistled shrilly into the train's riot of sound.

Sid, faintly hearing that signal, pushed erect and stepped onto the steel plates between cab and tender. His thumbs were hooked about the hammers of his guns, and there was a crooked smile on his face. He shouted above the pounding din of the locomotive's trucks: "Open 'er up, brother! Lay on the steam!"

The gray-mustached engineer reached back and pulled on the long throttle arm. The exhaust up front resumed its quick beat. The engineer's rheumy old eyes, staring back over Sid's head, came wide with surprise. His face hardened in stubborn anger as he saw the dull red front of the boxcar fall rapidly behind. He brought his hands slowly down, said — "To hell with you, stranger!" — and was turning and reaching for the throttle once more when Sid stepped in on him.

The gun in Sid's right hand rose and fell in a choppy stroke, the barrel striking the engineer a glancing blow above the temple. He started falling forward, but Sid reached out and pulled him back, letting him slump to the floor of the cab.

Sid wheeled on the fireman, who now stood white faced and in a paralysis of fear.

"Know how to run this thing?" he asked.

The fireman gulped, nodded.

Sid said: "Then burn some track as far as that switch up ahead. When you get there, throw on your brakes."

Turning the wheel to the hand brake on the catwalk of the car behind, Ed saw all this. Once, as Sid stepped in to slug the engineer, Ed's right hand had fallen to the butt of his gun, but the fireman made no try at Sid's back, and a moment later Sid had things in hand again. Below Ed, the brakes setting against the wheels screeched an inferno of sound. When the wheel would tighten down no more, he kicked shut the locking ratchet and turned and ran back along the car, jumping to the roof of the next. He set the brakes on that car, went to the next. Looking up ahead, he could see the cab light of the locomotive drawing away, already a hundred yards ahead of the first car.

Back in the caboose, Bill North had raised the limit on a pair of eights, his face set impassively and his long frame slumped down indolently in his chair. Runt, he saw, was a trifle nervous. Probably had a good hand. Bill was wondering if he should have passed the bet and left it up to Runt when he saw the conductor straighten from a stoop alongside an open locker at the rear wall and turn, frowning, to say: "Something's wrong up front! You notice anything?"

On the heel of his words, Runt sprang up out of his chair, kicking it from behind him and stepping back against the door to the platform. As he moved, his hand snaked in under his shirt and came out fisting a short-barreled .38 Smith and Wesson. He rocked it level with the table, moved it from side to side in a slow arc to cover Red and Bill, and said sharply: "Keep your hands on the table, gents, and you won't get hurt."

The conductor's sallow face froze in a look of bewilderment and wariness. As Bill straightened in his chair, drawling — "Watch it, Red!" — the conductor said: "By God, the engine's loose!"

Runt grinned wryly, his round face taking on an ugly look. "You guessed it, old-timer," he said. "We're goin' for a ride!"

Bill said: "A ride where?"

"Wait and see." Runt was smiling now, knowing that neither Red nor Bill were carrying guns.

Bill gave Red Huggins a brief glance, seeing that his partner's blunt and freckled face was set in an angry frown and that his hands were flat on the table, as though he was ready to come to his feet in a lunge. Knowing Red's quick temper, he cautioned once again — "Take it easy, Red." — and saw Red settle back into his chair.

Bill's casual glance judged the distance between table and door, where Runt stood. It wasn't more than five feet. The conductor stood to his left, backed against the closed doors to the row of wooden lockers. To the right of the table, immediately behind Red's chair, the sleeping brakeman lay on his side on the bunk chained to the wall. Ben, the second brakeman, had a moment ago stepped out onto the rear plat-form. Bill was thinking mostly of Ben.

Ten seconds passed slowly, Runt standing down headed and peering across at his three prisoners with a sardonic and twisted smile on his face. He started to say: "You won't have long to . . ."

Suddenly his head jerked up, and he lurched a half step forward. The door behind had abruptly pressed inward against his back. He turned his head, glancing briefly back over his shoulder and stepping to one side.

In the fraction of a second Runt's eyes left him, Bill North lunged up out of his chair, reaching down to take a hold on the edge of the table top. The table, he knew, was bolted to the floor. But it was old and wobbly and none too strong. He straightened his weight against it, putting all the drive of his body behind arms and shoulders.

192

The heavy solid top creaked under the upthrust. Runt was swinging around to face him again. All at once the near end of the table top came loose under Bill's driving thrust. He threw it up, against the leverage of the still-fast nails along its far edge, making a shield of it before his body. He pushed it out, stepping to one side as the gun at the door exploded in a welling burst of sound. Then, driving all his weight forward behind it, he left his feet in a dive.

The table top went up and over. Runt saw it swinging over at him. He tried to dodge out of the way, but the inswinging platform door caught him. He put all his weight against the door, tried to push it shut. It gave a foot, stopped. Then the slab of heavy wood was striking him in the chest, pinning him back against the wall. He rocked his gun up and thumbed two thought-quick shots upward and in line with Bill's stretched-out frame that was diving in on him. Then Bill's falling weight laid a crushing pressure against his chest, and his head rocked sideways under a glancing blow of Bill's fist.

His hand that held the gun opened weakly to let the weapon clatter to the floor. His head sagged, and his knees went back on him to leave him hanging there, wedged erect by the table top.

As Bill eased his weight to the floor and stooped to pick up Runt's fallen gun, Red Huggins got up out of his chair and let out his breath in a gusty sigh that looked like relief. He reached over and pulled up the table top. Runt fell to the floor. Red pointed to two bits of lead showing through the splintered underside of the slab of wood.

"All your luck don't come in a deck of cards today, Bill," he said.

CHAPTER
TWO

As the ruddy-faced fireman pushed forward the long brake arm to slow abruptly the locomotive out of its fast downgrade run, Sid backed toward the steps, his gun lined, drawling: "Stay set!"

He carried the long, paper-wrapped package that had been tied to his belt under his right arm now. He reached back, took a hold on the hand rail, and swung down onto the bottom step of the cab. Glancing quickly ahead, he saw the green glow of the switch's lantern a bare hundred yards away in the fan-spread, bright swath of the locomotive's headlight. The cross-etched ties were racing into that light at blurred speed. Sid called up sharply into the cab: "Brakes, damn it! Use your sand!"

He could see the upright switch arm now, sliding toward him along the embankment. Beyond it, in a gentle wide curve, arced the dull and rusted twin ribbons of the rails leading down the spur line.

A moment later a fine spray of blown sand made him squint his eyes, and the drive-wheels up ahead threw sparks as the sandbox lines poured sand against the rails. He felt the lurching weight of the engine slow against this new traction, and the cross-ties in the headlight's bright glare became distinct and separate under the slowing speed.

The green-lighted switch post dropped past him. Two seconds later, he rammed his gun into holster, took the package in his hand, and swung out and down. He lit in a half crouch, lost his footing in a forward sprawl, and rolled down the embankment, clutching the package to his flat chest. He stopped finally, crouched on his knees, his body aching. He looked down at the package in his arms, wide eyed and a trifle awed. Hanging from a torn end of the paper was a coiled three-foot length of fuse. The ends of four sticks of dynamite showed out of that tear.

Sid was a sober man as he came to his feet, being well acquainted with the peculiarities of dynamite that might have seen him blown to a thousand fragments these last three seconds. He glanced down the right of way to see the locomotive's cab light crawling slowly away. A muttering, rumbling roar behind him made him turn quickly and run the twenty yards back to the waist-high switch post. He laid down the bundle of dynamite, drew a gun, and shot the heavy padlock off the locked switch arm, the sound of the explosion drowned in the increasing thunder of the oncoming train.

He lifted the long arm and threw his weight against it as the high shadow of the first boxcar loomed out of the darkness a scant thirty feet away. The arm moved around stubbornly as the boxcar roared past him. He watched, fascinated, as the car hit the switch, halfway expecting to see it go straight on. But it gave an

196

unsteady lurch and swayed out onto the spur, the others racing in a long line after it. Sid breathed a sigh of relief.

In the next quarter minute, he moved down a few yards and crouched close in alongside the rumbling wheel trucks of the cars as they rattled over the near side of the switch. He unwound the coil of fuse and, shielding a lighted match in his cupped hand, lit the end of it. Then, scooping a hollow out of the gravel close in to the rails, he laid the package down and came erect and ran on down the spur a good twenty yards.

He had to stand there another ten seconds, listening to the blended rattle of the trucks and the bawling of the cattle inside the cars. The caboose's red lantern came toward him, struck the bend, lurched around it. He started to run with the train. As the caboose's hand rail rushed even with him, he reached out and jumped. He caught his hold, and his body was thrown inward so that he fell up onto the sharp-edged steps, bruising his thigh.

His first instinctive gesture was to reach down and draw the gun from the holster along his thigh. Crouching, he looked up onto the platform. It was empty. That sight reassured him. He went up onto the platform, thinking that Runt had done his job well. He pushed open the door and stepped through it, squinting into the glare of light from the lamp swinging from the ceiling.

What he saw during the next two seconds brought the breath sucking into his lungs in a sharp gasp. Runt sat in a chair, hands raised. Beyond him stood the man

197

who'd won most of the money in tonight's game of draw poker, Bill North. Beside North, boots spread wide against the violent swaying of the car, stood North's sorrel-thatched partner. And sitting on the bunk beside Red were the two brakemen and the conductor.

Bill North held Runt's ivory-handled .38 lined at the door.

It was sight of that gun that brought Sid to a sharp halt, halfway in through the door. His own gun was hanging at his side in his hand.

Bill said sharply: "Drop it, Sid!"

Sid's hold was relaxing on the gun when a sudden lurching of the car over the uneven roadbed thrust him hard against the door frame. Bill North staggered uncertainly. Red seemed to lose his footing. A split second later his heavy weight smashed solidly in against Bill. Red cursed, and Bill was thrown far off balance. There was a moment in which Bill's gun wavered. Then another jolt of the train threw Red into him again, this time harder.

Sid's gun rocked up and exploded, catching Bill reaching out instinctively with both hands to break his fall against the row of wooden lockers set against the wall. The sleeve along Bill's left arm showed a ragged tear where the bullet passed. Sid thumbed back the hammer of his weapon.

For the space of one suspended second, Sid thought he was going to have to shoot again. Then Bill, sensing that his gun was useless and a foot out of line now, opened his hand and dropped the weapon.

198

Sid stepped in, kicked the door shut behind him, and said: "That's better. Thanks for the help, redhead!"

Red glared at him in anger a moment, then turned to Bill to say in a lifeless tone: "You ought to kick hell out of me, Bill! But I couldn't help it."

Bill drawled: "Forget it. We'll get another chance." He eyed Sid with a steely, yet faintly amused, glance, as though he were enjoying this.

Sid noticed, then, that Runt had stepped in alongside him. He said sharply — "Get that iron!" — and held his gun lined as his companion crossed and picked up the weapon Bill had dropped.

Then, when Runt was alongside him once more, he said: "Get up and help Ed."

Runt backed out the door. He hesitated a moment on the platform, reluctantly eyeing the iron ladder that climbed to the roof outside the platform. While he stood there, an earth-jarring and muffled explosion sounded far back along the spur's right of way. That would be the dynamite blowing the switch. Still feeling an impotent anger at having been taken so easily back there three minutes ago, Runt forgot his caution and climbed the ladder and made the roof.

Four cars ahead he could vaguely see Ed turning the car's brake wheel. When he had covered that distance and told Ed — "Okay, so far." — Ed said: "Go on ahead. Get every other one. I'll be right behind."

The two of them, along with Sid, had planned this out days ago. How the crew in the caboose was to be held by one man while the other two cut the train loose, one man handling the engine crew while the other slowed the long line of cars by setting the brakes. It had called for accurate timing beginning at the top of the grade when Ed and Sid had made their excuses to leave the poker game. So far those few minutes when Bill North had called the turn back there in the caboose didn't mean anything. Sid's quick thinking and Red's carelessness had taken care of that. Now all that remained was to get the brakes off the slowing line of cars and let them coast on down the long grade of the spur. That grade ran for six miles.

CHAPTER
THREE

After Runt had gone out, Sid said: "Might as well sit and be comfortable, gents. This'll take some time." He had a moment ago heard the muffled explosion of the dynamite charge he'd left at the switch. The others hadn't noticed it.

The brakeman, who had been asleep until Runt's shooting had jerked him awake a few minutes ago, said: "What'll take some time? What's goin' on here, Ben?" He hadn't understood all he'd seen since opening his eyes.

The conductor said: "Can't tell yet, Mart. Better shut up." His eyes hadn't left Sid's rock-steady gun. He wasn't used to guns, didn't trust them, and was a little afraid now. The conductor said: "This is a penitentiary offense."

"What is?" Sid drawled, smiling bleakly.

"Breaking a train, threatening the crew with firearms!"

Sid laughed. "Wait and you'll have some more to add to that, old-timer." He eyed Bill and Red a moment. "You two're goin' to like what's comin'."

"What is comin'?" Red asked belligerently.

"It's too good to spill beforehand." Sid's smile all at once disappeared. "North, step over there out of the way of your partner."

Presently, Sid had them arranged to suit him, conductor and brakemen sitting on the floor, Red and Bill seated in chairs at the far corners of the small room, out of reach of the lockers. Sid himself climbed halfway up into the cupola, so that he could look down on them and cover them all with a two-inch move of his gun. He could raise his head without being seen and look from time to time out the front window of the cupola and down along the line of cars into the night's obscure blackness.

The cars were rolling on at good speed now, their motion telling Sid that the brakes had been released. Occasionally the steep banks of a deep cut into the side of a hill would crawl past. Sid knew every one of those hills and smiled as the train held its slow speed.

Five minutes after he'd gone to sit on the steps, he saw Ed walk toward him out of the shadows up ahead. He tapped on the cupola's window as Ed started climbing over it. Ed crouched, saw him, and waved. Forty seconds later the door below opened, and Ed came in.

He looked up, a confident smile on his face. "Better get goin', Sid," he said. "We're comin' up on the shed."

Sid climbed down out of the cupola and went to the door. As he opened it, he said: "Watch North. He's got ideas."

Ed nodded, drew both his guns, and sat in a chair to one side of the door, guns in his lap.

"How about the switch?" Sid asked. "I barely heard it."

"Blown to hell," Ed told him. "We ought to have until the middle of the mornin', dependin' on how smart that fireman is. It's about forty miles into the Wells, ain't it?"

Sid nodded, repeated — "Keep your eyes on North." — and went out onto the platform. Two minutes later he swung down off the caboose within a few yards of an abandoned tool shed set close in alongside the tracks. The shed was painted the same ugly red as the water tank back at Gody. Tied in back of it were three horses, standing saddled and the cinches loose.

He tightened the cinches and swung astride the blaze-faced sorrel, leading the other pair by their reins. In the mile and a quarter he covered, he rode a stretch of country that was gently rolling and dotted with sagebrush and a few scattered piñon. It was dry country, unfenced, and, from the highest point he crossed, he sighted no light winking into the night's obscure distance. The high vault of the star-studded heavens was shadowed to the north by a vague line of tall peaks, the Wishbones. Up there, Sid knew, people lived and scorned the waste of this near-desert country.

He was twenty minutes covering the mile and a quarter that brought him to the train, now stopped a few rods below a cluster of long unused cattle pens that had been the reason for the building of this spur line. He found Ed and Runt waiting impatiently at the near corner of the first corral. He smiled broadly at sight of the caboose's passengers, and drawled as he sloped out of his saddle: "Nice work, Ed. I wouldn't have thought of it."

Ed had somewhere found some rusty barb wire and used it to advantage. Bill North, Red Huggins, the conductor, and his two brakemen all sat with backs propped against separate posts that formed the line of the corral. They were tied to the posts by ample windings of the barb wire. Their hands were fastened behind the posts, and not one of them could move more than his legs without being reminded by the prod of the sharp-pointed barbs that to try and get loose was a futile task.

Sid focused his attention on Bill North, striding over to where Bill sat and asking: "Want anything?"

"A drink."

Sid turned and called: "Runt, get a canteen."

Each of the horses carried a canteen looped over the horn. Runt brought one across, and Sid gave each of his prisoners a long pull at it, telling Ben, who angrily refused it: "You'd better. It'll be hot as the hinges of hell down here in the mornin'." Ben finally drank.

Finished, Sid walked back to Ed, who was already in the saddle, waiting impatiently. "How about the locks on the cars?" he asked.

"Busted 'em open," Ed told him. "Hell, let's get started! You act like we was goin' home from a church social."

Sid climbed onto his sorrel. He lifted a hand, looked across at Bill and Red, and called: "Thanks, you two!"

Bill called back: "We'll be seein' you."

"Not if I can help it," Sid said with a dry chuckle. He and the others moved off into the darkness down the line of the spur. In another quarter minute the sounds of the boxcar doors grating open on their rusty hinges blended with the bawling of the cattle.

For the next quarter hour, Bill North listened to the sounds that slurred across the night's stillness, building a mental picture of what Sid and the other two were doing. Occasionally, he heard Ed's or Runt's voices high pitched in curt yells. There came the sounds of heavy planks being rigged from car platforms to the ground, runways for unloading the cattle. And always, insistently, rose the plaintive bawling of the thirsty cattle.

The sounds moved farther away as the near cars were emptied and the three 'punchers worked on toward the head of the train, pushing the cattle already out of the cars along with them. Finally Bill looked across at Red, who was wired to the next post, fifteen feet away. He could make out the faint outline of Red's face without being able to catch his partner's expression. Red was looking at him. He smiled mirthlessly and drawled: "We've been wastin' our time playin' nursemaid to a bunch of critters, Red. We should have thought of somethin' like this!"

Red said savagely: "If I could get my feet under me, I could work this post loose!"

"Save yourself the trouble," Bill told him. "We're licked for now, fella."

Red was silent for a moment. "I'd cut off my left leg to have that to do over again! It's my fault, bumpin' into you the way I did back there when you had the gun on him! We'd have had 'em if it hadn't been for that."

"Our luck was due to run out. If it hadn't been that, it'd have been something else."

There was an awkward ten-second silence. Then Red said: "We'll have to let our option on the layout run out, won't we?"

Bill gave a laugh that lacked all amusement. "And start all over again."

Ben, the brakeman, said from where he sat at the post behind Bill: "Is it that bad?"

Red told him dryly: "It's worse than that. About this time last year Bill had a fair herd built up on shares from roddin' one of the big outfits over west. All he needed was money. Then I come along. I had the money but no cattle, and knew of a sweet layout we could lease for two years with an option to buy. We went in together as partners on the Bar Eighty-Eight. This is the first sale we've made."

"Only we didn't make it," Bill said. "Five hundred and twenty head at around twenty-two dollars a critter. Figure it out for yourself."

Ben said: "Something over eleven thousand you've lost, then, ain't it?"

"Correct as hell!" Red growled. "But it's Bill that holds the sack, not me, damn it! All I lose is the fifteen hundred I laid on the line for this year's lease. I'm damned lucky we had to wait until I got back to put up the money for next year."

Bill drawled quietly: "We shouldn't have shipped the whole bunch, Red. Not that I'm blamin' you, understand."

"My ideas are always half baked," Red said reluctantly. "But I still say we could have sold this bunch and come back and bought stuff locally and made a nice profit."

They fell silent, each sobered by his own thoughts, by this sudden and unalterable destroying of each man's hopes.

At length, Bill said: "Maybe we can get 'em back again."

In this past minute he'd listened to the herd, his herd, moving away from the far end of the train. The distant rumble of the animals on the move came steadily now, a sign that the train was unloaded and that the herd was being driven off.

From beyond Red, the conductor called: "You won't have a chance to get 'em back. This is tough country, Bill. Your critters are headed for the Wishbones, them peaks across there to the north. You could lose half the cattle in New Mexico in those cañons up there."

Bill considered that, saying finally: "How about it, Red? Want to make a try?"

Red shook his head. "Not the way I figure it now. If I get back in a hurry, maybe I can sell our under-age stuff before winter sets in. That's the only chance we stand of gettin' out of this with even our undershirts. The bank ought to give us something for what improvements we've made. We'll get maybe a thousand apiece out of it. You work it at this end if you want. I'll work from the other."

"What'll I be up against, Red? You're from over here somewhere, aren't you?"

"From right here in the Wishbone country," Red told him. "That's what I don't like about it. It's like John, here, says. The country's tough, the people in it tougher. My guess is we won't get far."

Once again a silence held them. Bill knew that Red was listening to the fast-fading sounds of the herd moving out across the flats toward the hills, knew, too, that it was hurting Red as much as it was him to sit here helpless under a fifteen-foot length of rusty barb wire.

"How about money?" Bill asked, at length. "Runt took mine. I'll need a horse and a hull and an iron if I'm to stay."

"Better wait until I get back," Red said.

"How far's the nearest town?"

"Forty miles."

"I could get work."

"You could," Red admitted, "but it'd be two months before you'd earned enough. By that time the Wishbone country would be under two feet of snow. Our critters would have healed over their new brands, and we'd stand as much chance of findin' 'em as we would a mother lode. Better come home with me, Bill."

"Uhn-uh. I'll stick around." He turned and called back over his shoulder to the conductor: "Will your outfit charge us fare back to town?"

John said in mock solemnity: "They never give out any free tickets I know of."

CHAPTER
FOUR

At eleven the next morning a repair train coasted down the spur and ground to a halt at the loading corrals. The crew brought the news that a sheriff with a twelve-man posse was headed out for the Wishbone country, having guessed that the trainload of cattle had been stolen. But, since the fireman who brought in the freight's locomotive last night couldn't tell the sheriff what brand to look for, and since broken country was making him ride a hard eighty miles before he could reach the Wishbone foothills, the chances were pretty slim that he'd ever smell the herd's dust. There were a dozen rocky cañons within thirty miles of here that would blot out the herd's sign and cover the rustlers' back trail.

Bill and the rest hadn't suffered much except for cramped limbs and lack of water. The train crew cut them loose, fed them, and gave them water, then hooked onto the empty freight and pulled it the six miles out the spur to the repaired switch on the main line. They were in Apache Wells by two that afternoon.

Red took the first train west two hours later. Those two hours he and Bill spent arguing with the division superintendent in the railroad's local office. It was finally agreed that the superintendent would allow them sixty dollars against the advance freight payment they had made on their cattle shipment. Red needed forty-three dollars for his ticket home. Bill was thankful to get the remaining seventeen.

That night, late, Bill sat in on a stud game at one of the town's three saloons. It started out as a small-stake game and picked up at two in the morning to a two-dollar limit. Bill was nearly even with the board when the stakes went up. An hour later he had a hundred and thirty dollars in blues and reds stacked before him on the table, in a run of luck much the same as yesterday's. At four, when the game wound up, he was better than two hundred the winner.

He slept until ten that morning, ate breakfast, and started spending his money. A hundred and sixty of it went for a four-year-old quarter-strain Thoroughbred chestnut a circus had left with the livery-barn owner two months ago in payment for a feed bill. The animal was short barreled and leggy and mean eyed. Bill would have given his last nickel for him. He bought a used saddle, an Andersen, for forty-three dollars and paid twenty-two more for a .45 Colt, nearly new. Most of the rest of his money, nine dollars and eighty cents, went for a box of shells, two blankets, a frying pan, grub, and tobacco. His pockets were nearly empty when he rode the chestnut out the far end of the street at four-thirty that afternoon.

His camp that night was in a shallow coulée on the sage flats twenty miles to the northwest of Apache Wells. Three hours in the saddle had told him he hadn't been wrong about the chestnut, whose only faults were too big a heart and a habit of throwing his head. Bill squatted by his fire and made a hackamore before he turned into his blankets. He was up at the first light of the false dawn and in the saddle before sunup.

Two mornings later, high in the Wishbone foothills and his breath misty in the frosty air, he followed a twisting and narrow cañon a sheepherder had yesterday afternoon told him would take him into Valle Grande, a broad high valley that boasted half a dozen big ranches and a town, Mile High. The going here was slow, the cañon bottom centered by a foaming stream, the banks on either side choked for long stretches by thorn and scrub-oak thickets that grew rankly in the short open spaces unshaded by the towering cedars and gray-bark pines. Occasionally, where the walls opened out, he could look back and out and down to see the hazy horizon-reaching stretch of the flat wastes below. Far out there showed the faint straight line of the railroad embankment, the curving line of the spur leaving it to strike in toward the foothills.

Seeing the line of that spur reminded him grimly of his reason for being here and of the slim chance this long ride had in netting him any hope for success. These tangled hills formed a rustlers' paradise and a lone man, unacquainted with them, could depend on little but luck on such an errand as this.

He came suddenly out of a turning to see that the walls were falling sharply away. A hundred yards farther on, climbing stiffly, put him at the very lip of the cañon mouth. Beyond, in a vast thirty-mile stretch backed by the jagged snowcapped peaks of the Wishbones themselves, lay a broad and saucer-like valley.

Bill whistled softly and reined in on the chestnut, awed by the sight before him. He had never seen such an uninterrupted sea of bright, green, lush grass meadow, and his range-bred eye examined it with a near-worshipful expression. From here he could count six streams, like the spokes of a wheel, that flowed down off the valley rim and into a broad lake at the near center. That lake had once doubtless been a volcano's crater; the soil must be rich and deep, aged by long centuries of weathering. Dotting the lines of the streams were clusters of tree clumps, cottonwood and poplar mixed in with jack pine and cedar. And, always near the trees, he could make out on the near slope of the valley the sprawling buildings of ranches, some small, a few big. Immediately below, less than a quarter mile away, grazed a bunch of twenty or thirty sleek and fat shorthorns. Here was a cattleman's dream come true.

He saw the town last of all. It sprawled on the far side of the sky-blue lake at the valley's center, alongside a deep stand of timber. Immediately below it a lighter line along the lake-shore was made by high cliffs, Bill decided. He lifted the reins and put the chestnut out of the cañon mouth, striking obliquely east toward the faint line of a trail that angled down through a belt of timber.

Twenty minutes later he was riding that trail through the timber, pines, pin oak, and cedar, when a rider cut out of the trees a bare fifty yards ahead and started walking his horse in the same direction Bill was taking. The man's face was turned away, but Bill saw that his outfit was a frayed buckskin jacket worn over a wool shirt, faded Levi's, boots, and flat-crowned black Stetson. A carbine in a leather scabbard nudged the inside of his right leg. His horse was a gray, sleek, leggy. He didn't look back along the trail but rode on at a slow trot, apparently unaware of Bill's presence.

Bill lifted the chestnut to a faster trot and was within twenty yards before the man turned and faced him, pulling the gray to a stop and turning so that his rifle was hidden on the pony's off side. His face, Bill saw now, was old and grizzled with a gray longhorn mustache and beetling bushy brows. That face was distinguished looking but set in a grave frown, not quite hostile yet lacking any trace of friendliness.

Bill reined in three strides short of the man and drawled: "Howdy. Goin' my way?"

The oldster made no reply for a long awkward moment. Then, levelly, he stated: "That depends. Where were you headed?"

"For town."

The man's pale blue eyes fell to Bill's waist, taking in the holstered .45 sagging at his thigh. He said then — "So am I." — nodding on down the trail.

That gesture, since he made no move to lead the way, was eloquent of the distrust that had showed in his glance as Bill rode up. Bill understood, then, that the oldster didn't want to go first and run the risk of a gun at his back, so he put the chestnut on down the trail in the lead.

They rode in silence for all of three minutes, the old man holding the gray half a stride behind the chestnut and keeping to the far side of the trail.

Bill ended the silence by looking levelly at the oldster and saying bluntly: "Maybe I was wrong. I thought I wanted company."

A barely perceptible change of expression betrayed the man's surprise. "It was your idea," he stated. "You know who I am, Mark Shaw. You were waitin' for me back there. Get it off your chest, whatever it is!" His glance was openly hostile now.

Bill stopped, Shaw doing likewise. They measured each other for the space of ten seconds. Then Bill said: "I didn't know who you were, I've never heard of you, and I wasn't waitin' for you back there. Take it or leave it." He nodded on along the trail. "You goin' first, or am I?"

"You're a Bar Eighty-Eight man, aren't you?" Shaw wasn't asking a question but making a statement.

Bill's high frame stiffened at the surprise packed in Shaw's words. How could Shaw know him and name his and Red's brand? He said warily: "What about the Bar Eighty-Eight?"

"Bruce Schuveen's the only man hirin' strangers these days."

Bill thought a moment, drawled: "Is the Bar Eighty-Eight Schuveen's brand?"

"You ought to know," Shaw said with a straight-faced look that defied reading. "You were headed out his trail."

214

Bill understood two things instantly: first, that here, five hundred miles east of his own layout and in another state, he had found a man using a brand identical to his, and, second, that Mark Shaw wasn't taking much pains at hiding his dislike for the owner of that brand, Bruce Schuveen.

He had to get something settled here and now. He asked: "Is it a long bar or short? Are the eights lazy or straight up?"

Shaw said dryly: "What stall are you tryin' to pull? Did Schuveen send you here to . . . ?"

Without finishing his question, he turned and glanced warily up along the timbered aisle of the trail behind. Then, turning back again, his right hand dropped out of sight on the off side of his horse and rose again, swinging the Winchester saddle gun into line. He levered a shell into the chamber and said in a flat drawl: "Make tracks, stranger, and make 'em fast. You're on Double S land, and you're foulin' the air with your stink! Tell Schuveen for me that this trail's closed to his men from now on, that my crew's keepin' it closed."

Bill started to say — "Partner, you've got me wrong! Let me . . ." — when the hard glitter in Shaw's eyes told him that further argument was futile. He drawled — "Thanks for gettin' me posted on a few things." — and rode on down the trail. A hundred yards farther on, after he'd left the lower margin of the timber, he glanced behind. The trail was empty. Mark Shaw was no longer in sight.

In the two-hour ride it took him to make the distance on in to Mile High, he noticed but few details of the country he rode through for he was thinking back over the things Shaw had told him. He was only vaguely aware that the valley, close at hand, didn't show the even topography of his far look at it from the rim. The trail wound in and out among low hummocks and hills, some rocky and barren of grass. There were long stretches of open meadow, and in the distance the gradual climb of the slope was broken in places by ridges and out-croppings. The ranches he passed didn't all bear out their promise of prosperity and neatness. Some were workmanlike layouts with a profusion of steep-roofed sheds and barns and corrals, but there were more shabby spreads, one lone log shack alongside a roofless barn where wagons and tools stood exposed to and rusting in the weather. As he rode on, the sun became hotter, and he shed his coat and strapped it to the cantle of the saddle.

The lake changed in looks, too. It grew smaller, and, now that the sky was no longer directly reflected in it, he saw that it was a dirty mud color, that its edge was flanked on this near side by a wide bog where marsh grass and cattails grew in the backwater.

He came into the far end of the town's street abruptly, from around a high and rocky butte that ran along the lake's edge. What he saw destroyed the last of his illusions about the valley's richness. It had evidently rained here last night or yesterday, for Mile High's single street was fetlock deep with mud along its whole length. It was a narrow street, flanked on either side by small slab or log shacks at the outskirts and by gray-weathered frame stores at the center, buildings whose false fronts were painted with faded, garish signs as crude as those of the desert towns on the plains below the hills. There were no awnings over the walks as in a plains town and, except at the town's center, no walks at all beyond the packed mud at each side of the street. Mile High had a dismal, forlorn look of decay even in this bright sunlit morning. It seemed to ignore the pleasing vista of the lake whose shore lay less than a hundred yards behind the buildings to Bill's right.

A few saddle horses stood in the mud at the tie rails, down headed and tails switching at the insistent bite of late autumn's loggy flies. Half a dozen loungers stood on the walk, eyeing Bill with faintly curious and unwelcome glances. Bill picked the driest spot and turned in there, before the door of a saddle shop with one window dust covered and the other half broken out and boarded up. Two doors below was a saloon. Along the wall on the nearest side of the batwing doors stood three men, two with muddy low-heeled boots and the third, a short heavy-built man, outfitted in untidy black broadcloth vest and pants, a white shirt frayed and grimy at the cuffs.

Bill sauntered along the walk past the trio, ignoring them, and turned in at the saloon. The heavy-set man in shirtsleeves pushed indolently out from the wall, spat on the walk, and followed him in. He was apparently the saloon's owner.

Bill said — "Beer." — when the man stood across the unwiped pine bar before him. The saloon owner picked

217

up a cloudy glass from the drainboard below his counter and turned to fill it from a barrel set on two sawhorses behind him.

"Wash it first," Bill drawled.

The man turned quickly with a down-lipped and belligerent scowl on his flabby face. "Mister," he said, "do you want to spend your nickel here or across the street? If you're spendin' it here, you'll use the glass I hand you and like it."

Bill reached out lazily and picked up a bung starter lying three feet away along the counter. He hefted it in his hand. That gesture, along with the suddenly granite-hard expression of his eyes, made the saloon man's glance widen in alarm. He said quickly — "All right, I'll get a clean one!" — and did so immediately. He filled the glass, set it on the counter, and went on ingratiatingly: "No hard feelin's. I had a bad night."

Bill ignored him, taking a swallow of the beer. A wry expression twisted his face, and he turned and spat the beer onto the floor, then faced the saloon owner again.

The man held up his hands, palms out, and took a backward step, saying defensively: "I know! The beer ain't so good. But you didn't ask. Here, have some of this. It's on the house."

He reached around to the shelf under the cracked mirror and hastily took down a shot glass and a bottle of whiskey. He drew out the cork, wiped the neck of the bottle on his sleeve, and poured a drink. Bill took it without comment, tasted it, and nodded. "Better," he said.

218

The saloon owner smiled. "My own bottle," he confided. "These white trash around here won't pay for good whiskey. I haul it fifty miles in and sell it at a loss. Brother, I'm gettin' out as soon as I get rid of what's in the cellar."

"It ought to be a good town," Bill observed, his manner a little more friendly. "Why isn't it?"

"It used to be," the saloon owner agreed. "But not lately." He eyed Bill with a trace of suspicion in his glance, as though reluctant to explain any further.

"What's happened?"

The man shook his head. "Uhn-uh! You don't get me to make no statements."

"Why not?"

"You're on one side or the other. I ain't takin' either. I sell whiskey to both."

Bill was beginning to make a little sense out of the man's seemingly meaningless evasions. "Feud?" he asked, voicing his first guess.

Again, the saloon owner frowned. "Don't you know?" he asked frankly.

Bill shook his head. "I hit the country this mornin'."

"From which way?"

"Apache Wells."

"Lookin' for a job?"

"I might take one," Bill admitted.

"You wasn't sent up here?" came another insistent question that seemed to require an answer before the saloon owner would go on. "Schuveen didn't bring you in?"

"Who's Schuveen?" Bill asked, his curiosity over the name aroused for the second time in the past two hours.

The saloon man cast a furtive glance toward the street door, stepped over to lean closer against the counter, and said in a low voice: "You go out to see Schuveen. He'll give you work." He edged up until he could look over the counter and down at the gun along Bill's thigh. "That kind of work."

"Who said I wanted that kind of work?"

The man shrugged his heavy shoulders. "No one," he admitted. "But that's it, what you were askin', what's wrong with the town. It's Schuveen and Mark Shaw. And their fight'll go on after your kids has growed up."

"Cattle?" Bill asked.

"Cattle and land. For thirty years this country was a good one. Plenty of money around and no eagles screamin' from the pinch. Then those two big outfits up on the south rim started scrappin', the Double S and the Bar Eighty-Eight. Some say Mark Shaw started the ball rollin' by swinging a sticky loop on Eighty-Eight stuff. Some say Schuveen was a range hog and beyond his rights in homesteadin' that free graze between the outfits. I wouldn't know who's right. All I do know is that Schuveen has the strip under fence and that the buryin' ground's soon goin' to be too small to hold all the stiffs unless someone calls a halt. Ten men killed here this past summer."

Bill downed the rest of his drink, set the glass down on the counter. "How can two outfits fightin' each other ruin a whole country?"

The saloon owner laughed dryly. "Those two own near half the valley, boss it, too. Anyone livin' here has to be on one side or the other. Hell, this used to be a fine place. Now half the outfits are broke. Shaw's dam was dynamited and muddied the lake, and a man can't even make money sellin' fish."

"So all the outfits are mixed into the trouble?"

"Damn near all."

Bill made a smoke and lit it. "What's wrong with workin' for Shaw?" he asked.

"Nothin', only you'd be on the losin' side. Schuveen's bringin' in men to wind this up quick, I hear. I thought you was one of them."

"How would I go about gettin' work with Shaw?"

"See Nancy Shaw. She's in town today. Probably over at the hotel about now. She eats there when she comes in."

"Shaw's daughter?" Bill asked.

"Granddaughter. Her pa, Ed Shaw, was killed two years ago. Horse pitched him over a rim north of here."

Bill said: "What's she like?"

"Like all the rest of the Shaws. Guts aplenty and looks." His manner became sly and confiding. "Looks to spare. Only don't let a pretty skirt throw you off, stranger. The Shaws can't win the way the cards are stacked now."

Bill had a hard time hiding the unreasoning anger brought on by the smug inference in the words. He reached into his pocket and took out a quarter, exactly a third of his present cash resources. He flipped it onto the counter.

221

The saloon owner shook his head and said: "That was on the house."

"Keep it," Bill drawled. "I might want to borrow it sometime."

CHAPTER
FIVE

Mile High's hotel, the Lakeview, was an ugly
barrack-like building with a narrow verandah facing the
street. The small uncarpeted lobby was deserted. There
was no one in the four-table dining room adjoining the
lobby. Bill rang the bell on the desk. While he waited for
someone to answer, the smell of roast beef and onions
coming from the kitchen told him he wouldn't be
disappointed in one thing; cooking that smelled like
that would be good eating.

Presently, he heard a door open at the far end of the
dining room. A buxom, pink-faced woman wearing a
gingham apron appeared. She gave Bill a smile, wiped
her hands on the apron, and stepped behind the
counter to take a tattered register book from the rolltop
desk.

Bill said: "I won't need a room. I'm looking for Miss
Shaw."

"Nancy?" The woman's smile was warm at the
mention of the name. "She'll be here any minute now."
Some inner thought sobered her for a moment. "You
working for them? If you are, tell Sam Hart that
Schuveen's on his way in. I saw him and half a dozen of

his men coming down the trail a few minutes ago from the kitchen window."

"I'll tell him," Bill said.

"Staying for dinner?" she asked on her way back into the dining room.

He told her he was and went out onto the verandah to sit in one of the barrel chairs, propping his boots on the railing.

He had been there five minutes, cataloguing the things he'd seen and heard this morning, when all at once two things happened simultaneously. First, he saw a blonde-headed girl and a man come out of a store doorway directly opposite and start across toward him. Then, from down the street, came the quick-timed sound of several horses moving on at a trot. He looked down there to see six riders swinging abreast the first of the false-fronted stores.

He knew instantly that the girl was Nancy Shaw, for her tanned oval face with the brown eyes that made a striking contrast to her blondeness was exceedingly pretty. She wore a green and brown plaid wool dress under a short denim coat, and she walked erectly with a grace that held Bill's eye. The man with her would be Sam Hart, according to the information the hotel lady had imparted a few moments ago. He presumed, by the same authority, that the riders coming down the street were Bar 88, Schuveen's men.

The girl and the thin, middle-aged man with her seemed aware of the oncoming group of riders at almost the exact instant Bill first saw them. The man, Sam Hart, broke out of his stride and stopped abruptly,

224

and Bill caught the instinctive gesture his right hand made in lifting to the handles of a long-barreled Colt he wore at his thigh.

Then Bill heard him say flatly: "Get on across there, Nancy!"

Bill caught the look of sheer alarm that widened the girl's eyes. Then she glanced down the street, saw who was coming, and Bill heard her cry softly: "Sam, don't!"

Sam Hart said: "I'm through runnin', Nancy."

The girl's look changed. A lifeless sag came to her shoulders, and the strong excitement that had been in her eyes faded before a look Bill couldn't define, one akin to defeat and despair. She said in a low voice: "Please, for me, Sam. Don't do this."

"It can't be helped now," Hart told her. "Better get out of the way."

Strangely enough, she seemed to accept that. She looked at the riders, now slowing their ponies out of a trot as they neared. For an instant there was a bright look of defiance in her eyes. Then, as though she sensed that was futile, she turned and came on to the near walk and stood at the foot of the hotel steps, facing the street.

Bill picked Bruce Schuveen with an unerring instinct at recognizing a leader. Schuveen was the nearest of the first pair of riders. Bill had pictured him as being old. Instead, he was young, and his tallness made his big bay gelding seem an average cow pony. A genial, guileless smile was shaped on his narrow and handsome face. Fancy-stitched boots and a flowing black coat singled him out from his men. But what took Bill's attention was the man's slate-blue eyes. They reflected none of the geniality of his face. They, along with the pair of horn-handled guns worn high and butt foremost and showing under his coat, made him dangerous looking.

Schuveen's men reined in and bunched and let him walk his pony two strides ahead toward Sam Hart, who stood with feet planted apart, arms hanging loosely at his sides. Except for the time and place, his stance would have appeared indolent, relaxed. But Schuveen's presence gave Hart's posture a cocked, hair-trigger look. The Double S man's sun-blackened and hawkish face was set impressively, coldly.

Schuveen turned his pony so that he faced Hart obliquely across an interval of less than twenty feet. Bill took his feet down off the verandah rail and leaned forward in his chair as Schuveen's slow drawl laid its tones clearly along the street.

"Lookin' for me, Sam?"

"If you say so," came Hart's level answer.

Schuveen's smile didn't change, but now it lacked any hint of amusement and had taken on a mocking quality. "Want to take back what you said?" he queried, nodding to the far walk where eight or ten men had appeared in the last few seconds, standing comfortably near the protecting store doorways. "I'll be satisfied with your apology before these witnesses."

"I'll take nothin' back, Schuveen," Hart said with a touch of anger in his voice. "Not as long as it's so easy

226

to change a Double S brand over to a Bar Eighty-Eight."

"This is serious, Hart. You're namin' me for a rustler."

Sam Hart laughed softly. "You don't say."

On the heel of Hart's words, Schuveen's hands dropped the reins, his left spur touched his pony's flank, and his hands crossed at his waist. As his hands moved, his pony shied nervously aside. Sam Hart's right arm was streaking up along his thigh, and he was dodging to one side.

Bill saw all this, heard Nancy Shaw's low cry of alarm, and was instantly aware that one of Schuveen's men had moved along with the other two. Thought quick, he came to his feet and reached for his gun, seeing that the weapon of the nearest Bar 88 man was already out and swinging down into line with Sam Hart.

Bill hurried his draw, thumbing back the hammer of his .45. He barely had time to rock it into line and squeeze the trigger, aiming at Schuveen's man. The explosion of his gun came at the exact instant he saw flame stab from the muzzle of the Bar 88 man's weapon. The sound of his shot was drowned out by the concussion of others, three of them so closely spaced that they sounded as one. The echo was prolonged, deafening, and, as it racketed down the cañon of the street, the Bar 88 man swayed in the saddle and fell loosely on the off side of his pony. The man alongside him reached over and steadied him, pushing him erect again. The wounded man grabbed the saddle horn, dropping his gun, and would have fallen but for the steadying hand of the man alongside. He coughed once, thickly, and blood flecked his lips.

Bill's glance swept over to Schuveen and Hart. Schuveen was clutching his right wrist with his left hand, his face gone pale with bewilderment and anger in his eyes. His gun lay four feet out from his pony's front feet. Sam Hart was the way he had been two seconds ago, standing with boots wide apart. Only now he was bent at the waist in a crouch, and the smoking gun in his hand was moving in a tight arc to cover the men behind Schuveen.

Two of the Bar 88 men had started to reach for their guns. Bill's sharp — "Hold it!" — froze them in strained, cocked attitudes. Slowly, they raised their hands, along with the rest.

Schuveen shot Bill a surprised glance, then looked back at Hart.

Sam Hart drawled: "You satisfied, Schuveen, or do I have to kill you?"

For the space of five seconds, Schuveen glared balefully back at Hart. His men behind were not watching Hart but, instead, had their eyes on Bill. Finally, Schuveen let go his hold on his numbed wrist and lifted his reins, turning his pony around.

He looked back over his shoulder, drawling: "There'll be another time, Sam!" His glance swung across to Bill. "For you, too, stranger!" He gave a curt-nod, and his men wheeled around and fell in behind him. They went out the street slowly, taking their time and with the arrogance of men who won't admit they're beaten, the wounded man moving loosely in his saddle and braced by the crewman alongside who had an arm about his shoulders.

Bill dropped his gun back into leather as Sam Hart's glance swung over to him. Hart drawled: "You've taken out a first mortgage on me, stranger. I won't say thanks. It's too weak a word."

Nancy Shaw stood looking up at Bill. Her finely chiseled face had gone white, and there was a blending of surprise and fear in her eyes. She breathed in a voice raised barely above a whisper: "You shouldn't have done that. Why . . . why did you?"

"It was between Hart and Schuveen. I like the odds even."

Sam Hart had come over to the walk. He took the girl by the arm and moved with her toward the steps. Her eyes didn't leave Bill as she came up onto the verandah. Bill noticed that the onlookers said nothing but eyed Hart and the girl with faint hostility.

"Who are you?" Nancy Shaw asked, when she and Hart confronted Bill.

"Bill North . . . you've never heard of me."

She hesitated a moment, her face regaining some of its color. For the first time her glance seemed reluctant to meet Bill's. She said quietly: "I'm like Sam. I don't know how to thank you."

Bill said — "Forget it." — thinking that the combination of ash-blonde hair and brown eyes made her as striking looking as any girl he could remember.

Sam said: "I missed it, until I saw Mayhew's gun fall. How come he had it out?"

The girl put in: "Don't you see, Sam? It wasn't meant to be a fair fight. Schuveen would never go against you alone."

"Don't know as I can blame him," Bill drawled, "if that was a sample of your everyday shootin', Hart."

Sam's face colored a trifle. "Lucky," he said. His glance went beyond Bill and up the street. "Here comes your granddad, Nancy."

The girl looked away to see old Mark Shaw turning in at a tie rail two buildings above the hotel. She waved to him, and he seemed to see them for the first time and came on with his horse, swinging stiffly from the saddle directly onto the hotel steps. He ground haltered his horse and crossed the walk unhurriedly, his face gathered in a worried expression as he asked sharply: "What did those guns mean, Sam?"

"It was Schuveen," Nancy told him as he came up onto the verandah. "They were after Sam, six of them. This man shot Mayhew when he made a try at Sam behind Schuveen's back."

Mark Shaw's grizzled face took on a dogged, uncompromising look as he eyed Bill. "You again!" he said dryly. "Where do you fit into this?"

"Mark!" the girl said accusingly, addressing him by name instead of as her grandparent. "After all, he helped us."

"Why?" the oldster asked, his glance not leaving Bill's.

Bill shrugged his wide shoulders. "They ganged up on Hart, and I didn't like it."

"Then you're not a Schuveen man?"

"No. I tried to tell you that this mornin', but you wouldn't let me."

"You were comin' from Schuveen's place."

Bill said: "If I was, it was by accident. I came in along a cañon above that patch of timber. Three nights ago I was in Apache Wells."

Shaw's look changed subtly, losing its suspiciousness. "Then Schuveen didn't send for you?"

"No one sent for me. I'm here on business."

"And you needn't ask him what his business is," Nancy put in reproachfully. "Mark, you don't trust anyone any more."

"I've learned not to," Shaw stated. Then, generously, he thrust out a gnarled and ropy hand. "You have my thanks for what you've done, stranger."

"His name is Bill North," the girl told him as Bill took the proffered hand.

"And I'd like a job," Bill said.

Sam looked surprised but drawled quickly enough: "You're hired."

"What kind of a job?" Shaw asked, ignoring Sam's remark.

"Any kind."

"We've only one kind to offer. We'll pay you to use your gun for us."

Bill gave a brief nod. "I was expecting that. I'll take it."

CHAPTER
SIX

Over his second cup of coffee in the dining room, Mark Shaw told Bill: "So you see, we've been pushed into a corner. Schuveen waited until he had the money and the men to make his play stick . . . waited nearly six years. Then he moved in on me, sent his men in to homestead that strip of free grass both of us needed. He has title to it, legally. And I can't get along without my share of it."

"Who started the fight?" Bill asked. He was aware of Nancy's presence in the chair beside him, had been all during the meal. He hadn't much opportunity to look at her, since the talk had been mainly between him and old Shaw and Sam.

At his question, Mark Shaw breathed a long sigh of resignation. "They all say my boy, Ed, Nancy's father, busted things open. The day Schuveen strung his fence across that free graze last fall, Ed met him in town. Schuveen wasn't packin' an iron. Ed wasn't a big man, but he was tough. He named Schuveen for a range hog and invited him out into the street. Schuveen was in bed for three days afterward. Maybe you noticed that his face was a little crooked when he laughed."

"He wasn't laughin' today," Sam said meaningly.

"Ed broke his jaw," Shaw told Bill. "I wish he'd've killed him."

"What happened to Ed?" Bill asked.

Shaw shrugged his stooped shoulders wearily. "One of those freak accidents. He was forkin' a salty horse one day last winter and got pitched over the rim north of here. The fall broke his back."

For a long awkward moment they were silent. Bill asked finally: "That started it. What's happened since?"

"The usual." It was Sam who spoke this time. "Schuveen's thinned down our herds, brought in some hardcases to scare off our men, 'gulched a few who wouldn't quit. Two weeks ago the dam to our big reservoir was dynamited. When it went out, it washed a lot of muck down into the lake."

"Isn't there any law here?" Bill asked.

Sam looked guilty, and Nancy said: "The last sheriff we had was a man Schuveen brought in and voted into office. One day he came out to the place and tried to arrest Mark on a rustling charge." Once again the girl called her grandfather by name. Bill liked the way it sounded, more intimate and friendly than plain granddad. "Sam was there. The sheriff tried to pull a gun on him. They buried him the next day, and since then we haven't had a sheriff." The girl told it calmly and in a matter-of-fact way.

Bill was once again impressed by Sam's casual manner, realizing for the second time within the last hour that the Double S ramrod was one of those rare individuals who possess an unbeatable swift gun and don't parade it. He had the feeling that if it hadn't been for Sam the Double S would long since have been a forgotten brand.

"What's to happen now?" he asked.

Mark Shaw shook his head slowly in a hopeless gesture, and Sam said quietly: "We'll get along."

"How?" Bill asked.

"There's one way," the girl said quietly. "Sell out to Schuveen and leave the country. We're licked, Mark."

Mark Shaw's gnarled fist smote the table in a blow that rattled the silverware on the plates. "Damned if I will! I was the first man in here, the first man to cast a vote in this county. I won't let a snarlin' pup bark me off my own place."

"You think we ought to go, don't you, Sam?" the girl insisted.

Sam drawled quietly: "I'll do whatever Mark says."

Once again there was a silence, awkward for Bill, meaning something different to the others. They had their problem, and for the moment he had no place in their thoughts.

Finally, Sam pushed back in his chair and said: "Better be gettin' home, hadn't we?"

Bill had spent the last quarter minute turning an idea over in his mind. He said: "Wait a minute. I think I've got something."

Sam pulled his chair back to the table. "Let's have it."

"I'm new here," Bill told them. "No one's ever seen me before, and I have my reasons for wanting to stay. How would it look if I went to Schuveen for a job?"

Mark Shaw's eyes glinted in abrupt anger, and Sam's look was narrow and suspicious. But Nancy's glance showed a quick understanding, and she said: "You mean you'd be helping us?"

When Bill nodded, the two men shed their brief hostility, and Mark Shaw said: "Say that again. You think Schuveen'd hire you, after you shot up one of his men?"

"Leave that to me. I'll think of a way to explain what I did. But if I could hire on to him, I could keep you posted on what he's doing."

As they considered this, Bill was himself considering the wisdom of his suggestion. It had been prompted by the idea that he might discover something about his own stolen herd at Schuveen's, since the Bar 88 must be the hangout for men on the outs with the law, men like Sid and Runt and Ed. By working for Schuveen, he could accomplish two things — help Mark Shaw and maybe help himself.

At length, Sam said with conviction: "That's not a bad idea, boss."

"How can we . . . ?" Mark Shaw began, but bit back his words.

"Be sure of him?" Nancy finished for him. She gave Bill a look that was warm and trusting. "I think we can, Mark."

"So do I," Sam said.

Shaw nodded slowly. He said, in apology: "I'm an old man, North. I've had the props knocked from under me so hard Sam can tell you I've even suspected him." In that moment he was a broken old man, but that look passed an instant later, and his eyes, the same shade of brown as Nancy's, took on a fierce light of hope. "It might work," he breathed, moving his head in a brief nod of conviction. "It *will* work, if we use our heads."

Sam said: "You'd better let us get a head start on you, North. Then go back along the same trail you came in on this mornin'. Go as far as that trail takes you, and you'll be standin' on Schuveen's doorstep."

CHAPTER
SEVEN

Bruce Schuveen's Bar 88 headquarters sprawled high toward the rim of the broad saucer-like valley, looking down on it from the south and facing the majestic snow-mantled peaks of the Wishbones. It was as though Schuveen had chosen the spot expecting some day to be overlord of all the broad sweep of land that lay within his vision. The house, low and hump roofed, was of huge cedar logs, chinked with white plaster. It was big and squat, with two short wings jutting out at each end. Behind it, at less than a hundred yards, ran a belt of timber that gave it a naturally beautiful setting. Barns, sheds, corrals, and crew's quarters were to the west of the house and above it, half hidden by a jutting neck of timber. A lane led up to a low white-painted pole fence fronting the house.

Bill had ridden beyond the end of the lane and was crossing the broad yard before the house toward the fence when he saw a pair of men move out from the shadow of a doorway centering the house's main stem. One was Bruce Schuveen.

He blinked at the sight of the other, unbelieving, dumbfounded. For that man was Red Huggins! And Red was standing there, blandly smiling at him.

Bill had a bad moment, then, not knowing what to do. Why was Red here? How had he gotten here? To cover his confusion, he swung down from the saddle to one side of the center opening of the fence, throwing his reins over the top bar. Then, facing Red and Schuveen again, he was about to call out to Red when he caught the sorrel-thatched 'puncher's slow shake of the head. Barely in time, he swallowed his words and watched Schuveen, who evidently hadn't noticed his recognition of Red, stride halfway out to meet him. Schuveen stopped twenty feet away, Red coming on a stride behind him. The rancher's right wrist was neatly bandaged and held stiff by two small wooden splints. Sam's bullet, knocking the gun from the rancher's hand, must have sprained his wrist. Schuveen wore the same broadcloth suit and stitched boots Bill had seen earlier that day.

Behind Schuveen, two more men stepped out the door. They separated, coming out across the yard until one stood close to each wing of the house and on a line slightly behind the rancher.

Bill stopped just inside the gate, drawling: "Do I get a chance to talk first?"

Schuveen's handsome dark face betrayed the hint of a smile and his eyes a grudging admiration. "Talk about what?"

"A job."

Schuveen laughed softly, and Bill saw that the line of his jaw was crooked, shaping his smile so that one corner of his thin lips made a down-curving line.

238

"Mayhew died on the way out here," Schuveen said. "Want me to thank you for savin' me his wages?"

"I didn't know the set-up," Bill told him. "The way I saw it then, it was forked."

A three-second silence passed slowly. Red smiled vaguely, and Bill thought he saw his partner give an encouraging nod.

Bill said finally: "I still want a job."

"Why didn't Mark hire you?"

"He tried to. But I had asked a few questions in town first. I turned him down. I never pick a loser."

Schuveen's look changed. The smile disappeared, and his glance was shrewd, critical. "So it's like that?" he drawled.

Bill nodded. "They say you're hirin' guns. I can use your money as well as the next man."

All at once Schuveen laughed again, this time louder. He turned and nodded to his men, saying: "Take him to the bunkhouse, Slim."

One of them, the one who had held Mayhew on his horse on the way out of town, asked incredulously: "You mean . . . you're hirin' him?"

"Why not? He's got his guts sewed in tight or he wouldn't be here, would he?"

Slim said softly — "I'm damned." — and jerked a thumb over his shoulder, indicating to Bill that he should head for the outbuildings.

Bill said: "I'm not through yet." He was looking at the Bar 88 owner. "Schuveen, they tell me you want to wind this thing up fast. What's my pay?"

"Hundred and fifty a month." Schuveen was frowning now, and puzzlement was beginning to show on his face.

"For five hundred in cash, half now, half when the job's finished, I'll pick a scrap with Sam Hart the first time he sets foot in town," Bill drawled. "For twice that, I'll take some men and go across and get Shaw for you."

Schuveen's face didn't show the surprise Bill had expected at his arrogant statement. He knew, then, that something had gone wrong, something he couldn't yet define. The rancher waited out a long moment, then said noncommittally — "You'll get your chance." — and turned and walked back into the house. Red followed him.

Slim said caustically: "You ain't Billy the Kid come back from the grave, are you, stranger?"

Bill smiled thinly, wondering at Schuveen's strange behavior. "Maybe I am," he drawled. Then he asked: "Where do I turn this horse in?"

"Up above," Slim told him, and walked over to a side gate in the fence, followed by the second man.

Bill expected what he found at the bunkhouse: unfriendliness. Two men idling there recognized him and gave him hostile looks as he threw his possibles onto an empty bunk and followed Slim out to the blacksmith shed, where two men were helping a third heat and straighten the tines of a hay fork. Slim said caustically: "Meet one of the James boys, gents. He's brother to Jesse. Just signed on."

Again he was recognized and stood under the scrutiny of bleak, hard stares. One of the trio asked

Slim in sarcasm — "Did Sam Hart hire on with him?" — and Slim replied blankly: "No. The boss is sendin' on for Sam later."

For the next half hour Bill was ignored as blandly as though he'd been a snubbing post or one of the chickens in the cook's hen roost. Slim hadn't mentioned work, so Bill sauntered over to the corral where his chestnut was munching a feed of oats and sat on the top pole, chewing an alfalfa stem and trying to piece together the puzzle of Red Huggins's being here.

He was no further than he'd been at first sight of his partner when, at the end of that half hour, Red came along the path from the house. Red saw him and walked over to the corral.

When he stood below Bill, looking up at him, his blunt and freckled face took on a disarming grin and he drawled: "Go ahead! Call me anything you want."

Bill said: "You've got your reasons or you wouldn't be here."

A relieved sigh escaped Red. "I thought you'd be sore, Bill. But after I got on the train down at the Wells, I started thinkin' things over. I told you I was from this country. Not exactly from here but from one of the outfits on the other slope. I know this valley, 'most every man in it. I happened to remember something."

"It must've hit you hard to bring you up here."

"It did. I remembered this brand, the Bar Eighty-Eight. I hadn't connected it before with what happened to us."

"You're further along than me, Red. I can't tie it up even now."

"I was the one that picked our brand, wasn't I?"

Bill thought a moment, then nodded.

"And you remember me tellin' you that I'd once seen it back here, that I liked the way it looked on a cow's hide?"

"Something like that. A man can have some queer reasons for likin' one particular brand."

Red went on: "It's a pretty brand, and I've always thought so. This is the outfit I remembered, the Bar Eighty-Eight, when I picked it. Only I saw it as a kid, when it belonged to the Blairs and my old man used to drive his stuff over here for summer graze. We camped here at Blair's place long before Schuveen came in and threw up that log palace of his."

Bill laughed. "It is sort of big for one man."

"So when it came to a brand of my own, I picked the one I'd always liked. Thinkin' back over that was what made me jump the train at Gody and come up here. I thought it wouldn't hurt to work on an idea."

"What idea?"

"That Schuveen had stolen our critters and run 'em in with his own."

Bill said: "Then we're thinkin' along the same lines. That's why I'm here."

Red seemed pleased. "We'll work together," he said. "Only don't let on we know each other."

"How about now? You come straight here, and you're talkin' to me. Slim and those others are watchin'."

"Let 'em watch. Schuveen sent me. He's made me his right bower, since he knows who I am. Says he can't trust the rest of those hardcases."

"What does Schuveen want of me?"

"He's decided to take you up on your offer to go after Mark Shaw." Red frowned speculatively. "Were you serious about that?"

Bill shook his head. "I'm workin' for Shaw. It was my idea to come here and watch things. I'll let Shaw know of any play Schuveen gets ready to make against him."

Red grinned, asked: "You gone soft on the girl?"

Bill's lean face took on a shade of color. He smiled, although he felt a strange resentment at the implication in Red's words. "She hasn't given me the chance." He climbed down off the top pole, asking: "Does Schuveen want me down at the house?"

"No. You're to go out after the rest of the crew. Bill, this may be our chance."

"Chance for what?"

"I've tried to get away from the layout since I got here yesterday, but Schuveen keeps an eye on me. I have a hunch he may know who I am. I've also got a hunch that he's holdin' our herd in one of those cañons over the rim. Men keep coming and going out that trail." He indicated a well-marked trail that cut off into the timber beyond the corral. "I've tried to make an excuse to follow it, but he always gives me something to keep me here close. This time he's sendin' you out. It's a chance to see what's in that cañon."

A small excitement took its hold on Bill. It was overridden by a sudden suspicion. "Why's he sendin' me?"

"He says he's going to give you your chance to go after Mark Shaw. It'll be tonight. He's sending Slim along, to take you to where the rest of the crew seems to hole up most of the time, out that trail. He wants you to pick two good men and bring 'em back here." Red's look went serious. "Watch Slim! He was Mayhew's friend. And if you run onto our herd, come back here and get me. Between the two of us, we can raise plenty of hell for Schuveen."

CHAPTER
EIGHT

The trail wound crookedly along the aisles of the timber, climbing slowly toward the rim a half mile above the Bar 88. Slim, alongside Bill, maintained a sullen silence.

Once Bill asked: "Where we headed?"

Slim answered curtly — "You'll find out." — and ended any further attempt at conversation.

Five minutes of easy going brought them to the upper margin of the tree belt. The trail led obliquely out across a rocky open meadow that rose sharply to the near horizon. Beyond the rim, Bill knew, a maze of cañons ran downward into the far-flung foothills. It was one of these, one to the west, that Bill had followed this morning.

The late afternoon sun threw their shadows in elongated streamers far ahead of them as they followed the trail upward. Where the way led between outcroppings and huge imbedded boulders, they rode single file. And always, when they came to these places, Slim pulled in on his horse for Bill to ride ahead.

Bill began watching Slim's shadow, thrown out ahead, whenever the lanky man was behind and out of sight. They had ridden through two narrow stretches on the trail and were approaching a third, near the top of the slope, when Slim slowed again and let Bill lead the way in between two waist-high shelves of rock. Slim's shadow made a forty-foot-long pattern across the uneven ground ahead and to Bill's left. Studying that shadow, Bill could see the man's lifted elbows, the lines of his reins, the bobbing head of his pony.

Suddenly, he saw the shadow of Slim's right hand fall to his side. An instinctive surge of wariness made Bill turn his head and look around. An instant later he was kicking his left boot from stirrup and throwing his high-built frame into a quick roll that carried him out of the saddle. For his glance had met Slim's gun swinging up into line with his back.

As Bill rolled clear, Slim's gun exploded from behind in a hollow burst that laid a burning pain across the bunched muscle that capped Bill's right shoulder. He reached out with his hands, broke his fall, and rolled in behind the chestnut. His right hand snaked to holster and palmed out his gun. The chestnut shied away at Slim's second shot. The second bullet hit the rock ledge a foot to Bill's left and ricocheted away in a shrill whine.

A fraction of a second later, the chestnut had moved out of line, and Bill was swinging his gun down on Slim. The thin man's gesture was exactly timed to Bill's. Bill squeezed the trigger as he threw himself to one side. The guns exploded in a precise double concussion that echoed back off the rim.

Falling, Bill fired again, and again. Slim all at once stood erect in the stirrups. His hands clawed open, his

246

gun dropped with a thud to the rock shelf. Then, slowly, the tall man tottered and slumped sideways in the saddle, hands clutching his throat. His pony shied and threw him. He lit on his back, head snapping back against the rock shelf. The pony, gun shy and crazy with fear, lunged into a run, dragging him by one boot caught in the stirrup.

Bill let out his breath in a low whistle, sitting down on the shelf to rock open the loading gate of the Colt and punch out the three empties. As he shucked fresh loads from his belt and dropped them into the weapon's cylinder, he was wondering how wise it would be to ride back and tell Red what had happened.

In the long seconds he sat there, his glance holding sharply to the point where the trail left the timber below, he decided against going back. Bruce Schuveen had no way of connecting him with Red, and for the present Red would be safe at the Bar 88. What was more important was to follow Red's hunch that their herd was being held down one of the cañons below the rim.

Bill spent half a minute tying his bandanna about the shallow bullet gash on his shoulder. Then he walked over to gather up the chestnut's reins, seeing that Slim now lay a hundred yards below and to the right of the trail and that his pony had wandered a few rods away, dragging trailing reins and a broken stirrup leather. The pony, trained to stand rein haltered, wouldn't head for his home corral until hunger or thirst drove him there. If anyone at the layout was curious enough about the shots to come and investigate, they couldn't get there until Bill was out of sight over the rim. Schuveen had, of course, mistrusted him all along. He'd sent Slim along to bushwhack Bill; he would be waiting for Slim's return.

Three minutes after he had climbed into the saddle, Bill was looking over the rim and across the gradual downslope beyond which emptied into the shallow mouth of a cañon half a mile away. A quarter hour later, he was riding between those cañon walls, walking the chestnut, keeping to one side of the trail. Faintly, from far ahead and below, he once thought he heard the bawling of cattle. His pulse quickened its beat, and he rode on warily, right hand resting on the butt of his .45.

Half a dozen times in the next hour he had to cut back to the trail momentarily to ride through a narrowing of the cañon or to get through a thick tangle of brush. Each time he scanned both lengths of the trail and made sure they were empty before he showed himself. Now he could plainly hear the cattle far below. He hurried the last ten minutes, for the gloom of dusk was settling into the cañon's steep-walled notch, and he wanted to have his look at the cattle before darkness caught him. He could hear the animals plainer as he went on, their thirsty bawling and the absence of any stream in the cañon making him wonder how they could be held here on dry feed.

As the shadows were becoming too obscure to give him clear detail, the chestnut lifted his ears, raised his head, and tried to whicker. Bill leaned over the saddle and clamped his hand quickly about the animal's nose.

248

Then, coming aground, he held the reins short with one hand, the other ready to stop his horse's signal, and walked off to the left toward the line of the trail. He came to it abruptly, and looked down at it.

There, still within sight in the thickening darkness, was an open grassy pasture, narrow but long. Dotting it were shifting bunches of cattle, thickest around a shallow basin that showed signs of recently having held water. The basin was churned into a thick soupy mud now, and two riders circled it, keeping back the thirsty cattle. Bill knew that the basin must be fed by a spring and that it would give enough water to keep the cattle alive. Otherwise, Schuveen wouldn't risk holding them here, for the herd represented money to the Bar 88 owner.

He saw two more riders drifting on the edges of the herd, one nearby, the other toward the foot of the narrow pasture. The threat of the nearest man was enough to decide him not to go down there and try to get a look at the brands on the closest animals. Instead, he tried to pick out some animal that was familiar to him.

Once he caught a glimpse of a heifer with a peculiar white belly-band marking that he was on the verge of recognizing. But she was gone, hidden by other animals, before he could be certain. Then, as he was trying to get another look at her, an old bald-faced range bull, minus one long horn and with toes turning outward from age, waddled slowly up the pasture and in toward him.

He knew, then, that these cattle were his, for that bull represented the beginnings of his herd. Ten years ago, working for the rancher who had eventually made him foreman, he had bought that bull and twenty heifers out of the small heritage left him at his father's death. Good luck, hard work, and his savings had built the herd to its present size. A third of the steers down there had the bald-faced old bull's blood in their veins.

Soundlessly, taking his time, Bill walked back up the trail and around the nearest turning. He climbed into the saddle and started back up the cañon. Now he followed the trail, trusting to his hearing and his horse to warn him of any rider coming toward him.

The moon was topping the line of foothills to the east as he made the mouth of the cañon and topped the rise behind the Bar 88. He looked off toward the opening in the timber where the trail cut downward but saw no one moving down there. Then, reining the chestnut out along the line of the rim, he struck into the east with Mark Shaw's Double S as his goal.

CHAPTER
NINE

Nancy knew her grandfather well enough to recognize the change in him shortly after they left Bill North and started the ride home. The old man's look was at first a dogged one. Then she saw signs in him that had been long familiar, the sag to his shoulders, the curtness of his speech, and the long, gloomy silences that had become a habit with him since Ed Shaw's death. These signs told her that, if Mark Shaw had an hour ago believed Bill North could help them, he didn't believe so now. He was perhaps even regretting that he'd trusted Bill North with the few small confidences he had given the man.

Mark Shaw had taken such a beating these past few months that it would take more than a stranger's encouraging words to change him back to his old self. Her grandfather was a harassed and discouraged old man, witnessing the crumbling of a cattle empire he had spent his life in building. Nancy was sorry for him; and now, seeing that he wasn't putting much faith in this stranger, Bill North, she knew it was futile to try and argue him back into his good mood of this noon.

Sam Hart, riding the buckboard seat beside her, understood the signs when Mark Shaw rode on ahead and alone along the trail. He said: "Don't you worry, Nancy. We may come out of this yet."

She had to be satisfied with that small encouragement and her unfounded belief that somehow, in some way, Bill North was destined to see them through their trouble. She wasn't yet ready to admit that she was more than casually interested in Bill, or that she was attracted to this tall 'puncher whose smile could prompt a feeling in her that was foreign to anything she'd ever before experienced.

Nancy and Sam drove in to the Double S ranch yard shortly before three that afternoon. And once again, for the hundredth time these past few months, she was half angered and half sobered by the look of her grandfather's ranch. Last fall, when she'd left for Denver to go back to school, the trouble had already started with Schuveen. But the Double S had then been a real home, the bunkhouse full for the roundup and her father's deep bass laughter ringing in the high-ceilinged main room of the log house. And, like Ed Shaw, Mark had then been a hale and hearty man, a big man, looking twenty years younger than his seventy-three.

Then, one day shortly before the start of the Christmas holidays, Nancy had received a telegram. It told of her father's death. She had packed her things and taken the first train home, to Gody. Sam Hart had met her there, and on the drive in, alongside their fire that first night when they'd camped out on the flats below, he'd told her of the changes the past months had brought to the Double S and to old Mark Shaw. If she hadn't been warned of that, she couldn't have stood it. For old Mark was but a shell of his former being, a failing old man. And the cheerful life at the Double S was a thing of the past. Sam had moved out of the bunk-house and was living in her father's room. He and Mark hadn't opened the big living room since the night Ed had been buried.

She tried at first to bring back the old normal run of things. She had failed, dismally, and now the Double S seemed a deserted, haunted layout. They had tried hiring new men in the spring. Men came, and went, not wanting to stay and run the risk of getting shot even at high pay. Now only one man used the bunkhouse. He was a gangling youth of seventeen, Fred Kerney, who saw to the chores, the son of one of the loyal neighbors who had been dragged down in this fight along with the Double S. Nancy did all the cooking. Machinery rusted in the ranch yard, waterholes needed cleaning, and the last cutting of hay lay rotting in the fields. Sam and Mark and Fred couldn't do it all alone.

That evening, as she prepared supper, Nancy tried vainly to put down the feeling of restlessness that took possession of her. She tried not to think of Bill North but couldn't help it. He represented their one hope now. Sam and the threat of his guns had held off the Bar 88 through the summer. But sooner or later Sam would be cut down, probably by a bush-whacker's bullet, and that would be the beginning of the end. It would be the end unless her hunch about Bill North proved out.

Supper was a silent meal, with old Mark going to his room shortly afterward and Sam sauntering outside for his evening prowl. Nancy and Fred did the dishes. It was while Nancy was drying the dishpan that she heard the sound of a running pony coming in along the back trail. Ten seconds later Sam's low voice was calling out its flat challenge somewhere out there.

It was Bill North who answered Sam. She immediately knew the sound of his voice. It wiped out all the disappointment and hopelessness that had been in her. She went to the door, threw it open, and, when Sam and Bill walked into the light shining through it, she smiled gladly and said on impulse: "I was hoping you'd come."

Afterwards, when Bill stepped in and looked at her, his lean face set in a good-natured smile, she was confused, not knowing why she had said what she had.

"North's got some news," Sam told her.

The inner kitchen door opened, and Mark Shaw stood there, soberly eyeing Bill. Nancy pulled a chair out from the wall for her grandfather, then one for Bill. But he wasn't looking at her. His glance had gone to Mark.

"What news?" Mark asked.

Bill said: "It'll take some time tellin'. It's about the business that brought me here. I'd have told you this noon if you'd asked what it was."

Sam put in: "We don't aim to pry into your affairs, North."

"There wasn't much point in botherin' you with them. Now there is," Bill said. Then, briefly, he told them what had happened in the last four days, how his and Red's Bar 88 herd had been stolen, how he'd come up here on the chance of finding it, what he had found down the cañon this evening.

They heard him out without interrupting. Once again, as at noon today, a spark of hope seemed to burn alive in Mark Shaw. But, as Bill finished, that hope cooled once more, and into the following silence the old man said: "There's only three of us. I believe what you say. But we've got no proof and couldn't do anything about it if we had."

"There's four," Bill reminded him. "You're forgettin' Red. He's worth two ordinary men. And Sam here can take care of himself."

"Bruce Schuveen has a dozen men, two dozen if need be," Mark said ominously. "He makes his own law. Even if I could arrest him, no judge in this country would have the nerve to try him."

"Then we'll go about it another way," Bill drawled quietly. Their glances went to him sharply. "I've thought of all that," he said. "So we'll fight him his own way, not out in the open, but by hitting him at his back. Tomorrow night Sam and Red and I will run off that herd. We'll drive it down out of the hills and over into the next county, where there's a law to back us. If Schuveen tries to follow, Red and I can prove ownership. If we raise a big enough stink, we'll have railroad detectives in here investigating the theft of that train. They'll bring in federal men. Schuveen will last only long enough for them to get proof. Once he's crowded, his men will give him the double-cross.

Sooner or later we'll turn up the three men who raided the train. That'll be the end of Schuveen and the Bar Eighty-Eight."

There was a long-drawn-out silence, until finally Sam breathed explosively: "By God, Mark, it'll work!"

The old rancher's eyes were alive with a fire Nancy and Sam hadn't seen in months. He nodded, not trusting himself to voice his hopes.

It was Nancy who broke the brief silence. Bill had turned so that she could see his other side, and now she noticed that his shirt was torn at the shoulder, that there was blood around the tear.

"Bill, you're hurt!" she cried.

Sam saw the dark stain on the shirt for the first time and said sharply: "How'd that happen?"

Bill hadn't mentioned the shoot-out with Slim. Now he had to tell him.

Sam heard him out, then said: "What is it Schuveen knows about you?"

Bill shook his head. "I'd feel a lot better if I could tell you, Sam. He may have had some way of knowing what was said in the dining room there at the hotel today."

"That couldn't be," Mark Shaw put in. "Missus Robbins is one of the few friends I have left in town. She wouldn't let a Bar Eighty-Eight man into her kitchen for love or money."

Nancy said: "You can talk that over tomorrow. Right now, I'm going to fix Bill's shoulder, and you're all getting some sleep."

She did, washing the wound and putting on a clean bandage. In the bunkhouse, reclining on a bunk, Bill couldn't get the girl from his mind. It wasn't until Sam, who had decided to stay in the bunkhouse tonight with Bill and Fred, reminded him — "Think hard, Bill. What would Schuveen know about you?" — that she left his thoughts.

He considered Sam's question a moment, once again trying to see behind Schuveen's attempt at a bushwhack. Finally he had it. He said: "It must be that one of the jaspers who ran off our herd was there and recognized me."

"Then why didn't he recognize Red?"

Bill couldn't answer that. He fell asleep trying to.

CHAPTER
TEN

Bill rode down to Mile High early the next morning. Sam could find only half a dozen shells for the only two rifles on the place, and they would need their guns. It was finally decided that Bill would go in for a box of .30-30 shells.

Mile High's street had the same drab and deserted appearance of yesterday. Bill saw four ponies tied at the hitch rail before the saloon. Closer in, he made out their Bar 88 jaw brands. A man loafing on the walk saw him and stepped into the saloon. Bill chose the opposite side of the street and came down out of the saddle a few doors short of the saloon at the general store. Crossing the walk, he glanced back over his shoulder and saw Red coming out of the saloon doorway. Red saw him, hesitated, then went down along the walk without giving any sign of recognition.

It was two minutes before the lone clerk in the store finished with another customer and came to wait on Bill. Bill asked for his box of shells and watched the clerk go back to get them. His glance traveled casually down along the aisle and to the back doorway that opened onto a loading platform. Red was standing there, just outside the doorway, and beckoned him.

258

Bill waited for the shells, paid for them, said — "Think I'll go out the back way." — and walked down along the aisle and out the door.

Red stepped from behind a woodshed twenty yards away along the alley. Bill went over to him, and they stepped back out of the alley and in behind the woodshed.

Red said: "They found Slim along about dark last night. What happened?"

Bill told him.

Red whistled softly, drawling: "A bushwhack, eh? Did you follow the trail on over the rim?"

Bill nodded. "And found our herd, Red. It's down there three or four miles. Tonight we're going to drive it off." He went on to explain what he and Sam and Mark had planned to do.

Red's blue eyes took on a bright light of interest as Bill talked. Knowing that sign, Bill said: "Want to come in with us?"

"Did you think I'd sit around wearin' out the seat of my pants and let you do all the work?"

It somehow made things better for Bill to see that this red-headed man was still the same carefree, reckless partner he had gone in with only a year ago. This was the old Red, the fighting Red he'd sided through a tough winter and a busy summer. He said: "What's your idea on it, Red? Want to come along with me now?"

"Give me time to get my jughead," Red said, and started around the corner of the woodshed.

"What'll Schuveen say?" Bill called after him.

"Probably plenty. But who cares? Meet me on the trail out of town."

An hour and a half later they were riding in on the Double S. Red's look sobered at sight of the layout. "The old man's pretty well licked, ain't he?" he queried.

"He was yesterday, but not today. If we swing this, Red, he'll be on his feet again."

Sam was cordial on meeting Red. Old Mark was more reserved, but Bill could catch the approving glint to his glance as he inspected Red's solid frame and noticed the way he wore his guns. Nancy, strangely enough, wasn't overly cordial. Later, Bill went into the kitchen to ask her about it. She was alone.

Before he could put his question, she said: "Bill, how long have you known Red?"

"A year. Why?"

She shrugged her shoulders. "That's it. I don't know why, but I don't like him. I keep thinking I've seen him before."

"He'll do to ride the river with, Nancy."

She smiled at him, seeming to put aside her seriousness. "If you think that, I'd better start doing the same."

She made it a point during the noon meal to make up for the bad impression she'd given Bill. She was polite to Red, went out of her way to talk to him. But still Bill caught her once or twice in an unguarded moment when she gave Red that same half-questioning, half-distrustful glance of their first meeting.

He forgot about it soon afterward. They were starting shortly on the long circling ride that would take them down into the foothills and to the cañon before dark. Sam judged they would come to the pasture where Bill's herd was being held sometime near midnight. They were taking blankets and enough grub to last three days, packing an extra horse. Mark Shaw was restless and excited, not satisfied with leaving Nancy and young Fred Kerney alone until he'd made the girl promise not to set foot outside the yard during the day and had taken Fred aside to warn him to keep a loaded shotgun within his reach and not to get out of sight of the house. "That girl's all I have left, Fred," he said. "Don't let anything happen."

Finally Mark was ready and climbed stiffly onto his bay horse. Nancy watched them ride out of the yard. As they trotted through the gate, she called: "Careful, all of you! Bill, come back!"

Alongside Bill, old Mark smiled and said meaningly: "Wish I was fifty years younger. You're a lucky cuss, Bill."

It was the first real show of friendliness the old rancher had demonstrated. Bill nearly missed the meaning behind the words at his gladness over hearing them.

CHAPTER
ELEVEN

By eleven that night the moon had topped the cañon rim to wipe out the unrelieved blackness of the pasture where Bill's Bar 88 herd was being held. He and Mark and Sam and Red lay belly down on a high rock outcropping at the foot of the pasture, looking out along the quarter-mile-long stretch where the bunches of cattle moved slowly in and out from the dark scar of the spring's muck hole. Surprisingly, no riders circled the spring tonight to keep the cattle away.

When Bill was sure of this, sure even that no rider was at the far end of the pasture, he said: "What do you make of it, Red?"

"They're gone," Red said.

Sam grunted: "I don't like it!"

"Why not?" old Mark asked. "Makes it easier, don't it?"

"Means they're up to some other devilment." It wasn't necessary for Sam to add that the Double S might be the scene of that trouble.

But the tone of Mark Shaw's voice when he said gruffly — "Let's get on with it!" — showed that he realized what Sam had been thinking. He, like Bill, was made grim by the thought that they'd made their choice and couldn't change things now.

They walked back down the cañon to where they had left the horses. When they had come upon the pasture again, Mark said: "Bill, you come with me, and we'll swing across. Sam, you and Red take this side. We'll meet above and push 'em along."

Bill and Mark crossed the foot of the pasture to the opposite wall, and rode slowly up along it, past the spring and to the upper end of the meadow. Across the way, they occasionally caught a glimpse of Sam's and Red's shadows moving parallel with them. Presently, they were swinging in toward the pasture's center at the timber margin above.

When Sam and Red rode up out of the shadows to join them, Sam growled once again: "Mark, I don't like it!" He stood up in the saddle and turned to scan the impenetrable blackness of the timber upcañon.

Suddenly, from out of the trees close at hand, Bill caught a whisper of sound. It might have been the jingle of a spur chain, or the metallic grating of a bridle chain. But, unmistakably, it was a sound foreign to the night, one that shouldn't have been there.

For a half second it struck a keen paralysis of wariness through Bill. Then, roughly, he was wheeling his chestnut around and into Mark's gray horse, pushing him sharply to one side. And as he moved he called stridently: "Back, Sam! Look out, Red!"

Hard on the heel of his call came the explosion of a gun, followed sharply by another. Bill, looking into the trees as he raked the chestnut with his spurs, saw those gun flashes. His right hand dipped to his thigh and lifted the Colt from holster. He swung it into line as his horse was lunging into a run. He thumbed two thought-quick shots at the target of those flashes, hearing either Sam's or Red's weapon explode off to his left. Then, bent low in the saddle, he followed Mark Shaw hard away from the spot and down across the open pasture.

They covered fifty yards, sixty, at a hard run. All at once the sharp reports of rifles smote the stillness behind, the echoes racketing loudly back and forth between the walls. Bill saw the gray horse ahead break his stride for an instant, then run on again smoothly. He thought Mark Shaw's body wove uncertainly in the saddle.

A hot and blinding rage had taken him these past few seconds, anger at his helplessness, hatred for Bruce Schuveen and the cunning the rancher had used in setting this trap. Schuveen must have known about him and Red all along; and today, in town, Red must have been seen coming across to talk to him. The report of Red's seeing him had gone to Schuveen, who had undoubtedly made a shrewd guess on what was to happen when Red failed to show up later at the Bar 88. The trap had been set, and they had ridden into it blindly, not even stopping when the absence of the guards on the pasture should have warned them off.

Bill looked back over his shoulder toward the timber, bracing himself against the chestnut's swerving run as the animal dodged in and out of bunches of cattle shifting nervously at the sound of the guns. Off to his left, riding almost even with him, he could see Sam. But Red was nowhere in sight.

Real fear was in him, then, fear that Red might be lying back there with a bullet through him, or that Red had been cornered and was fighting it out.

On sudden impulse he drew rein, calling — "Keep goin', Mark!" — and struck off toward the nearest flanking buttress of the cañon's climbing wall. The upper end of the pasture was indistinct now in the shadows. A rifle up there sent an even-spaced racket of fire down the cañon. Bill could have drawn his own Winchester and targeted those powder flashes. But killing one Bar 88 man wasn't important now. Finding out what had happened to Red was.

He rode silently in on the outthrust spur of the wall and came out of the saddle, clamping a hand about the chestnut's nose. He stood there, listening for long seconds after the rifle had ceased its firing. He heard the echo of a man's derisive laugh, the low-toned speech of another voice made unintelligible by the distance.

A minute dragged out its seemingly endless space of time. Another passed, and Bill was about to walk farther up the pasture when he heard the slow muffled hoof thud of a pony coming toward him. He backed farther into the wall's shadow and waited, one hand holding down the chestnut's head, the other fisting his .45.

The shadowy shape of a pair of riders drifted by less than forty yards away. When they were about to fade from his sight, they stopped and one of them called: "Nothin' over here, Sid! They vamoosed!"

Sid would be one of the trio who had held up the train, Bill decided. So the man had been at the Bar 88, after all, had probably seen him ride in on the layout yesterday and then leave later with Slim on the attempted bushwhack. Here was one more item of proof against Schuveen. But what about Red?

He was trying vainly to fathom out his answer when he heard a voice he recognized as Sid's say: "Hell, they're gone! No use followin' and invitin' a dose of lead poison. Let's gather up the gang and get back to the boss. He'll want to know about this."

"Yeah!" answered the other in sarcasm. "Won't he love it when he finds out they got away!"

They struck out across the pasture and presently were out of sight. Seconds later, Bill heard them call out and summon the other Bar 88 crewmen who had ridden down the far side of the cañon. The sound of their ponies in the next three minutes told him that the crew met out in the pasture and then rode up to the head of it and along the trail that cut up through the trees. Finally, nothing but the night sounds and the restless shifting of the herd out in the pasture came to him. Only then did he let go his hold about the chestnut's head and try and think out what he must do.

Sam and Mark would take the long way home. They would wait, but go on without him when he failed to appear. Red might be with them; he might by lying up there near the trees with a bullet in him; or . . . Bill refused to let himself think of the last alternative, that Red had been taken a prisoner.

It was while he was climbing into the saddle that another thought came to him. Schuveen, having failed to trap Mark and Sam tonight, might do the next best thing, strike at the Double S while it was undefended except for a boy and a girl. The idea struck Bill so forcibly that he used his spurs on the chestnut as he rode to the upper end of the pasture. There was no need for hurry, he knew, since he couldn't run the chance of overtaking the Bar 88 men while they were in the cañon. But the thought of Nancy in danger filled him with an urgency, a need to be with her that was strong enough to bring up a recklessness in him.

He spent ten long minutes riding the margins of the timber and searching the outermost brush thickets for sign of Red. But his partner had vanished, probably siding Sam, and the mystery of his disappearance would have to remain unsolved until later, until he knew that Nancy was safe, and that the Double S wasn't threatened.

He started up the cañon, sure now that the Bar 88's crew had ridden straight for Schuveen's layout and wouldn't bother to leave a man guarding the trail. He covered the distance to the rim in forty minutes, using little caution to hide his approach to the upper end of Bar 88's meadow. He swung into the east along the rim, lifting his pony to a lope.

Fifty minutes later he was sloping down on the Double S, his fears quieted by the deserted look of the place.

As he came across the yard, Fred Kerney's voice sounded from a darkened window of the house: "Sing out, stranger! Or I let this thing off!"

"It's all right, Fred," Bill answered. "Show a light."

He off saddled and turned the chestnut into the corral. The kitchen door opened as he came up across the yard, and Nancy's tall figure was outlined by the light of the room. She was wearing a flannel wrapper. Her blonde hair caught the lamplight and framed her oval face with a halo of spun gold. Her eyes, dark and bright with excitement, held a question he hated answering.

But he had to tell her, so he said: "Nothin' to worry about. They baited us, and we traded a few shots. No one was hurt. Mark and Sam took the long way back. They'll show up soon."

He could see the hurt and disappointment come into her eyes. But, then, she was smiling. It was a brave smile, one that wouldn't admit of defeat or despair.

"You'll want some coffee," she said quietly, and went to the stove to lay a fire.

Bill helped her, carrying in an armload of wood and a handful of chips.

When the fire was going and the granite coffee pot was sitting on the stove, she turned to him to say abruptly: "Bill, we mustn't let Mark down. This will mean the end for him unless . . . unless you can think of something. Please try, won't you?"

He nodded, trying to appear confident. But he wasn't. She had asked him to fill a big order, and he didn't know how to set about doing it.

CHAPTER
TWELVE

Two hours later they heard a pair of horses coming in along the lane. Fred went outside, and presently Mark's voice hailed him. Nancy, sitting in an armchair near the stove with her legs drawn up under her against the chill night air, gave Bill a pleading glance that was eloquent for the lack of words to back it. In these two hours they had tried to think of something, anything, to tell Mark. They had failed, miserably, and Bill's feeling was one of guilt and self-loathing. The Double S's troubles had grown to mean more than his own. This girl was looking at him as a last hope, making him the slender thread that held Mark Shaw from dropping into the pits of ruin. And in two hours that thread had weakened until now it looked like it might break. Bill's feeble attempts at planning a move against Schuveen hadn't netted them one concrete hope.

Sam's boots pounded the doorstep outside. The door swung open, and the frail-bodied ramrod stepped into the room, Mark coming directly behind him. Sam's face was set in a dark frown. Blood matted his shirt wetly to his left side, high along his ribs. When he saw Bill, he stiffened, drawling: "So you're back again!"

Nancy said: "Sam, you're bleeding. Let me see what's wrong."

Sam ignored her. Mark came in and closed the door. A tension ran through the room, building up a feeling within Bill of wariness and puzzlement. For Sam's words had been gruff and accusing.

Nancy said: "What's wrong?"

Sam didn't answer. His glance clung to Bill in that same unwavering, accusing way.

It was Mark who finally broke the prolonged silence. He said in a voice edged with bitterness: "You said this afternoon you'd seen Red before, Nancy. I said you were wrong. You weren't. I remembered him on the way back here. He was that deputy Schuveen's sheriff hired two summers ago. The one that shot that kid your father brought in to work as blacksmith."

Bill, eyeing Mark, heard Nancy's quick indrawing of breath. Something was happening here that concerned him yet was going over his head. At length, catching Sam's hard glance on him, he queried: "What about Red?"

Sam's thin lips curled down in a sneer. "Supposin' you tell us," he drawled. "You ought to know, since you and him framed us."

"Framed you?" Bill echoed hollowly. "I don't get it, Sam." He was trying to ignore the warning light in Sam's eyes now, that and the slow dropping of the man's hand until it hung along his thigh, close to the handles of his gun.

Mark said: "North, you're a Schuveen man. You made up that cock-and-bull story about losin' your cattle. Schuveen planted that herd down there so we'd swallow your yarn. You were sent here to trap us, to toll us down there into his guns."

For the space of three long seconds, Bill's thoughts raced madly, trying to put reason behind the rancher's accusing words. Then Sam abruptly said: "Red's the man that gave me this." He brought his arm across his body to the bloody side of his shirt.

The last prop was knocked from under Bill's understanding. What Mark and Sam were saying was sheer insanity, without logic or reason. Yet he heard himself asking calmly:

"How do you know Red shot you?"

"It had to be him," Sam said. "The angle of the shot, the sound of it."

Nancy said quickly, in a hushed voice: "Sam, you could be mistaken."

Momentary indecision showed in Sam's eyes. Then Mark said: "How else could they have been waitin' there for us?" He lifted a hand and made a disparaging motion that indicated Bill. "Look at him. He wasn't even scratched. They had their try at me. My horse stopped a bullet, barely managed to limp home, and Sam's lucky that bullet didn't go two inches farther in."

Sam breathed abruptly: "To hell with all this talk!"

Bill had been watching him, knowing for sure what was coming. At the first tightening of the muscles along Sam's right arm, he was throwing himself to one side in a lunge, raking his hand up along his thigh to lift out his .45. He palmed the gun up, rocked it into line with the lamp on the shelf behind the stove.

His move took Sam by surprise. In the split second it took him to thumb back the gun's hammer, Bill saw Sam's arm arcing up with blurred, sure speed. As he squeezed his gun's trigger, his stomach muscles hardened against the expected crushing slam of a bullet. The hollow burst of sound made by his own gun was deafening, punctuating the precise instant the lamp chimney sprayed apart, and the flame guttered out.

A split second after his gun spoke, a second explosion and a lance of powder flame marked the spot where Sam stood. Bill felt a light blow strike him alongside the face, the air concussion of Sam's bullet streaking past his head. Then he was lunging the two quick strides that took him to the window in the side wall of the room.

Passing the table, his hand grasped for a chair and found it. He swung it up and out, ahead of him, straight at the window. It went through the glass with a shattering crash, knocking out the crossframe that divided the two sashes.

He threw his body after it in a long, rolling dive. A shard of glass caught him on his left thigh, ripping a rent in his pants and sending a stab of pain up his side. He held his hands out in front of him as he fell, trying to remember how far he had to drop. Then his hands struck the ground, and his arms took up the driving weight of his body. He turned one shoulder, hit hard on it, and curled his body in a long hard roll that drove the wind soughing out of his lungs in a painful, choking gust.

272

He was on his feet even before his lungs had sucked in air again, running around the corner of the building and toward the corrals. Halfway across the yard he saw the two horses tied to the hitch rail forty feet away. He changed his stride and ran over toward them. A shot echoed hollowly from the kitchen's doorway, and the bullet laid a whisper of sound in front of him. He lunged in under the tie rail, putting Mark's gray horse between him and the house. Jerking loose the reins of Sam's pony, he slapped the animal on the shoulder, turning him out toward the lane, vaulting into the saddle as he took his first full stride.

His boots rammed down and into the stirrups. Another shot beat the still air in the direction of the house. Bill gathered up the reins with his left hand as the animal broke into a run, thrusting his Colt into holster with his right. Then he was bent low in the saddle, reining the horse from side to side down the lane. No more shots followed him away.

Beyond a low rise at the foot of the lane, he pulled the horse to a quick stand and sat listening for five seconds. No one was coming behind, which meant that Sam was probably ignoring Mark's wounded horse and would be headed for the corral for a fresh one; either that, or they weren't going to try to follow him.

When he went on again, he headed straight west, toward the Bar 88. It never occurred to him to ride anywhere else but toward Schuveen's place. For there at the Bar 88 lay the answer to this riddle, the answer to what had happened tonight. And enough had happened since, added to the trap they had ridden into, that one and only one thought was uppermost in Bill's mind. He was in some way going to come face to face tonight with the man who had undermined his whole existence, his future. That man was Bruce Schuveen.

He suddenly remembered Red and the story Sam had given of Red's having shot him. Sam was mistaken, of course. Those first shots out of the timber had come with too startling a suddenness for Sam to remember clearly what had happened. Bill himself couldn't clearly bring back those first few seconds, when he had pushed his horse into Mark Shaw's and tried to save the rancher from stopping a bullet. Sam had been just as confused, just as bewildered over Bill's rapidly timed warning shout. He might have thought that the bullet that hit him came from Red's direction. It probably had, from the gun of a Bar 88 man hidden in the brush beyond Red.

It was clear now that Red had either been shot or taken a prisoner. He might be at the Bar 88, probably wounded. Once he decided that his partner was in Schuveen's hands, Bill had one more reason for pushing Sam's horse at its hardest run. Schuveen had several things to answer for: the theft of the herd, the dragging down of Mark Shaw and the Double S, the laying of tonight's trap, and whatever had happened to Red, and, last of all and most vital to Bill, Schuveen was the cause of breaking the trust of the only people, aside from Red, Bill cared for — Mark, Sam, and, above all, Nancy.

As he rode bent low in the saddle, scanning the short reaches ahead that came into sight in the moonlight, he knew that he would never live to see a hope he only now recognized come into being. That hope centered about Nancy Shaw, and he realized suddenly that he loved this girl. She represented all that was clean and fine that the future might have held for him. He didn't pause to consider whether or not she shared his feeling; he simply knew that, had things turned out differently, this girl would have formed a vital part of his life. She was the kind of girl a man could spend half his life searching for and, even then, not be sure of finding. He remembered vividly each change of expression on her oval face, the sometimes grave and sometimes laughing way her dark eyes regarded him. And deep in him rose up a hurt and a bitterness over the thought that she might never know how wrong Sam was in accusing him of betraying Mark Shaw's confidence.

By the time he sighted the far-flung spur of timber a half mile short of the Bar 88, a change as sure as the adding of ten years of hard living to his life had come to him. He was cool and nerveless, without a trace of fear for what he was headed into. His gray eyes were steely with a predatory light, and there was in him a quality akin to the cold-bloodedness of a hunting animal. When he sloped out of the saddle barely inside the margin of the trees and tied the horse's reins to the branch of a scrub oak, his movements were sure and fast, cat-like with an economy of motion. He was a killer, for the first time in his life, unfeelingly setting about the stalking of a human quarry.

That quality stiffened within him as he walked on toward the Bar 88. He paused to reload the Colt only when a light from the side window of the huge log house showed winking through the trees. From there on, he walked soundlessly, nothing but a moving shadow in the deep gloom of the timber.

The light came closer, and soon he could make out the rectangle of the window.

Across the fifty-foot stretch of open yard, he could look in that window and see a man's broad back tilted in a chair before a desk along the far wall of a paneled room. He recognized Schuveen's back instantly, and, when he saw that the window's lower sash was raised all the way, a mirthless, shadowy smile eased the hardness of his lean features.

He glanced carefully to either side, making sure that the yard was deserted. Then he walked soundlessly out across it toward the window. He was within ten feet of it, the room broadening out before his vision, when a voice came out to him.

"Hell, Bruce, why crab about it? You made this deal a year ago. I came through with my end of it. Now it's your turn."

Like the slam of a hard blow full in his face came the drawling sound of Red's voice. And along with that was the stunning implication behind Red's words, the familiarity of long acquaintance with Schuveen, the positive statement that he and Schuveen were in this together, that it had been planned for a year. His short acquaintance with Red fell into a clear pattern now.

Then, as though the two men in the room beyond the window sensed his presence in the night outside and were explaining all that had happened, Schuveen's voice said in an even-toned drawl: "It's not my turn. The play's still up to you. Mark Shaw's still alive. What's more important, so's Sam Hart."

"Listen, Bruce," came Red's patient, unangered voice. "I had this idea in the beginning, didn't I?"

"No. It was mine. You never would have thought of running Shaw off this range."

"I don't mean that. I mean this other, my goin' out of here and findin' a ranny with a fair-sized herd who needed money to start a layout. It was my idea to find such a man and go partners with him, put up a few hundred on lease money for a half share in a small outfit. It was my idea to brand the stuff Bar 88 and then to bring a big shipment through this country so your crew could steal a trainload of critters, wasn't it?"

Bill, closer to the window now, caught Schuveen's brief nod. He could see Red clearly. His partner was slowly pacing one end of the room. A cigarette drooped from a corner of Red's thick-lipped mouth, and he was eyeing Schuveen narrowly, squinting against the curl of smoke from his cigarette.

"All right. All that was your idea," Schuveen said. "We were to split even on it. At present prices, that'll mean your share is something like seven thousand. I'll write you a check for that amount now, and push that herd up onto my graze and in with my other stuff. You can hightail and no one'll be any the wiser."

"What about Shaw? I went to the trouble of framin' it so your crew would get a chance at Shaw and Hart and North, all three, tonight. Is it my fault you hired a bunch of poor shots?"

277

"It's not your fault. But when we went in as partners on this Double S deal, gettin' rid of Shaw was your job. That was the agreement. You were to get Shaw and Hart for a half interest in the Double S, and I was to keep your split on that other. Now you kick like hell because I want to send you over there with a crew to finish the job."

"I'll go if you will."

Schuveen moved his head in a negative, turning slightly in his chair so that Bill could catch the twisted smile on his dark face. "That wasn't in the bargain. If this falls through, I don't want Shaw to have any proof against me. No, thanks. I'll stay clear of it."

"That's final, Bruce?"

Bill saw Red's hand move up along his thigh as he put his question. The tone of his voice made Schuveen swivel around in his chair. By that time Red had lifted his gun out and rocked it into line. Schuveen stiffened, his hands clenching the arms of the chair until his knuckles showed white, and after a second he breathed: "You can't get away with this."

Red's smile stiffened to a sardonic grimace. "I'm not goin' to kill you, Bruce," he drawled. "But you're goin' to open that safe and count me out fourteen thousand, the sale price on that herd I stole for you. You can have the Double S, all of it. Did you think I'd stick around and let you slip my neck in a noose?"

From far behind him, beyond the timber, Bill caught a hint of sound, that of horses coming on at a full run. He knew immediately that it would be Sam and Mark, that tonight the Double S was fighting for existence the

278

same as he was, that Mark and Sam had made a decision something like his own, to throw caution aside and settle things once and for all.

The sound of those running horses made Bill straighten and come closer to the window. His hand fell to the handles of his Colt, waiting for the signal that the men inside had heard the oncoming riders. And his glance clung to Red now, instead of to Schuveen.

For in these last three minutes a sudden and violent hatred for the sorrel-thatched man had risen up in him. All the blame he had heaped on Schuveen was now directed toward the man really responsible for what had happened — Red Huggins. He looked back over his year with Red and remembered the confidences they had shared, the deceitfulness Red had never betrayed by one word or action.

Haunted by Red's brazen defiance of all the codes of friendship, he forgot Schuveen and wanted nothing so much as the chance to get his hands on Red, to beat his ruddy face to a shapeless pulp, to blow by blow exact a small revenge for the ruin Red had left behind him. Common sense told him that neither he nor Sam nor Mark could win tonight even though they could fight together. Schuveen's crew was within call, and the odds were too great. Schuveen, and probably Red, would never answer for what they had done.

Schuveen was rising stiffly from his chair under the threat of Red's gun. Red said suavely: "Better hurry, Bruce. I want to be out of here before sunup."

As Schuveen moved out of his line of vision, Bill edged over to one side of the window. He could see

Schuveen again. The rancher was kneeling before a small black safe in the corner of the room. Red's back was to the window.

Bill all at once decided that he would never have a better chance than now. He lifted his gun from holster and stepped up to the window. He heard the hoof echo of the running horses nearer now, wondering idly as he reached out for the window sill why Red hadn't noticed it.

He crouched, swung a boot up, and vaulted in through the window, saying sharply as he moved: "Hold it, Red!"

His boots touched the floor inside, and he leveled his gun as Red swung around at him. Red's body turned first before his gun arm. He saw Bill, looked into the .45's round bore, and let his gun fall to the floor. Schuveen spun around at the sound of Bill's voice. Then, with startling swiftness, he leaped to one side. As he moved, the hand hidden behind him, the one that had been reaching into the safe, came into view. It was fisting a double-barreled Derringer.

Schuveen cried: "Jump, Red!"

Bill saw the Derringer come into line with him and instinctively let his knees buckle. He squeezed the trigger of the .45 and threw himself into a falling roll. The Derringer exploded in a concussion that matched the .45's. The double charge of buckshot whistled over Bill's head and chopped into the window frame, sending out a spray of flying wood splinters.

Before the sound of that explosion had died out, Red had reached down and snatched up his fallen weapon.

Then, with a wide sweep of his other arm, he knocked the lamp from the desk. It hit the floor with a crash, its flame spurted up for a moment, and then Red trod it out as he moved across the darkened room.

For two seconds a settling silence ran over the room. In that brief interval Bill came to a crouch and moved three steps to one side, away from the window and along the wall. Schuveen called in a low voice — "Are you with me, Red?" — and Red answered dryly — "Sure, Bruce!" — in a way that made it plain he wasn't.

From out front, in the yard before the house, came a man's strident shout and a hollow-beating shot. Bill realized then that he could no longer hear the running horses below the spur of timber. He wondered if Sam and Mark were, after all, the ones who had been riding those ponies. As if in answer to his question, three more rapid, close-spaced shots exploded against the night's stillness, and he knew that it could be no one but Mark and Sam.

A boot scraped the floor across the room in the direction of the safe. Once again Bill was tempted to shoot but held back. He straightened up along the wall and moved another step toward the corner.

More shouts sounded from the front of the house, followed by a few ragged shots. Suddenly there was the solid tramp of boots in a corridor beyond the room's doorway. And, just as suddenly, Schuveen was calling: "Stay out!"

His call was a split second too late. The door opened, letting in a widening rectangle of light and outlining a burly short figure Bill recognized as Sid's, one of the three men who had held up the train.

Two things happened instantly. Bruce Schuveen, crouching in that fan-spread swath of light by the safe, leaped to his feet and took one lunging stride toward the door and the man in it. Across the room, at his back, a gun exploded once.

Bill didn't see the flash of Red's gun. He was looking at Schuveen, seeing the rancher's legs give way, seeing his head tilt back as a piercing scream welled up out of his throat. Red's bullet had taken him in the spine.

Sid saw Schuveen leaping at him and started back. When the shot crashed out, Sid turned, pulled the door shut, and ran back down the hall.

Once more the room was shrouded in total darkness. The air reeked of coal-oil fumes and the acrid smell of gunpowder. There was the sound of Schuveen's labored breathing, but no sound came from the front yard. Bill stayed where he was, rigid, listening for something that would betray Red's moving toward him. The light hadn't fallen on him when the door opened, and he knew he was safe from the threat of one of Red's bullets.

Five seconds dragged out, then ten more. Abruptly, Red's drawl came from over near the safe, from a position at least ten feet from where Bill had thought him to be: "How'd you like it, Bill? Nice shootin', eh?"

Bill didn't answer for a moment, thinking his voice would give Red a target. But then, knowing Red's temper, he said acidly: "Not bad. Ever line your sights at a man's front?"

Strangely enough, Red laughed. "Schuveen wasn't worth an even break," he drawled. "He was as big a sucker as you were that night on the train when I pretended it was an accident that I bumped into you and spoiled your play against Sid. Bigger maybe. I've planned this getaway all along. There's fifty thousand in that safe, and I'm taking it with me."

Bill knew now the approximate spot where Red stood. It was within three feet of the safe, probably beyond it in the direction of the door. But he had to be sure.

He groped for a moment in search of something to mention that would get Red to talking again. Finally he had it and said: "What happened to Ed Shaw, the old man's son?" He moved immediately away from the spot where he'd been standing, out from the wall two strides. And, as he moved, his left hand went to a pocket of his shirt and took out two matches.

Red's laugh came again. "He didn't fall off that rim by himself," he said, and his voice came from the same spot as before, beyond the safe. He waited a moment while a rattle of gunfire sounded from out in front of the house and across toward the line of timber. When it died out as suddenly as it had begun, he went on: "That was Sid's job. Schuveen paid him five hundred to follow Ed up onto the rim and shoot his horse from under him. It was lucky they didn't dig the horse out from under the slide that buried him. They'd have found the real reason if they had."

Bill changed his gun from his right hand to his left. Then, holding the matches flat in his palm, he brought his arm back. His arm cocked, he spoke once again, wanting to make sure Red hadn't moved: "I'm comin' out of this alive, Red. You aren't."

Red's answer was a derisive — "Like hell!" — and Bill took one more step toward the room's center, sure that Red hadn't moved.

He brought his arm arcing up over his head in a wide swing. Then his palm, cupping the matches lengthwise, slashed down and out toward the uncarpeted floor in the direction of Red's voice. He brought his arm back sharply as the impregnated end of one match burst into flame. His gun flicked across from left to right, and his thumb hooked over the hammer. The match's sudden flare showed Red crouched back against the wall, his side to the safe. His head was turned slightly, and his squinting eyes were looking away from Bill.

Then, suddenly, Red saw him. As the match died out, Bill had a fleeting glimpse of Red, lunging out from the wall, his gun swinging into line. Bill triggered his gun at that moving target. The flash of the weapon, and that of Red's answering shot, lighted up the room. Bill fired again, as a crushing blow took him high on the left shoulder and spun him around. He braced his boots wide apart and thumbed back the hammer of the Colt once again. He emptied his gun at Red and thought one of his shots drowned out a stifled scream.

Suddenly there was silence in the room, Bill's ears ringing to the concussion of the shots. A throbbing ache lanced into his shoulder as he moved his left arm. Then he forgot the shoulder as, close to his side, the swivel chair crashed over and onto the floor. A soft and yielding weight rolled against his right boot, and a hand closed on his leg. He lost his balance and fell heavily on his hurt shoulder. A body's weight rolled onto his legs, and now a hand clutched at his shirt front. He brought his gun up and slashed it down in a hard blow that raked the hand down off his shirt. A groan, half a choked death rattle and half a scream, rode out across the room's momentary stillness. Then the weight slacked off his legs, and he pushed away from it, crawling to the outside wall until he sat with his back against it.

Outside the window he heard the thump of boots striking the ground. He looked toward the window in time to see a man's head and shoulders show against the moonlight. He swung his empty gun up until the head was notched in his rear sight. His thoughts were vague as he thumbed back the hammer of the weapon and squeezed the trigger. The hammer pin clicked on an empty shell case at the exact moment he recognized Sam Hart as the man who stood there.

He let out his breath in a long sigh of relief and said: "Stay back, Sam. He may still be alive."

The next few minutes, after Sam's sharp exclamation — "I'll be damned! It's Bill, Mark!" — came to him, and Sam backed away from the window, were afterwards vague in Bill's memory. He was aware that no more shots came from the yard out front, and he thought he heard horses going out the lane, away from the house, at a hard run. There were sounds in the hallway outside, then the sudden opening of the door. He could see a lantern sitting on the floor in the center of the doorway, its glare bright and blinking. Squinting against the light, he thought he saw shapes moving beyond it.

Then Mark Shaw was standing beside the lantern, picking it up off the floor and saying: "There's Schuveen and Red, or what's left of 'em. Where . . . ?" Mark saw Bill at that moment and hurried into the room. "Here he is, Sam. Get in here! He's hurt!"

It was Sam who lifted him to his feet and picked up the overturned chair and eased him down into it. And it was Sam who found the full bottle of whiskey in a desk drawer and poured three swallows of it down his throat.

The room stopped spinning before his eyes. He looked down to see Schuveen, lying face down over near the door, Red lying on his back and staring upward at the ceiling with glassy eyes, near enough to the desk so that he could have reached out and touched him. Abruptly, from out in the hallway, sounded quick steps. Then Nancy was standing in the doorway, looking in at them. Her face was pale, and her eyes wide in fear and alarm. She saw Schuveen, then Red, and tears of relief welled into her eyes as she threw herself into her grandfather's arms, sobbing: "Mark, I thought they'd killed you!"

Sam stepped around her and into the hall, coming back carrying two small rugs. He threw them over Schuveen and Red, then stood before the desk, looking down at Bill and saying: "Feel like lettin' us in on it, Bill? We ride hell for leather across here after your hide and find this." He indicated the two bodies. "It's a cinch they didn't blow out their own brains."

Nancy said: "He doesn't have to talk now, Sam. Look at his shoulder." She came across and knelt on the floor alongside the chair, tearing away the sleeve of Bill's shirt. And the glance she gave him was warm and trusting.

"Anything you say, Nancy," Sam said. "But I'd like to hear it. All this shootin' back here in the office was what decided the crew that the place was surrounded and they'd better get out. We let off a few shots and hurried 'em a bit, but Bill pulled the trick. What happened, Bill?" he asked, this time insistently.

He held out the bottle of whiskey. Bill took another swallow of it and then told them what he'd heard through the open window, how Red had killed Schuveen, and finally: "Then Red and I had it out. I was lucky."

"Lucky, hell," Mark Shaw breathed, smiling broadly as he looked down at Bill. He nodded to indicate the whiskey bottle. "Some day I'm goin' to fill you full of that stuff and find out what happened. But right now all I need to know is that you're alive, and I can thank you for what you've done."

Sam said: "I reckon that goes for me, too. I have a few things to take back."

"Mark, go out and find Fred and send him into town for the doctor," Nancy cut in severely. "Bill knows how grateful we are."

After Fred, who had hitched the buckboard and driven Nancy across here from the Double S, had left for town, Sam and Mark carried Schuveen and Red out to the deserted bunkhouse. Back again, they ran errands for Nancy, getting a basin of hot water from the cook shanty and tearing up some clean sheets for bandages.

"We could have saved Fred the trip," Sam observed, after inspecting the wound in Bill's shoulder and watching the way Nancy dressed it. "The bullet went through clean as a whistle. You'll be a well man in two weeks, Bill."

"And after that, what happens?" Mark Shaw asked.

Bill said: "Guess I'll play nursemaid to that herd on the way to Kansas City. That's what I started out to do."

"What you start out to do and wind up doin' is two different things," Mark said. There was a shrewd gleam in his eyes and the hint of a smile on his face. "Take me, for instance. I started across here tonight to throw some lead through you and likely get killed doin' it. I wind up owner of half this valley and with no crew to run the layout."

Nancy turned slowly to face him, her eyes wide in surprise. "Half the valley?" she echoed.

Mark nodded. "That's what it amounts to, with the Double S and the Bar Eighty-Eight thrown in together."

"But you don't own the Bar Eighty-Eight," Nancy said.

"Who says I don't?" Mark bridled. "If I say the Bar Eight-Eight's mine, who's there to argue against me?"

Sam let out his breath in a low whistle. "Not bad, Mark," he drawled.

Mark went on: "We'll do it up legal, hire men to come in here and homestead Schuveen's graze, like he homesteaded that free grass last summer. He died without any heirs, which means that finders are keepers. We'll sell off enough of his critters to square accounts with the other small outfits he's driven to the wall. Then, maybe, there'll be peace around this valley."

"You're pretty old to start out on a job like this," Sam said pessimistically.

"Who said I was goin' to do it?" Mark's smile broadened. "Bill's young. He's got a head on his shoulders. He's already got his brand registered over in Arizona as Bar Eighty-Eight. We'll have it recorded here. He and Nancy can move right into this house and not have the bother of buildin' a new one."

Nancy gasped, and her face took on a shade of color. "Mark, you . . ." She got that far and no further, dumbfounded by her grandfather's statement.

Bill's face had gone red, too. He looked at Nancy. Something he saw in her eyes as they swung around to meet his made him say: "I wouldn't have asked any man to propose for me, Nancy. But it's a fact."

"What's a fact, Bill?" Nancy asked softly, a warm light shining in her eyes.

"That I want you to marry me."

Sam reached over and nudged Mark as Nancy knelt beside Bill's chair and impulsively kissed him. Out in the hall, after he'd pulled the door shut, Sam said: "You've got more guts than ten mules, Mark. Them two kids could have swung it on their own."

"I know," Mark said irritably. "But I'm in a hurry. I'm an old man, and, if I'm goin' to see this thing squared away and start rollin' before I die, I can't wait around for things to happen. I've got to make 'em!"